STRANDED

K.L. HAWKER

STRANDED

www.facebook.com/klhawker

www.klhawker.com

This is a work of fiction. The characters and events portrayed in this novel are fictitious.

Any similarities to real people, living or dead, business establishments, events or locales is

entirely coincidental and not intended by the author.

Stranded / K.L. Hawker

ISBN-13: 978-0-9917257-2-4

Cover Design by Conrad Visual Concepts

www.conradvisualconcepts.com

For Kate, my little miracle.
I love you.

"Discretion will protect you,
and understanding will guard you." ~ Proverbs 2:11

STRANDED

K.L. HAWKER

PROLOGUE

IT WAS EXHAUSTING knowing that every move I made was being mirrored by Nick and Noah—Jake's orders. When would Claudia and Rachel be back? I needed to go the washroom.

"You okay?" Nick asked, his gaze locked on my bouncing knee as we sat on the outdoor patio of a quaint café in Italy.

"Have you heard from Jake? And when will Rachel and Claudia be back anyway?" I pointedly ignored his question.

"Do you need to go to the washroom, Anna?" And he pointedly ignored mine.

"Yes."

"Claudia and Rachel will be back soon. They just need to show Eli and Mark where to patrol."

Yes, Eli and Mark—more bodyguards insisted by Jake. I sighed heavily.

"Get used to it," Nick said, a bit of playfulness now

gone from his voice. I rolled my eyes so he couldn't see.

Up to this point, Noah had been quietly sipping his coffee. "He just wants to make sure nothing happens to you while he's gone."

I nodded, fully understanding, although not entirely appreciating the importance of it yet.

My knee began bouncing again.

"Okay, up you go," Nick said, pushing his chair back and pulling at my arm. "I'm taking you to the washroom."

"No, you most certainly are not," I challenged.

"Anna, stop being so stubborn. Claudia and Rachel may not be back for another twenty minutes."

I frowned, considering how much longer I could hold it. "Fine!" I gave in, annoyed. "But you're not coming in this time."

Nick laughed. "Noah will go in first to make sure it's clear, and then we'll wait out by the door."

I whimpered. There was nothing I hated more than being followed and watched and guarded all day, every day.

Once the washroom was safety-approved, I headed in and enjoyed a moment of peace while I stared at my reflection in the mirror. No Claudia. No Rachel. No bodyguards. Just me. But now I missed Jake. At least when Jake was near, the others backed off a little.

I knew he'd be deep into training right about now, but I just needed to talk to him. Or at least read his

words. I dug out my phone from my clutch and sent a
text to him:

> ~ *I miss you. I hope training is going well.*
> *Come back soon and safely. xo*

I waited a minute, staring at the phone and willing
for it to buzz. Nothing. I sighed and continued to the
washroom stall.

The door opened and Noah called in, "Anna? You
okay?"

"Geez, Noah!" I shouted. "I'm not planning an
escape. I'll come out when I'm ready to be monitored
again." Rage boiled inside of me. *What do they honestly
think is going to happen in here? There's not even a window
for Pete's sake!*

When my phone buzzed, I hurried out to the sinks
to read my text as butterflies danced inside of me.

> ~ *I miss you too, baby. Training's going well. Only a few*
> *more hours. Hope the guys are taking good care of you.*

And the butterflies froze. *Seriously? Is that all he cares
about? That the guys are taking good care of me?* I wanted
to write something brave back. Something that would
show him that I didn't need protection. But what? What
could I possibly say? Maybe I'd tell him that I was
enjoying a long walk along the beach by myself. Maybe

I'd tell him the others went to lunch and left me alone in the hotel room. Maybe I'd tell him . . . my thoughts and brilliant ideas started getting foggy and I had to clutch the sink for stability as the room began to spin. My eyes scanned the room around me, trying to make sense of what was happening.

"Nick?" I tried to call, but my voice was weak and hoarse. I slumped to the floor. "Noah?" I tried again.

The room was darkening around me when the door opened and Nick said, "Don't get mad at me, Anna. I just need to check on you."

I couldn't answer.

"Anna!" the door opened hard and that's the last I registered.

"JAKE CAN'T FIND out about this," I heard Noah say as my thoughts started slowly collecting again.

"I agree," Rachel added.

"That's not a good idea," Nick argued. "He'll be pissed if he finds out and we didn't tell him."

"I don't know, Nick," Claudia chimed in. "He'll be even more pissed if he finds out we nearly killed her."

"I should never have let her go in there alone," Nick mumbled.

"It doesn't much matter how it happened. Jake can't find out. He'd lose his mind," Rachel said.

"I don't know," Nick said.

"She's right," I heard myself say, my throat raw and

sore. "He can't find out about this." My eyes opened and I found myself lying on my hotel bed with my four friends surrounding me. I wasn't exactly sure what Jake shouldn't find out about, but I did know that whatever it was would only cause him to become more of a constrictor—never leaving my side for even a minute.

"How are you feeling?" Claudia asked, removing a facecloth from my forehead and replacing it with a cold one.

"What happened?" I asked, trying to piece together the events.

"Carbon monoxide poisoning," Rachel answered. Nick and Noah both hung their heads. "It came in through the vents. We had no idea."

"I felt dizzy and then passed out," I recalled.

"Doctor just left. He said you'll be just fine. He had you on a breathing machine for oxygen therapy for a couple of hours—to clean the poison out of your blood," Claudia explained.

"Do we know who did this?" I asked. "I assume it wasn't an accident."

Noah shrugged. "There's an investigative team on it now. But, yeah, it wasn't an accident."

I looked at each one of my friends, each carrying a portion of guilt. "This is not your fault," I said. "And I agree that Jake can't know about this."

"He's been texting me," Nick said. "Apparently he's been texting you and not getting any answers."

I remembered back to when I had texted Jake in the washroom to tell him I missed him, but then he had responded with a comment about how he hoped I was being protected. It had made me angry. And before I had a chance to respond, I had collapsed.

I dug through my clutch and found my phone. Eight new texts since our last exchange. Three missed phone calls.

I read the texts first:

> ~ Well?? Are they?

> ~ Are they taking good care of you?

> ~ Why aren't you answering me?

> ~ I just tried to call. Anna, mess off and answer me.

> ~ !!!

> ~ Anna, I'm coming back if you don't answer me!

And then there was a reply from me, which I knew I hadn't sent, so it must have been Rachel, Claudia or Noah. Nick wouldn't have been so bold. It read:

> ~ I'm fine. I love you.

"Who sent that?" I laughed, surveying their innocent faces.

"Rachel," Claudia grinned. "It kept going off while we were with the doctor so we had to shut him up. Last thing we needed was for him to come back before you were better."

I continued reading the texts.

~ Okay, good. I love you too.

And then the last text, which was received within the last half hour, read:

~ Nick and Noah aren't answering my texts or calls. What the hell is going on there? I don't feel right about this.

I looked up at the guys. "Did you answer him yet?"

They both shook their heads.

"This isn't right though. He should know," Nick said.

I couldn't stop the tears that pooled in my eyes. "Nick, if you tell him, I won't hear the end of it. I already feel suffocated with all the security on me as it is. I can't handle more. Nick, *please*."

Claudia reached across the bed and took Nick's phone from his hand. "I'll tell him Anna was tired and so we're back at the hotel resting. It's not a lie."

"It's not the truth," Nick pointed out.

"But it's for the best," I said. "He'll be no good if he has to worry about me all the time. He needs to focus too. Just like the rest of you."

"You know he'll find out one day," Nick said, "and when he does, there'll be hell to pay."

"And I'll pay it," I said. "It's my problem, Nick."

Suddenly the hotel room door swung open and Jake stood in the doorway, flanked by Eli and Mark.

"Jake!" I said as I sat up straight and tried to keep the evidence of my dizziness from reaching my face.

Nick and Noah stood to greet him, but he pushed past them and came right to me. "Are you okay? What happened to you?" Then he turned to Nick and Noah. "Why haven't you answered your phones?"

Before either could answer, I said, "Jake, I'm perfectly fine. Look at me. I'm just tired and not feeling that great." I clutched my stomach as evidence.

He touched the facecloth in my hands and then gave it to Claudia. "Get her a cold one," he ordered. Claudia did as she was told and went off to the washroom, pulling Nick with her.

"Lay down with me," I said as I rested my head back down on the pillow and patted the bed next to me. He didn't lie down, but instead sat next to me, leaning over me protectively.

"I missed you," I said, kissing his fingers softly, and hoping the diversion would be enough.

He nodded, clearly not yet in the mood to forgive

me for putting him through hell.

"Jake, don't be mad. I'm perfectly safe."

Our eyes locked and he took a deep breath. "I hate being away from you. I felt sick all afternoon."

I forced a laugh, but couldn't help but keep the irony from my voice. "Me too."

Jake looked back at the others standing near the door. "I'll take it from here, guys. Thanks for taking care of her."

Noah nodded and when Nick didn't answer, Noah said, "No problem, man. Anytime."

I sent a thought to Claudia: *Please tell Nick I owe him one.* She winked and they left, leaving me in the arms of my protector as I contemplated a strategy to prove my independence to him.

Chapter 1

SOME PEOPLE BELIEVE that, before you are even born, you are the writer of your own destiny. You assist God in creating your own challenges, assigning your own personality traits, and even deciding when and how you will die. All of the obstacles that you create are designed to bring you to your purpose in life. It is also believed that déjà vu is a reminder to your inner self that everything is going according to God's plan. Your plan.

I PULLED UP on the plastic shade covering the tiny airplane window and looked out over the ocean as we soared tens of thousands of feet above it. What a fantastic summer vacation—spent with my closest friends, on an amazing continent, making incredible memories.

Anna was sleeping soundly beside me with an adorable glimmer of drool at the corner of her mouth. A smile formed at the corners of my mouth. So angelic and peaceful.

Reaching up, I brushed a strand of blonde hair from her eyes and tucked it behind her ear, then softly kissed her forehead. I was the luckiest guy in the world. No doubt about it.

"Should I take offence to that?" Claudia whispered, breaking the silence.

I leaned forward and caught her grimacing from the middle seat on the other side of the aisle. Although her mind reading skills could be quite useful at times, she seemed to find more enjoyment in reading *my* mind than anyone else's.

"That's because you're the most messed up," she laughed.

"You'd know," I chuckled. "And what do you mean, should you take offence to that?" I searched my head for my last unguarded thought.

"You were just thinking that you are the luckiest guy in the world," Claudia whispered, "but I'd like to think that Nick is." She turned to face her boyfriend, who was sound asleep in the window seat beside her.

"Yeah, yeah. Nick's pretty lucky too," I gave her.

"Damn right he is." She playfully tossed her brown curls over her shoulder and laughed.

Now go back to sleep! I thought.

Claudia giggled and settled back into her seat.

I was just about back to sleep when I heard Rachel's

voice: "Jake? You awake?"

My eyes instinctively rolled beneath my pinched eyelids and I considered pretending I was asleep to avoid the inevitable one hundred and one questions or never-ending one-sided conversation that Rachel was notorious for.

Rachel sat in the aisle seat next to Claudia, and across from Noah. Over the summer Rachel and Noah had become pretty close. Still not an official couple, but close enough that she had good reason to be upset when she caught him kissing another girl while we were at a training camp in Paris. I had a hunch that this is what she wanted to talk about.

"What is it, Rachel?" I answered, deciding to play nice.

"Oh, nothing really. Just wondering if you were awake," Rachel lied. You didn't have to be a mind reader to be able to read Rachel Riley.

I sighed and sat forward, giving her my undivided, albeit reluctant, attention. "Are you sure, Rach?"

She fiddled with the button on her blazer, which reminded me of how insanely brainless her dress code was in Europe. We were there to "backpack" and appear as tourists while attending several undercover training camps, and she couldn't resist packing her high-heel shoes, skirts, and stark white blazer. I was actually surprised it was still white after all it had been through this summer. I had a strict 'no white' rule in my closet. Nothing stayed white for more than an hour after I put it on. Might have something to do with Abby who was always giving me little sister hugs while sporting chocolate-covered hands or juice-stained lips. Rachel didn't have any siblings, so that made it easier, I decided.

"Spit it out, Rach, before I go back to sleep," I threatened.

"Okay. So I was just wondering if you think Noah"—she paused and waved her hand in front of Noah's face—"was actually *attracted* to that girl in Paris?" The sound of disgust plagued her soft voice.

It took everything inside of me not to roll my eyes and tell her to give it up, but I could see she was still struggling with it, so I put on my therapist hat.

"Rachel, I am sure Noah found her attractive," I began and then paused to watch her horrified reaction, which I found amusing, "but I am also sure that he finds you *extremely* attractive."

Rachel stared at me with uncertainty. It wasn't what she was expecting to hear, I could tell.

"Jake?"

"Yes, Rachel?" I laid my head back on my seat again hoping the end of the conversation was near.

"You suck at giving advice."

I laughed and felt satisfied with that. Perhaps she'd stop using me as her sounding board for her problems.

"So why do you think he did it then?" she

whispered, leaning further across the aisle.

My smile faded as I came to the realization that this conversation wouldn't be over until either Noah woke up or we landed in Halifax, which was another four hours.

"Rachel, Noah is a guy. Guys like girls. It's just how it works." I felt like I was getting better at the therapist thing.

Rachel didn't. "And *that's* why I don't want a boyfriend. You're all the same." She sat back in her seat, folded her arms and frowned.

"Hey now! Don't be like that. Noah is a fantastic guy. And I know for a fact that he wouldn't have kissed that girl if you hadn't just rejected him for the hundredth time that week. Noah would be completely, one hundred percent devoted to you if you'd just let him."

Rachel looked down at her blazer button, which was now hanging loosely from its threads. "Do you think?" she asked, biting her lower lip.

"Give him a chance and find out," I coaxed.

"Maybe. I'm just nervous."

"About *what*?" I heard myself say as I pressed my head back into my seat hoping that it would swallow me up and take me away from this conversation.

"About—" she stopped suddenly as Noah stirred and began waking up. "Never mind."

Thank you, Noah! I pressed my eyelids closed and

reached for Anna's hand. Once her warm hand was held securely in mine, I drifted off to sleep.

"JAKE? JAKE!"

My body was being shaken, bringing my discombobulated self quickly back to earth. "What! What's going on?" I tried to jump up, but was restrained by my seatbelt.

"Relax, it's just me," Anna whispered as she covered my mouth with her hands. She was giggling and obviously amused by my reaction.

It took a few seconds for my heart to begin beating regularly as I assessed our surroundings and realized that no one was in danger . . . mainly Anna.

"You scared me," I admitted.

She giggled. "I know."

I relaxed and raised her hand to my lips, taking in the lavender scent of her skin.

"What time is it?" she asked, resting her chin on her free hand and puckering her lips for a kiss.

I leaned in, touching my lips to hers, then reluctantly withdrew to check my watch and answer her question. I suddenly remembered the gift that I had specially made for her in Italy. A gift that would help me keep an eye on her at all times, even when it wasn't possible to be near her. "That reminds me! I have something for you!" I shimmied past her and dug through the overhead compartment for the little brown bag deep in my backpack.

"What is it?" she asked with a big smile as she clapped her hands together in excitement.

I smiled at her child-like enthusiasm. "Open it," I directed, handing her the box wrapped in brown paper.

Anna ripped off the paper and slowly opened the box. Her eyes reflected the sparkles of the diamonds that adorned the edges of the bracelet. "Oh, Jake, it's beautiful!"

She carefully took the bracelet out of the box and ran her fingers over the intricate detail.

"It's so beautiful with the little circle accents and the sparkly diamonds. Where did you ever get something so beautiful?"

I thought carefully before I answered. "I had it made for you in Italy."

"Italy! But when did you ever find the time to do that?" she questioned with only a little interest as she studied the bracelet, which also doubled as a watch.

"Do you like?" I asked, hoping.

"I love," she answered, leaning in for a kiss. "So Italy? Is that when you left me behind with all those guards for the whole day because you had to do some sort of 'special training' on your own? Did you *lie* to me, Mr. Rovert?" Anna played.

"No, I did not *lie*, Ms. Taylor! I actually did have some special training that I had to take care of, but I also had this made in the meantime. And it wasn't like I left you with an army of bodyguards. It was just Noah and Nick and a couple other trusted friends." I helped put the bracelet on Anna's arm and watched her admire it.

"Well, it sure felt like an army. They wouldn't even let me go to the washroom by myself—they called in re-enforcements every time I had to go," Anna begrudgingly reminded me.

It wasn't something I enjoyed doing—leaving her alone. But when it had to be done, I had to be sure she was going to be safe in my absence. I wasn't going to risk losing her again.

"Re-enforcements!" I laughed. "You mean Rachel and Claudia?"

"Stop laughing, Jake! It's embarrassing being followed around everywhere you go!" Anna wrinkled her eyebrows in disapproval.

"It's not my fault you're a rare commodity, babe. Anything could happen to you at any time. I can't risk letting my guard down. I can't risk losing you." I shuddered as my mind let in a flood of memories from her kidnapping just a few short months ago.

Anna looked satisfied with my answer, but bothered, nonetheless. I knew she was.

"And I said I was sorry," I continued. "But now you know why I really had to go. I wanted to have something special made for you, my little miracle."

Anna relaxed in her chair and ran her fingers over

the bracelet again. "Well, I'm glad you did because I love it. And it will match pretty much everything so I should never have to take it off."

"That's the idea," I said, kissing her lips.

"Although I probably should only wear it on special occasions," Anna said as she unclasped the bracelet and slid it off.

"No," I answered too quickly. "No, you have to wear it all the time."

She shot me a questionable glance. "Why?"

"To cover your mark," I said, running my fingers on her freshly branded wrist.

"But I could get a cheap little wristband for that. This is too beautiful to wear everyday," she protested.

"No, it really wasn't that expensive," I lied. "I want you to wear it all the time . . . please."

"Jake, why are you being so insistent?" Anna demanded.

"Anna, you need a watch. You are always asking me what time it is." She gave a weak smile and I guessed that she was a little offended. "It's not that I *mind* telling you what time it is, I just think that a watch is a practical thing to have, and this one compliments your beauty."

"You're so full of it, Jacob Rovert," she accused. "Are you sure I should wear it *all* the time?" She ran her fingers over the face of the watch.

"Positive. Even in the shower." I draped the bracelet

over her wrist again and re-clasped it. Then I rested my head back on my headrest and struggled to keep my eyes from closing.

"Three," Anna whispered a minute later. I almost didn't catch it as I was starting to drift off.

"Three what?" I asked, confused.

"It's three o'clock at home right now. Remember? I wanted to know what time it was?"

"Oh yeah. We should be landing in a couple of hours. We should get some sleep because you know our parents are going to be expecting a debriefing of our whole summer vacation," I reminded her.

"They sure are, although my parents are in Uganda so my debriefing will be easier than yours," she bragged.

"Well, my mom is going to be expecting to see you too, so you'll have to come over, you know."

Anna smiled as she touched her new watch. "I wouldn't miss it."

She rested her head on the backrest. "Jake? I really do love the bracelet." Her eyes started to close.

"Anything for you, my love," I replied. Anything.

I watched her drift off to sleep and thanked God for Anna Taylor and for keeping her safe all summer. I wasn't looking forward to the months to come where she'd be thrown into the battlefield with the rest of us. Hopefully her new bracelet, also known as a tracking device, would help keep her safe. Completely water and fire proof, the bracelet had over three thousand sensors with an integrated state-of-the-art computer chip that was able to assess her needs by sensing her heart rate and body temperature. I knew I would rest easier tonight.

CHAPTER 2

STANDING AROUND THE luggage belt, I could barely keep my eyes open. Rachel, Anna and Claudia did all the talking and reminiscing while Noah, Nick and I stood quietly watching the bags go around and around.

The airport was busy, even at the early hour of five o'clock on a Sunday morning. I was finding it hard to watch for our luggage while keeping an eye on Anna and her every move. It wasn't hard to tell she noticed because of all the annoyed looks she was shooting in my direction.

Anna hated to be under surveillance all the time. She had such an independent personality that the idea of everyone making a fuss over her was wearing thin on her. I think she thought it was flattering at first, but as the summer wore on and she realized that not only me, but *all* the Gifted Ones, made her the centre of observation, she started feeling claustrophobic.

"That's yours, Jake!" Anna broke into my thoughts,

pointing at the large red backpack approaching me.

I hauled it off the conveyer belt and realized my bag was the last one we were waiting for. We headed out into the brilliant sunrise and inhaled the sweet smell of home. A refreshing hint of the ocean, mixed with the coolness of the early morning fog. There was really no place like it.

"BUBBA!" ABBY CALLED as she ran down the hall toward me, arms wide open and ready to leap.

I had barely opened the front door and stepped inside. "Abby!" I braced myself, caught her swiftly and swung her around. "What are you doing up so early?"

Abby's smile stretched from ear to ear as she helped me take my jacket off. "I set my alarm so I could be the first to see you when you got home!"

Abby was something else. Not your typical little sister, but someone I could count on like a best friend. Being seven years younger, there was never much animosity between us. She was more of an ally than a sister.

"Where are Mom and Dad?" I asked as I laid my backpack by the front door and headed down the hall to the kitchen. Abby followed closely behind.

She pulled out a chair for me at the table and answered, "Still sleeping."

I looked around at the spotless kitchen, tidied living room, the sparkling floors and the polished cupboards.

"Been cleaning again, Abs?" I teased, catching her slightly embarrassed expression.

"I know, I know. It's totally not cool to be a clean freak, but I can't help it. I like organization," Abby defended.

"Well, you've always been so much older than you are. And definitely not average," I said, reaching over to mess up her hair.

Abby swiftly fixed her hair and then rested her head on the table, watching me carefully. "So tell me about Europe. I didn't get to talk to you much. Every time you called I was in bed," she scolded.

"Yeah, sorry about that. I really wanted to talk to you, but by the time we got back every night, it was always past your bedtime. Forgive me?" I always felt bad about not being able to talk to Abby when I called. Since Dad was away on business trips so much, I sort of felt like it was my responsibility to be that role model for her.

Abby laughed. "It's okay, Jake. Really, Mom needed to talk to you more than I did, anyway. She was a little lonely without you. I tried hard to fill your shoes, but your shoes are big," Abby remembered with a smile.

"Well, I'm home now." I leaned back in my chair and stretched. "But I think I'll head to bed for a few hours. Can I tell you about our trip later?"

Abby followed me up the stairs. "Sure. Oh yeah, and we're having a barbeque this evening for you and

Anna. Is that okay?"

"Sounds good. 'Night Abby." I threw her a wink as I closed my bedroom door and crashed hard on my comfy pillow and plush bed. I pulled my phone from my pocket and laid it next to me on the pillow, making sure the GPS tracking was working and the volume was all the way up in case Anna needed help.

I WAS HAVING the best dream ever. I was lying in a field, and Anna was hovering over top of me. Her silky blonde hair tickled my face as the wind tossed it around. She slowly lowered her body to meet mine and touched her smooth lips to my ear. Her warm breath tickled as she whispered, "I want you . . ."

". . . to get up, Jake. Wake up," Anna's voice echoed in my ear as I slowly came to the realization that I wasn't dreaming anymore. Anna was sitting on the edge of my bed tickling my face with her fingers.

"What? What's going on?" I stuttered as I sat up.

Anna laughed. "You're so adorable when you sleep." She reached over and fixed my hair. I closed my eyes and kissed her hand as she stroked the side of my face.

"How long have you been here?" I demanded, somewhat embarrassed.

"Only about twenty minutes. I watched you sleep for a while, but then I had to wake you. Supper's ready. You *have* to get up now." Anna pulled my arm, leading me out of the room.

"Supper? What time is it?"

She checked her new watch, proudly, and answered, "Five o'clock. You've slept the whole day away."

I shook my head, trying to make sense of everything. I remembered going to bed around seven o'clock this morning, but I was sure Mom would've woken me up by nine. I couldn't believe I slept another ten hours!

"JACOB!" MOM PUT down the salad tongs and greeted me with open arms, followed by a long hug. "It's about time you got up. I wanted to wake you this morning, but your father wouldn't let me." She scowled at Dad who was carrying in a plate of grilled steaks from the back deck.

"Oh please, Joanna! You *tried* to wake him, but when he didn't wake up to the cold glass of water you poured over him, I merely suggested you let the poor kid sleep." Dad laughed, placing the plate of meat in the middle of the table and motioned for us to sit down.

I looked down at my damp shirt—evidence of the cold glass of water—and shook my head. "Thanks, Mom!"

"Sorry, sweetheart." Mom smiled as she stroked my cheek with the back of her hand. "I'm just glad you're home."

"Well, thank you for letting me sleep," I said, sitting down in the chair next to Anna. "I didn't get much shut-eye on the plane."

"Oh, Jake, I've missed you so much," Mom sulked. "You are the man of the house when your father is away, and Abby and I had to do it all on our own."

Dad rolled his eyes. "Joanna, dear, this is about Jake and Anna." He turned to me and said, "So Jake, tell us about your trip."

I swallowed my steak and looked to Anna for assistance. "Well, we had a great time. Did lots of touristy stuff, stayed in some hostels. That sort of stuff." I had to be careful not to lie, so being evasive was my best option.

Anna picked up, "My favourite part was Venice. We took a gondola ride down this beautiful canal and had a really great time there."

Anna wasn't dishonest. Venice was amazing. The best training camp was there and we stayed in a well-appointed hotel in the city centre.

"How did you like Germany?" Dad asked, leaning over the table as his fork played with a piece of steak.

Germany was where we spent most of our time. It was the main centre for our training. Really intense training with some of the best Gifted Ones in the world. We didn't do any sightseeing in Germany because there wasn't any time with all the training, so I really had nothing I could say about it. But how did *he* know we went to Germany? I hadn't told Mom that.

"Well, I mean, *did* you go to Germany too?" Dad corrected.

Something wasn't right about that. He *knew* something. "Yes, we went to Germany," I answered cautiously.

Anna squeezed my leg under the table. "Germany was lovely," she answered pleasantly.

Abby jumped in. "Oh! Did you get to see the Eiffel Tower in Paris?"

I took this opportunity to change the subject. "Yup. We saw that too. I have some pictures on my camera that I can show you later. We have one of us in front of the Eiffel Tower."

"Paris was very romantic," Anna added, sending a wink in my direction.

"How did you find your way around everywhere?" Mom asked.

"Oh, we hired tour guides a lot," Anna answered. "We had a fantastic tour guide for Paris. He took us everywhere for like pennies."

"Oh yeah, he was great. What was his name again?" I scrunched my eyebrows in an effort to look deep in thought. "Something like Mr. Mar . . . Mr. Mart . . . What was it?"

Dad joined in, "Martinez?"

Busted! I *knew* he knew too much. Just as I was about to ask him how the hell he knew so much about our trip already, he quickly said, "It's a common surname in France."

"It *was* Mr. Martinez!" Anna laughed with amusement. "Mr. Rovert, you're good!"

"Lucky guess." Dad shoved a forkful of steak in his mouth while I studied him cautiously. Mom continued asking Anna more about Paris, and I eventually turned my attention back to the conversation, with the resolution that I would look into my father's peculiar attitude later.

We continued telling stories over dinner, making our once weekly visits out as tourists seem like daily events. Finally, dinner was over and we started clearing the table.

"Oh, David, could you please go into the garage and get the ice-cream cake out of the freezer, please?" Mom asked.

Dad pushed his chair from the table. "Yes, dear," he answered before heading out into the garage.

When he was gone, Mom handed me a smelly box of leftovers. "Jacob, could you please take this box out to the green bin?"

"No problem," I answered, dutifully, following Dad's tracks to the garage.

I opened the garage door and stopped abruptly. Across the room, Dad was standing with his back to the door and lifting the freezer off of the floor, effortlessly, with one hand.

"Dad!" I gasped, not quite comprehending what I was seeing.

Dad quickly set the freezer back down and spun around. "Jake! What . . . what are you doing out here?"

I scanned the room, expecting some sort of danger. Something was out of balance and didn't make sense. "What are *you* doing, Dad?" I finally asked.

"Oh, yeah, of course. That probably looked really strange. Well . . . you see, there was a leak," Dad explained, pointing at the water pooled at his feet, "and I was just trying to figure out where it was coming from."

Almost convincing. "But you lifted the freezer . . . with one hand." I cautiously stepped toward him, still scanning the room for anything out of the ordinary.

Dad sighed and lowered his head. "I'm so sorry, Jake." He slowly stroked his chin with his fingers as if he was contemplating something.

"Dad? What's going on? Who *are* you?" My heart started racing, my palms already sweating. All the signs that something paranormal was happening. I slowly backed up until my back was against the door. I kept reminding myself that Anna was in the house. Alone. Unprotected.

CHAPTER 3

"JAKE," DAD BEGAN as he took a few steps toward me, "I don't know what you think you saw, but believe me when I tell you that it's no big deal."

As much as I wanted to believe him—my father—I just couldn't. Something about it was a lie. Something evil and downright mixed up. But how could that be? How could the man that I called my father since I was three years old, be a fake? What *could* he be?

Dad lowered his head and let out a deep chuckle. It sent a shiver down my spine, then he took another step toward me, extending his hand out to me.

"Stay right there!" I warned, searching the room for something that I could throw between us. All the summer training in Germany on mind movement was about to pay off. I spotted my BMX bike in the corner of the garage and considered hurling it toward Dad.

He stared at me, eyes wide and somehow pleading innocence. No matter how hard I tried, I couldn't look away. Was this some sort of mind trick? Or was it just my upbringing that told me not to look away from my father. As we locked eyes, I suddenly saw a flicker of something in his eyes that made me relax and take a bigger look at the picture. It really wasn't that bad, actually. I *think* I saw him lifting up a freezer a foot or two off the ground. But really, it *could* have been empty. Maybe freezers aren't that heavy after all. Who was I to second guess my father, anyway?

The garage door suddenly opened and Mom stood in the doorway with her hands on her hips. "Trouble finding the freezer, David? And the green bin, Jacob?"

I was finally able to look away.

Dad spoke first. "Sorry, dear. We're on our way in now."

"Did you need more time alone?" Mom asked sarcastically, although that would have been nice.

"No, sweetheart. We're done here. Right Jake?" Dad shot me a look that I wasn't able to challenge.

"I guess so."

I turned to follow Mom into the house. Dad caught my arm and pulled me a step back. "Are we cool, big guy?"

Big guy. That was Dad's nickname for me when I was growing up. He hadn't used it in years, so I took this as his whole-hearted plea for something.

"Yeah, we're good," I lied. But really, what was I supposed to do? Question my father? Wasn't how I was brought up.

I TOOK MY own car to school the next morning, instead of catching a ride with Noah. Pulling into Anna's driveway, I fixed my hair and popped in a stick of gum. Anna came skipping down her walk, a large smile across her face.

"Good morning!" she piped as she hopped into the car.

"You're in a good mood," I noticed, leaning in for a kiss.

"I'm always in a good mood when I'm with you."

"Suck up. What do you want?" I laughed.

"You to love me forever," Anna said, reaching for my hand.

"Is that it? That's like asking me to breathe," I said, giving her hand a squeeze. "As long as I'm alive, it's impossible not to."

Anna sighed. "I'm so happy."

"Me too, babe."

"Hey, do you think anyone will notice my new arms?" Anna rotated her arms in front of her and admired their defined muscular shape.

"I don't care if the girls do, but the guys better not." I cocked my eyebrows at her as she half-heartedly rolled her eyes.

"You have nothing to worry about. I'm all yours."

WE PULLED INTO the school parking lot and headed to the front doors. We were immediately surrounded by a group of friends who we hadn't seen all summer.

"You're back!" Lexie shouted, throwing her arms around us both.

"How was your trip? Tell us everything!" Monica chimed in.

I noticed Eric, Anna's biggest fan, eyeing her up from behind the crowd. I casually put my arm around her waist and pulled her in for a kiss on her forehead.

"We had such a great time!" Anna beamed.

"You two look fantastic!" Monica noticed, giving Anna's arms a squeeze.

Perhaps she should've worn a long-sleeve the first day back.

"We did a lot of rock climbing and some skydiving while we were in Europe," I said, trying my best to divert their inquisitiveness.

"You went skydiving? Tell me all about it!" Lexie gasped. The diversion seemed to work.

"Oh, it was amazing! So, so scary, but really fun!" Anna said.

Someone grabbed my arms and shook me from behind. It was Noah.

"We're here!" he announced.

Lexie nearly pounced on Noah, draping her arms around his neck and squeezing hard. "You look awesome, Noah! I mean . . . uh . . . you have a great tan, and . . . and your *muscles*!" She squeezed Noah's bicep as she leaned in closer.

Everyone chuckled as Lexie flirted with Noah. Everyone but Rachel, that is.

"Okay, break it up," Rachel finally said, pulling Noah from Lexie. I was somewhat surprised, actually. I mean, I knew she'd be internally jealous about it, but I didn't think she'd actually do anything about it.

Anna piped up, "I think what Rachel is trying to say is, the bell rang a few minutes ago so we should get to class." She grabbed my hand and we led the way down the hall.

Noah was still in shock. I looked back to see him standing there with a smirk on his face. I think he was pleased that a catfight nearly broke out over him. This could make for a very interesting year.

"Where are we going first?" I asked Anna, pulling out my class schedule.

"Biology," she answered awkwardly.

"No, that can't be right," I disputed. "I have math on mine." I checked my schedule against Anna's and confirmed that our class schedules weren't the same. "I'll be right back. . . . Noah, watch her," I said as I headed down the corridor and barged into Ms. Peters's office.

"Ms. Peters? What's going on here?" I demanded as I closed the door behind me. I had caught her off guard as she spun around in her chair to face me. "I thought you were going to put Anna and me together?" I threw our class schedules on her desk.

"Jake, please sit down." Ms. Peters motioned toward one of her big leather guest chairs.

"No. Tell me what's going on!" I insisted.

Ms. Peters put her cup of coffee down on the table and leaned back in her chair. She chose her words carefully. "When she's not in your class, Jake, she is with either Rachel or Noah. She will be fine."

"What's going on here?" I could tell by her evasiveness that there was more to this than a scheduling error.

"Okay, but you have to promise not to make an issue out of this."

"I'm not promising anything," I held.

She sighed, but continued, "Anna called me a few weeks ago and asked if I could make some changes in her class schedule. She accepts the fact that she has to be monitored, but she thought it would be best for your relationship if you weren't the one monitoring her the whole time."

I took a stunned step backward. "She *said* that?"

"Jake, if she's feeling suffocated, then this is a safe way to give her some independence."

"She *said* that?" I repeated, feeling my heart cracking just a little.

"It's a lot for her to take. If it's not you, then it's Noah or Nick always on her all the time. Yes, she needs surveillance, but you might want to give her some of her independence back, Jake."

"I let her sleep in her own house at night," I pointed out.

"You had an alarm system hooked up to her house and you have security cameras covering every inch of her home. I hardly consider that giving her freedom."

"Okay. So I'm a little paranoid, but do you blame me? Last year she almost died. In front of my eyes. I am *not* willing to let that happen again." I stormed out of the office still feeling hurt that Anna would feel smothered, and angry that Ms. Peters didn't tell me sooner. As far as I was concerned, she still owed me for how she kept Anna's gift a secret from me last year.

Anna met me in the hallway outside of the Principal's office.

"Jake, I'm so sorry," she said, reaching for my hand.

I pulled away and clenched my jaw. "What do you *want* from me, Anna?"

She seemed caught off at my outburst. "I . . . uh . . ."

"You have *no* idea how hard this is for me, do you?"

"For *you*?" she said quietly, her eyes begging for understanding. And that's when I realized that it really wasn't all about me.

I took a deep breath and relaxed a little, letting my head hang back and my eyes rest on the ceiling tiles. "I'm sorry I've been smothering you. I'll back off," I said, slightly defeated.

"It's not that, Jake. It's just I'm afraid that if we spend every minute of every day together, then you'll get . . . *we'll* get . . . tired of each other." She reached for my hand again and I let her take it. "I love you, Jake. So much. I want to grow old with you. I want you to love me forever. I don't want you to get tired of me . . . yet."

"Anna, I will never get tired of you. You are stuck with me forever." I sighed and pulled away from her. "Now get to class. I'll see you at lunch," I grumbled, walking away in the opposite direction and leaving her in the care of Rachel who was quietly waiting for her.

CHAPTER 4

RUGBY TRY-OUTS WERE held on Thursday after school. While in Europe, Nick had convinced Noah and me to join the team because it was a great way to exert energy and keep fit. Since Nick had come back from graduation to be the rugby coach this year, I assumed Noah and I would be guaranteed a spot on the team and be able to skip the try-outs, but apparently not.

My main concern was leaving Anna during the practises and games, but Claudia and Rachel promised to keep a close eye on her so I agreed. Claudia also decided to come back to coach the cheerleading squad and was still working on getting Rachel and Anna to join her squad, which I thought was hilarious. Anna was definitely not a cheerleader. Kickboxer, yes. Cheerleader, no.

I struggled to keep focused on the drills. Anna was safely sandwiched between Claudia and Rachel on the bleachers, although I knew they wouldn't be as alert as

I would be. Still, I thought I owed it to the girls to trust them. After all, they did an alright job watching over her during the summer when I couldn't be right there with her.

We weren't fifteen minutes into the practise when Nick's head snapped to the side and his stance became firm. Being gifted with Discernment, Nick's sense of good and evil was acutely defined. The look in his eyes was something I'd seen many times, and I knew it wasn't good. I followed his gaze to the bleachers, and saw four large guys standing in front of the girls. Before I could formulate a reaction, the three of us were sprinting toward the bleachers.

My senses heightened. My arms bulged as my heart thudded like a steel drum. I grabbed the first guy I reached and hurled him into the field. Nick and Noah were now standing between the girls and the three remaining guys, who appeared quite alarmed.

"Nick!" Claudia warned. "Let go of him." Claudia slowly pulled the outsider's shirt from Nick's fists. "I'm so sorry," she said sweetly to the other guy.

I paced my breathing as I surveyed the situation. First things first—Anna was safe, and still sitting on the bench next to Rachel. She looked annoyed, but I didn't care—she was safe.

Rachel stood up and coyly said to Noah, "I can take it from here." She looped her arm through the arm of the guy Noah was guarding and led him away. Calling back to the others, she said, "Follow me, guys. I'll show you where the basketball game is."

"The basketball game?" I repeated, realizing that everyone on the field and any spectators were now watching intently.

"Yes, Jake." Anna rolled her eyes. "They were asking for directions to the gym."

"Oops," Nick said, followed by a smack from Claudia.

"You guys have to start trusting Rachel and me. We can take care of Anna. We'll call you if we need help. Trust me," Claudia pleaded. I was sure the urgency in her voice was in part due to reading Anna's thoughts, which I knew were raging at this point.

"I just . . ." I began, but gave up. "Ugh!" I threw my hands up and headed back to the rugby team, waiting in the middle of the field.

It was completely irritating how I wanted so badly to give Anna her freedom and not smother her, but there was just something inside me that couldn't. Something that *knew* if anything happened to her, I'd lose my mind . . . literally.

IT WAS A long forty-five minutes, but when the try-outs finally ended, the girls were calmed down and laughing about something as we approached.

"What's so funny?" Noah asked, tossing the ball back and forth between his hands.

"We were just talking about those basketball guys," Claudia said with a grin.

"What about them?" Noah mumbled.

"One of them asked Rachel for her number," Anna said, nudging Rachel.

You could've roasted marshmallows with the heat coming from Noah. The muscles in his jaw were throbbing and his breathing was heavy.

"Did you give it to him?" I asked Rachel, for Noah's benefit.

Rachel looked up at Noah and smirked. She was enjoying his discomfort. "I don't give out my number."

Noah relaxed a little.

"So I took his instead," she added, deceptively.

I watched Claudia who I knew would be listening to Noah's thoughts. Her troubled expression caused me to create a diversion.

"So guess who made the rugby team?" I said, snagging the ball from Noah and gathering everyone's attention.

"Congrats!" Anna said, jumping up to give me a warm hug. "Go Bedford Blues!"

I swung Anna around in the air and leaned in for a kiss. A change of mind at the last minute had me biting her lower lip instead.

"Ouch! You little!" Anna shouted as I quickly dropped her and started running down the field. I was pacing myself in case there were spectators. No need for anyone to see me sprinting faster than a car on the highway. Anna quickly caught up though, and tackled me, sending us both sprawling on the ground.

"Don't hurt me!" I laughed, trying to hold her back.

I finally let her get in close enough to wrap my arms around and hold her tight as she struggled.

"Damn you and your super strength, Jake!" she growled between struggles.

"You're not believing you can beat me. If you think you can . . ."

"Yeah, I know. If I think I can beat you, I can. Whatever." She gave up and sat beside me on the ground, throwing an elbow into my side, which only hurt her. "Ouch!" she bellowed.

The rest of the group came jogging over.

"Is she okay?" Noah asked, bending down beside her.

"Of course I'm okay!" Anna snapped, caressing her elbow.

I rolled my eyes at her liberty then took her elbow in my hands and rubbed it gently, healing it to its initial perfection.

"It was just my funny bone, Jake!" Anna scowled as she pulled her elbow from my hands.

I laughed, planting a kiss on the top of her head. "Relax, darling. You'll beat me next time."

She shook her head in defeat and turned her attention to Claudia and Rachel instead. "So when did you girls want to go shopping?"

I struggled to keep my lips closed. What had they planned? Did Claudia and Rachel honestly think I would let them take Anna for the whole day anywhere other than within my reach?

Claudia looked at me and rolled her eyes.

Seriously, Claudia, I can't handle it, I thought.

Claudia shook her head then turned to Anna. "How about next weekend then?" she offered.

What? Didn't she just get my last message? *Don't do it, Claudia!*

"Next weekend sounds good to me," Rachel chimed.

"Are you sure next weekend works for you, Claudia?" I prompted, giving her an opportunity to change plans and help me out a little.

Claudia smiled and then said slowly, "I'm one hundred percent positive that next weekend works for me, Jake. Thanks for checking, though."

I was seething! I could feel my jaw muscles throbbing as my teeth fought hard at merging. Words couldn't express the anger I felt toward Claudia at that very moment. *Traitor.*

I knew she was reading my thoughts, so it was no surprise when she muttered, "Control freak."

Anna stood up and brushed the dirt off her pants. "I've got to go to the washroom."

"I'll take you." Claudia jumped up before the words

were even out of her mouth.

"No, *I'll* take her," I argued, stepping between Anna and Claudia.

"Claudia and I can take her, Jake," Rachel added, pulling Anna from me.

"Rachel, stay out of it," Noah warned.

"What the hell is your problem, Claudia?" I shouted, finally letting my anger escape.

"My problem? *My* problem?" Claudia squared off in front of me and challenged my every word. "*I* am not the one with the problem, Jake! *I* am not the one who is smothering Anna! *You* are being way too overprotective! Never letting her do anything for herself. Never trusting anyone but yourself. She won't learn survival skills if you're always doing everything for her, Jake!" Her finger was jabbing into my chest at this point, and her voice was raised loud enough for anyone in the field to hear, had there been anyone left.

I pushed Claudia's hand aside and stared her right in the eyes. "When you've gone through what I went through last year with Anna. When you've almost lost everything that was important to you. When you've gone through something like that, *then* and *only* then can you give me advice on how I should guard her."

"Yeah, that's right, Jake," Claudia taunted, "blame everything on that one time. You do know that she is a miracle worker, right? You do know that she can help herself now, right?"

"No, she can't, Claudia!" I yelled, finally understanding why she had been so careless. "She *can't* help herself. Didn't you know that? Miracle Workers *can't* help themselves. Only others. She is vulnerable. Defenceless. You can use your gift to help yourself. I can use mine . . . but she can't!"

Claudia paused and took a step back. "What?" She looked uneasily at Nick, then Noah, then Rachel.

"She's defenceless, Claudia. She needs us," I said more softly now. I watched her hands tremble as she brought them to her lips. I turned to Anna, but she wasn't there. "Where'd she go?" I panicked.

"She . . ." Claudia stumbled back. Nick caught her. "She got fed up with the fighting and left for the washroom. . . . I didn't know, Jake. . . . I'm so sorry."

Before she was finished, I was sprinting across the field toward the school. I didn't care that there *could* be witnesses to my speed. I just needed to get to Anna. Nick and Noah followed closely behind. By the time we got to the washroom, Rachel and Claudia had caught up. I kicked open the washroom door and hollered, "Anna! Anna, are you in here?"

Nick and Noah darted down the corridors, searching empty classrooms while Rachel and Claudia checked under all the stall doors.

I caught something out of the corner of my eye, by the washroom sinks. It was Anna in the middle of drying her hands; mouth ajar.

"Are you freaking kidding me?" she finally shouted. Probably it did look a little intrusive with me standing in the middle of the girl's washroom and Rachel and Claudia looking under the stalls.

"Baby, I'm so glad you're okay!" I pulled her in and held her close, taking a deep breath of relief. I felt Anna's body tremble, and then heard her sobs. "Are you okay?"

She pulled away from me, taking one last look into my eyes. Her defeated expression wasn't hard to read. She ran from the washroom as tears streamed down her face. Claudia grabbed my arm, pulling me back from following Anna out the door.

"Jake, I'll go. She's really upset."

"*You'll* go?" I said, disgustedly.

"I made a mistake. I understand now. I won't leave her side. Let me go, please!"

I waved my arm in agreement and watched as Claudia chased after Anna.

Rachel slowly came next to me and put her arm around my waist. "She'll get over it, Jake. She just needs some time."

Why was it so damn hard for people to understand the seriousness of Anna's safety? Why was it so hard for *Anna* to understand? Didn't she know her life could be taken in an instant if she were left unprotected? Didn't she even *care*? I felt my neck getting hotter and my breathing getting heavy. What if Claudia couldn't find her? What if those basketball jerks got their hands on her?! My eyes were burning, although I was barely conscious of it. I had to settle myself down. Now. I took enough training sessions on controlling my emotions, that it should've been easy. But it wasn't.

"Jake! Break out of it!" It was Nick. I could see him, red in the face, shaking me. But I couldn't feel it. I could hardly hear his voice. Mostly just white noise.

I saw Noah's fist come at my face, but felt nothing when my head jerked back and my eyes met with the ceiling.

"Noah! What should I do? Should I go get Claudia and Anna?" I heard Rachel shout.

"No! Just guard the door, Rachel!" Noah ordered. "Damn this mind movement shit!"

I needed to know where Anna was. If Claudia had reached her. If she was safe. I needed her to know why I had to be so protective. Why was this so damn difficult?!

"JAKE!" Nick's deep voice again penetrated my thoughts. "Anna is SAFE!"

The white noise seemed to fade as the words repeated in my head: "Anna is safe . . . Anna is safe . . . Anna is safe." Squeezing my eyes closed, I fought to let my senses regain control of my body. Suddenly the burning sensation in my eye became noticeable, causing me to flinch.

"I'll get some cold paper towel," Rachel said

rushing to the sink.

"Careful of the glass," Nick said.

"My . . . my eye?" Confused, I touched my swollen eye and felt the blood trickle down my face.

"I'm sorry, dude," Noah apologized. "I thought if I punched you, you'd snap out of it."

Rachel gently placed the cold paper towel over my eye as I surveyed the room with my good one.

"Crap!" I groaned. Every one of the six mirrors was shattered on the floor. Toilet paper was strewn all over the room. Two stall doors were hanging from their hinges.

"We really need to come up with a way to break you out of that," Rachel said.

"Yeah? How about never letting Anna out of your sight," I suggested. "Keep her safe and I'll have nothing to complain about."

Rachel pursed her lips. "I'll go find a janitor."

I PACED MY bedroom all night, waiting for a phone call from *someone*. When my phone finally rang at half past two in the morning, I was relieved to see it was Anna.

"Hey, you," I answered in my drawn-out apologetic voice.

"We need to talk."

The four worst words in the English language.

CHAPTER 5

ANNA REFUSED TO have the talk over the phone. She wanted me to meet her down at her dock on the water. I quickly got dressed and crept out of the house.

"Anna?" I called into the darkness as I approached the dock.

"I'm down at the end," her smooth voice answered back.

I sat down next to her and watched as her feet made circles in the water.

"Jake, I hate this," Anna began. "I hate feeling like this. I hate feeling like you're stuck to me all the time because it's your job. I hate that I can't even go to the washroom by myself."

I sucked in a deep breath of the cool evening air. Was she going to break up with me? I pinched my eyes closed and slowly let out the air.

"Anna, I am so sorry. I hate how I've upset you." I ran the back of my hand down her smooth arm.

"I've been crying all night, Jake. Do you know why?" She looked up at me with swollen, red eyes that glowed in the moonlight.

"I have an idea." My heart hurt to see her like this. I wanted to throw up.

"Jake, I love you. I really do. But I don't want to spend the rest of our lives like this. With everyone smothering me. With *you* smothering me. I wish . . . sometimes I wish . . . I didn't even have this gift."

Her words stung like alcohol in an open wound. I remembered saying those exact words—I wish I didn't even have this gift—when I first found out that I wasn't able to be with Anna, an ungifted one, because it would put her in danger.

"Anna, I need you to understand why I am so protective. I can tell you that I will back off and give you more freedom, but I honestly don't believe that I can do it." I paused and took a deep breath. "Last year, when you were kidnapped,"—I felt Anna stiffen beside me—"I really felt like my life was over. I literally knew that if anything happened to you that day, I could not go on in this world without killing every single person that hurt you that day. I had so much hatred toward those bastards when I saw them taunting you and holding that gun to your head. I really don't know how I found the strength to hold back from killing them all in that moment."

Anna was watching me intently. We had never

talked about that day before now.

"I can never go through that again, Anna. I love you even more today than I did back then, and I can't imagine living without you."

She wrapped her arms around my waist and laid her head on my shoulder. "I'm so sorry, Jake. I never knew it was that hard for you. You always played so tough."

"Anna, it almost killed me. If you weren't able to come out of that room alive . . . neither was I."

We sat for a few minutes holding each other at the end of the dock. I eventually laid down on the wooden boards and pulled Anna down next me, cradling her head with my arm.

"I love you, Jake. I just wish there was more of just you and me. And not everyone else, you know?"

"I know, babe. Me too." I leaned over her and gently licked the salt of her tears from her lips. She ran her hands through my hair, pulling me closer and slowly lifted her body into mine. I moved my lips down her neck and kissed her tenderly as my mouth made its way to her throat. My lips tickled from the vibrations of her moans and I knew then that it was time to slow down.

"No, don't stop. Please," Anna begged, nibbling on my ear. A trick she knew I was a sucker for.

I fought hard at steadying my heavy breathing as I rolled over onto my back and pulled her on top. She sat on me and flipped her head back, pulling her hair up into a clip. She looked radiant with the moonlight spilling in around her, illuminating her golden hair.

She interlocked her fingers in mine and pulled them above my head, pressing them against the dock, as she slowly breathed in my ear, "Jake, I need you."

The four best words in the English language.

THAT NIGHT AND the next morning, I thought a lot about Anna's wish for us to be able to spend some time with just the two of us. So I decided to plan a night away to our secluded island, just Anna and me. Of course I couldn't let anyone else know because the two of us on our own would be a sure target. And I would have to make sure I kept my distance from Claudia so she didn't read any of my thoughts.

"YOU UP FOR some golf this weekend?" Noah asked as we sat down at the lunch table.

Instinctively, I reached for Anna's hand. The idea of leaving her for several hours in the middle of a Saturday afternoon was enough to send my heart into palpitations. Then I remembered that Anna and I would be on the island tomorrow anyway, so I relaxed just a little. "Yeah, sure. Give me a call around eleven."

Was it wrong to make fake plans with Noah? Maybe, but it was the only way to keep suspicion away.

"Impressive," Rachel said, nudging Anna. "I can't

believe he's going to actually give you a few hours off."

Anna looked just as surprised. "Hmmm." She watched me suspiciously. "What gives?"

"Nothing," I defended, and then I realized how everyone was eyeballing me intensely. I guess it was a bit of a stretch for me. So I added, "On one condition, though."

"Oh, here it comes!" Rachel laughed.

"What!" Anna grumbled as she rolled her eyes.

"You and Rachel hang out at your house. Claudia too." I thought that sounded believable.

"What if I have other plans?" Rachel protested.

I laughed. "Yeah, right! Doing what? Getting your nails done?"

Rachel sneered at me, then answered, "My *hair*, actually."

"Good. Then you can take her with you," I suggested.

"Yaye!" Rachel clapped her hands excitedly. "You and me get to have girls day at the spa!"

Anna smiled and joined in on her excitement. "Are you paying, Jake?"

"I'll pay," Noah piped up, whipping out a hundred dollar bill from his wallet, "as long as you two stay clear of our golf game."

Rachel snatched the bill from his hand and held out her other hand. "It's going to be more than that."

I wasn't about to hand out my money considering I

knew Anna wasn't even going to be there, so I said, "I'll pay Anna's way."

"You don't have to do that, sweetheart." Anna kissed my cheek. "I make enough money to pay my own way." A nice subtle reminder that she was higher up on the pay scale with Interpol given her "rare and specialized" gift.

"Ouch," Noah said, shoving a mouthful of turkey sandwich into his mouth.

"I didn't mean it that way!" Anna quickly added as she flung an orange peel at Noah.

"Sure you didn't! But I guess it's okay. I'll let you buy my forgiveness, Miss Money Bags!" Noah teased.

Anna rolled her eyes. The money issue was a sensitive one for her. She never talked about money and was adamant about saving it for "a rainy day" or "a good cause." I guess when I thought about it, she was starting to rub off on me too; I couldn't remember the last time I wasted money. The last big purchase I made was her tracking bracelet, which set me back to almost zero, but it was well worth it.

AFTER SCHOOL, I headed to my bedroom and packed a duffle bag of clothes and grabbed my camping gear. Then I found a piece of paper and pen and scrawled a note for Noah. I knew he would be calling in the morning for our game of golf. If Anna and I disappeared without leaving a note, there would be hell to pay when we returned. The note read:

Noah, I'm taking Anna away for the weekend.
Sorry about the golf.
Be back Sunday morning around 9:00. We'll be fine.
Jake

"Abby!" I called across the hall.

"Yeah?" she yelled back.

I walked over to her room and handed her the folded up note for Noah. "Could you do me a favour and give this to Noah tomorrow when he comes looking for me?"

"Sure," Abby said, taking the note without looking up from her scrapbook.

"Oh, and if Mom or Dad asks, just tell them I'll be home sometime over the weekend."

Mom rarely ever asked where I was going. I'd often spend the night at Noah's or Anna's on the weekends, so I knew she wouldn't miss me. As for Dad—he only asked for me when he needed something done. The lawn was mowed, my room was clean—I should be good.

"Sure," Abby repeated, dutifully.

EARLY THE NEXT morning I walked into Anna's house, went straight up the stairs and knocked on her bedroom door. She opened the door wearing nothing but a towel around her wet body.

"Come on. Get dressed. I'm taking you somewhere," I said, shielding my eyes out of respect.

"What are you doing?" Anna laughed.

"Get a change of clothes for tonight and tomorrow. And a bathing suit," I instructed. "I'll meet you downstairs."

"Wait! Where are we going? What should I pack?"

"Just pack regular clothes. Can't tell you where we're going 'till no one is around to hear. Hurry, let's go!" I was nervous that Claudia and Rachel might show up. Then we'd be caught.

In a few minutes, however, we were on our way out the door and down the path in her backyard to the dock.

"We're going to the island? For the night?" Anna asked with a hint of excitement in her voice.

"That's the plan. I was thinking just the two of us, no one to bother us. It should be fun, right?"

"*Love* the idea!" she said as she skipped alongside of me. "What did the group say?"

"Uh, I didn't exactly tell them yet."

Anna came to an abrupt halt. "You didn't tell them?" she asked, eyebrows pitched.

"No, I didn't. I knew they'd object, citing various reasons why the two of us should not go out there unprotected. Plus, if any Defiers came looking for you, all they'd have to do is read Noah or Rachel's minds to know where we were." I wrapped my arms around Anna and kissed the top of her head.

"You did this because of me, didn't you?" Anna pouted.

"We need some alone time. . . . Yes, I did it for you."

She held me tightly and I nearly had to struggle to breathe. "This is so sweet. You're the best."

Within minutes we were in the canoe, paddling to our own private oasis. The bright yellow life jackets we'd been putting on for the last six years didn't quite fit anymore, but I still made Anna wear hers the best she could. I could hear her muttering obscenities about me as she begrudgingly loosened the straps to fit. It made me smile, though. This was how our trip to the island always went—me telling her what to do, and her resenting me for it all the way to the island. If all went according to plan, this was going to be one weekend we both wouldn't soon forget. But not everything goes as planned, and we know that all too well.

CHAPTER 6

THE WATER RIPPLED gently around our canoe as we
floated across the lake. Everything was silent, save for a
couple of birds who could be heard singing in the
distance. Within an hour we were manoeuvring our
canoe through the passageway to the private lake
which encircled our own private island.

"I can't believe we haven't been here since last
spring," Anna said as she hopped out of the canoe and
into the knee-deep water.

I crawled out behind her and started pulling the
canoe up onto the shore. "We've had some great times
here," I recalled.

Then I felt a splash of cold water over my back. I
dropped the rope and chased the giggling culprit
through the water.

"You are going down!" I warned as I caught up to
her and dove into the water with Anna in my arms.

"I should've known better than to mess with you,"

Anna laughed when we came up for air. She wrapped her wet arms around my neck and tickled my nose with hers. We waded in the cool water, holding each other as if there were no cares in the world. As if nothing else mattered.

Eventually, I grabbed our gear from the canoe and we headed into the island toward our special place. Still standing tall and strong, the leaves on the old oak tussled in the gentle breeze. The hill it rested on was overgrown with daisies and knee-deep grass. We found a relatively level spot in the field, close to the old oak tree, and pitched our tent. Anna had her sleeping bag, pillow and clothes all laid out neatly inside the tent before I even finished driving the last stake.

"This is going to be so much fun!" she exclaimed, twirling around in the field. I stopped unpacking and watched her spin. She bent over and started picking daisies from the grass.

"He loves me, he loves me not . . ." I heard her mutter as she skipped through the field, plucking petals from the flowers. She circled around the field, then made her way back over to the tent and looked up to find me watching her. "What are you smiling about?"

I pulled her close and took the petal-less stem from her hand. "Does he love you?"

Anna pouted. "No."

"Well, that flower must be broken." I pulled the stem from her fingers and tossed it away. "'Cause he most definitely loves you."

The corners of her mouth turned up again and a familiar look blanketed her eyes.

"What? What are you thinking?" My eyes flickered back and forth between hers. Claudia's ability to read minds would definitely be useful to have around Anna. What I would give to be able to know what she was thinking all the time.

Before I knew it, I was on my back with Anna standing over top of me. "Didn't see that coming, did ya, tough guy?" Anna laughed, looking a little too confident.

It took me a few seconds to get my bearings and to realize that she totally just took me down. Completely off my guard. Flat on my back. Impressive!

"Are . . . are you okay?" she asked with gentle concern. But before she could say another word, I swiped her legs and caught her in mid-air, cradling her in my arms.

"I'm fine," I said with a smirk. "How are *you*?"

She carefully relaxed and draped her arms around my neck. "Better now that I'm in your arms." She sat up and kissed my nose. Then, without warning, she launched herself up into the air and flipped over my head, landing behind me. "You know I could kill you right now," she whispered in my ear with one arm locked around my throat and the other hand pressed against the back of my head.

"I see you've been paying close attention in your self-defence classes," I observed. I considered showing her how one could get out of such hold, but decided to let her beat me instead. Otherwise, this could go on all night. I tapped my hand three times on the ground. "You win, babe."

She released her hold and danced around me in celebration. "You didn't see *that* one coming, did you?"

"Not at all. Where did you ever learn that flip technique? That was pretty Spiderman-ish!"

She laid down in the grass beside me. "Training with Claudia has its benefits. She's been showing me and Rachel all her cheerleading moves."

"Really? Impressive." I thought about Claudia and how, by now, she'd be cursing my name for running off with Anna.

"Do you think they're looking for us yet?" Anna smiled, obviously pleased with the fact that we had made a successful escape.

I checked my watch and, confirming it was close to noon, replied, "Definitely. Noah and I had plans to play golf at eleven." I stretched out on the grass next to Anna and watched the clouds float by.

"What do you think they'll do?"

"Oh, I'm sure they'll be pretty mad. I left a note with Abby so she'll give it to Noah when they come to the house looking for clues." I chuckled at the idea of all of them showing up with the intention of rummaging through my bedroom, dusting for fingerprints and checking for tire marks in the driveway.

"You didn't tell them where we are, did you?" Anna sat up quickly and stared at me accusingly.

"Of course not, my freedom-seeking princess," I teased.

"Did you bring your cell phone?" She wasn't yet done her interrogation.

"Are you kidding? Ms. Peters would have us tracked down in about thirty minutes or less. No cell phone."

She lay back down and closed her eyes, allowing the sun to bounce off her smooth skin. "Maybe this will show them we can handle being on our own more often. I mean, seriously, you're a healer and I'm a miracle worker—what could possibly happen to us?"

"Geez, Anna! Don't say stuff like that! A lot could happen to us, and more importantly, to *you!*" My heart began beating so heavily that I thought my chest might collapse.

Anna propped herself onto her side and placed her hand softly on my chest. "Relax." Her warm breath tickled my ear lobe. I closed my eyes and felt my heart resume a normal beat. Her fingers skimmed over my torso and down to my waist. Her hand slowly slid up my shirt and found its way back up to my chest. I felt her lips on my ear as she whispered, "You're hungry."

The corner of my mouth curled up. "You felt that?"

"Seriously? I think the animals on the island felt that." She stood up and dusted off her pants. "Why don't you cook us up some food while I go get changed out of these damp clothes."

Instinctively, I jumped up to follow. Two steps in, I remembered where we were and that tagging along wasn't really necessary. Anna's smile suggested she enjoyed exercising her freedom to be able to leave my side.

THE HOTDOGS WEREN'T gourmet, but we still managed to scoff down half the package. After lunch, we blazed a new trail down to the lake and sat on a large rock jutting out of the water.

"Jake, this is so perfect. I really needed this." Anna kicked off her sandals and submerged her feet in the water.

I nodded in agreement. "Do you miss Europe yet?"

"Ummm . . ." Anna began, "yes and no, I guess."

"How so?"

"I just mean that we had a lot of fun there this summer and I loved every minute of it, but on the other hand, I can't really miss a place if you're still with me."

"Well said."

"I do miss Portugal a little. That was so much fun," Anna recalled.

"That's because we hardly had to do any training there. It was the closest thing we had to an actual vacation," I reminded her.

"True. The only annoying thing was all the security on me all the time." Anna nudged me.

"Oh, come on! I had no choice, babe. You know that!"

"You, Nick, Noah, Rachel and Claudia would have been plenty! I really don't think those other three guys were necessary."

I rolled my eyes at her innocent stubbornness. "First of all, Nick and Claudia had bad vibes every time we went off the training camp. Secondly, Rachel had a vision of all of us sitting around at the beach, but you weren't there. And thirdly, my sweet, you were the hottest thing wearing a bikini within a hundred mile radius and there was no way I was letting anyone near you!"

Anna smiled. "Not quite." But not letting me interject, she quickly added, "Oh! Remember when Noah and Rachel got in that big fight in Paris? What on earth was that about? They were speaking French and I couldn't keep up."

"Yeah, that was pretty funny. That was the night of our big party with all the Gifted Ones from Paris, right? So this girl who had been flirting with Noah all week followed him to the washroom and apparently she stopped him and they started talking and then before he knew it, she was kissing him. But bad timing for Noah, Rachel walked around the corner and saw it all."

Anna's mouth was agape. "Are you kidding me? Who was it?"

"The girl? Oh, I don't remember. I think it was something like . . ."

"Was it Naomi?"

"Yeah, yeah. That's it. Naomi. Did you guys know her?"

"Yes! She was in our lip-reading class and Rachel did *not* like her one bit. We were doing this one drill where half the class stood on one side of the room and half of us were standing on the other side and we had to lip read what they were saying. They were all supposed to be mouthing this unified sentence 'no one will take my tunic,' but Rachel swears that Naomi mouthed 'Noah will be mine tonight.'

"Anyway, she was so sure of it but I just told her she must have read her wrong. I remember looking to Claudia for reassurance, but she didn't back me. She must have known." Anna shook her head as she pieced the puzzle together.

"Well, that explains why Rachel was all over Noah that afternoon. He couldn't figure her out. One minute she tells him that she doesn't want a boyfriend and the next minute she can't do anything for herself and needs Noah to tie her shoes for her."

"Wow, I did not know he kissed her. Why would he do that?" Anna asked, seemingly disgusted.

"What do you mean?"

"Well, he obviously knows how Rachel feels about him. Why would he kiss another girl?"

At the risk of adding fuel to a conversation that I didn't even want to have, I felt the need to defend Noah. "Noah didn't kiss *her*. *She* kissed *him*. And Rachel and Noah aren't even together. She keeps rejecting him. Is he supposed to wait around for her?"

Anna turned on the rock and looked at me straight on. "Are you serious, Jake? Together or not, Noah and Rachel *are* a couple. Everyone knows it. He likes her. She likes him."

"Then enlighten me, Anna. Why won't she just admit it and get on with it?"

Anna bit her lip and turned back toward the water.

"You know something, don't you?" I pried, craning my neck to read her face.

She struggled with something I knew she wanted to tell me, but obviously felt a sense of duty to withhold.

"Never mind. I don't care enough anyway. I'm just happy to be here with you and have this whole place to ourselves." I stood up and whipped off my shirt, throwing it to the ground. "Let's go for a swim."

Anna smiled with a look of appreciation. Girls and their secrets! I rolled my eyes and hopped in the water, pulling Anna in behind me.

THE CAMPFIRE LET off a good amount of heat as we sat on a log roasting marshmallows, lamenting over our last few waking hours on the island by ourselves.

"This was really great, Jake. Thank you." Anna rested her head against my shoulder.

I finished browning my marshmallow to perfection and slid it off for Anna.

"We should probably head to bed soon," she said, checking her watch. "It's only ten o'clock but I'm exhausted." She yawned, adding effect to her story.

"I'm ready," I agreed, dumping a bucket of water on our fire.

CHAPTER 7

THE HEAT OF the tent was enough to wake me several hours earlier than I was accustomed to on a Sunday morning. So as not to wake Anna, I quietly lifted my hand out of my sleeping bag to check the time. Seven o'clock. Seriously? On a weekend? There was no point in going back to sleep though—it was too damn hot! I slowly unzipped my sleeping bag and looked back at Anna to make sure I was being quiet enough. She wasn't there.

"Anna?" I called out as I quickly pulled on some pants. She didn't answer so I unzipped the tent door and headed out. No sign of her. "Anna!" I shouted into the field. Damnit! How long had she been gone? What happened to her?!

I immediately regretted not bringing my cell phone with the integrated tracking device. I went back to the tent and grabbed my Swiss Army knife from my backpack and headed across the clearing into the woods. "ANNA!" I shouted, but stopped suddenly when I heard a crackling noise coming from in the woods. Frozen, my eyes darted from this tree to that tree, looking for a sign of something. My adrenaline was pumping and I was now in rescue mode. Full alert. Full strength.

I took one careful step into the woods and sensed the closeness of something. Someone lurking. Waiting to attack. Then suddenly the bush behind me rustled slightly and a figure pounced toward me. Before it had a chance to attack, I let out a deafening growl and hurled the attacker thirty or more feet into the woods, causing its body to slam against a tree and crumple to the ground.

"Jake . . . help . . ." Anna's weak voice trembled from a distance. It took me a second to realize where her voice was coming from. . . . Thirty feet into the woods—at the base of the tree!

"No!" I gasped as I realized my presumed attacker was none other than Anna. I sprinted to her and picked her up in my arms. Blood trickled from the back of her head. "Anna! Anna, I . . . I didn't know. . . . I'm so sorry!" I cried.

She made a pitiful moan as she reached up to touch the back of her head. "Ouch."

What kind of monster was I? I could've killed her! I closed my eyes to concentrate on healing her. "Don't move, Anna. I'll fix you. I'm so sorry, baby." I covered her head with my hands and thought healing images. I prayed that I hadn't damaged her permanently in any way. I imagined her head completely healed, without spot or wrinkle. Next, I ran my hands over her body to absolve it of any bruises or imperfections. Right down to her toes, I made sure not to miss one inch of her body.

Feeling so ashamed, I finally looked up at Anna. She had a slight smile on her face. "You done yet? I was healed like ten minutes ago."

"This is *not* funny!" I scolded. "I could've killed you." I sat back against the tree and felt the tears leak from my eyes. Anna sat quietly beside me for several minutes.

"Jake, I didn't mean to startle you. I had just gone to use the washroom and when I came back up through the woods, I saw you standing there with your back to me, so I thought it would be fun to try and sneak up on you."

I didn't respond. I couldn't. Holding my head in my hands, I stared mindlessly at my feet. *What did I do?* If I had been gifted with Discernment like Nick and Claudia, I would've been able to discern good from evil and I would've known that my so-called attacker was not a threat. She could be dead right now. I looked down at the knife, lying on the ground between my feet. She could be dead right now.

"Jake?" Anna gave a gentle pull at my arm. "Are

you mad at me?"

I squeezed the last of the tears from my eyes and wiped them away with my palms. Taking a deep breath, I answered, "No, Anna. I'm not mad at you. I'm just struggling with myself right now."

"Why? It's not *your* fault. You were just acting on instincts. Protecting yourself."

"Yeah, and my so-called instincts caused me to almost kill the one girl who means the most to me in this world. I was protecting you, Anna. And in doing that, I almost killed you."

Anna sat down in front me and softly touched my legs. "How were you supposed to know? It was really stupid of me. I didn't realize you were on alert."

How was I supposed to know? She was right. If I had the gift of Discernment, then I would've known. But I didn't. So how could I? There was only one way to ensure that this would never happen again. . . . I needed that gift.

"Jake, let's just forget about it. I'm okay. See?" Anna stood up and did some sort of girly twirl.

I tried to force back a smile, but failed miserably, so I stood up and pulled her in close. "That won't happen again. I promise."

"Me too."

AFTER BREAKFAST, WE packed up our gear and headed back to the canoe. I was feeling better, knowing Anna was completely fine, although I wasn't ready to laugh about it yet, like Anna seemed to be able to do. We came to the shore of the lake and looked up and down for the canoe.

"Where'd we put it?" Anna asked as she set her gear down on the rocks.

Confused, I walked over to the fallen tree on the shore and sat down. "This is where we always tie it up. Right here."

"Yeah, I know." Anna put her finger to her lips. "I don't remember tying it up, though, do you?"

I thought back to the morning before and remembered getting out of the canoe and pulling the rope out to tie it up . . . but then Anna splashed me and I took off after her. "I didn't tie it up," I confessed aloud.

"Because I splashed you, right?"

"No, not because you splashed me. Because I forgot."

"Because you got distracted. Because of me, right?"

"Are you *trying* to cause a fight? It wasn't because of you. Now give it up." I scanned the lake to see if I could spot the canoe floating nearby. No such luck.

"Okay, so we just call Noah and give him directions to get here. He can take the neighbours' canoe," Anna suggested.

I smirked and looked up at Anna. "Didn't bring my cell phone, remember?"

"Oh yeah, right."

We sat in silence for a few minutes. Then Anna stood up and clapped her hands together. "Well, I guess there's only one thing left to do."

"We can't swim it, Anna," I guessed.

Anna pulled me up off the log. "We go have some fun. The group is bound to start looking for us by lunchtime. They'll somehow figure it out and find us."

Her sense of optimism was refreshing. "And how do you think they'll find us?"

"I don't know. They'll probably call in tracking dogs or something. Helicopters, maybe? Who knows. Who cares!" She grabbed me by my arms. "Jake! You and I are stranded on a deserted island. Let's make the best of it."

Sounded good to me.

WE LEFT OUR bags where they were and decided to take a walk around the island to make sure the canoe wasn't sitting somewhere close by. I loved this time of day, although I rarely took time to enjoy it. The sun was still making its debut while the loons in the lake began calling to each other. The water was still and life just seemed to be a whole lot simpler.

"I couldn't be happier right now," Anna finally said as she slid her hand into mine.

I stopped at a large, flat-faced rock and leaned up against it, pulling Anna into me. "Me too."

Anna pressed her face into my chest and I felt her inhale. "You smell so good."

"Really? 'Cause I need a shower," I chuckled.

"Then how about we go swimming?" And before I could suggest that we wait for the water to warm up a bit, she was stripped down to her bikini and running through the water. "Come on, Jake!"

I groaned. It was going to be cold. She disappeared under the water and I waited for her to come back up. I waited and waited. She was just trying to get me in faster, but could I take that risk? I dove in the water after her and frantically searched the water. I caught sight of her starring at me with wide-eyes and bubbles pouring out of her mouth as she laughed at me. Her hair floated angelically around her face.

Bursting out of the water, I shouted, "Anna Taylor, you are going to be the death of me!"

Her sneaky eyes peeked above the water and then she finally came up for air. "A minute and twenty-four seconds," she announced proudly.

"What are you—half fish?"

"No, but I'm lifeguard certified. You need to be able to do these things, you know."

"No, I didn't know. Thanks for informing me."

Anna swam over to me and wrapped her legs around my waist as she floated on her back. "This feels so nice," she moaned.

I held her smooth hips and watched the water lap

over her body. She giggled as she struggled to pull herself up. She draped her arms around my neck and I couldn't resist stealing a quick kiss, which lingered a little longer. I couldn't let her go. She fit perfectly in my arms. We stumbled our way through the water toward the beach area, and I rested her gently on a large rock, keeping my lips to hers.

She wrapped her legs around my torso and held me close, her fingers tangled through my hair. "Jake?" she whispered in my ear. "Remember when you said you'd do anything for me?"

"Yeah?" I breathed.

"I don't want you to stop," she said.

I considered her words as her fingers moved up my neck into my hair. I slowly pulled away and sat up, catching my breath and bringing my senses back to reality.

"We should walk around the island again. Maybe we can spot the canoe," I said, watching her carefully.

"What are you doing?" Anna sat up and kissed my neck. "I said I didn't want you to stop. I love you."

"I love you too, Anna. That's why I *am* stopping."

"That doesn't make any sense," she challenged, playfully biting my earlobe.

"I don't want you to regret anything." I had to close my eyes and focus hard on not giving in.

"Jake, I won't regret it. I promise." Anna sat back and held my face in her hands. "I know someday we'll be married."

"So let's wait for *someday*. Let's wait until we're married. It will be more special. Like our first real adventure as one." I smiled in an effort to rid the blanket of frustration on her face.

"Fine," Anna said as she turned away and pulled her hair into a ponytail.

"Don't be mad, babe. There is nothing I want more right now than to make you happy. But I think in the long run, this is best for you. For us." I stood up and took her hands. "I love you so much, Anna. I'd give you the world if I could. If I thought it was what you needed."

The lines in her forehead faded just a little, and the corner of her mouth twitched. "You really are the perfect boyfriend, aren't you?"

"I'm trying."

"Thank you."

"For?"

"Respecting me."

I laughed, relieved. "Thank you for understanding."

"Always."

CHAPTER 8

WE ATE THE last of our food by a cozy fire near the old oak tree as the sun started to set. We had spent most of the day on the shore, waiting for a sign of someone coming to our rescue, but the lake remained quiet.

"What if they can't find us?" Anna finally asked, hooking her arm in mine as we sat against the comfort of the oak's base.

I squeezed her hand. "I guess we'll have to build a raft. Or maybe the canoe will find its way back."

"Either way, I think this all happened for a reason. I think God wanted us to spend more time together." Anna seemed pleased with her theory.

I smirked. "Probably."

"You don't believe that, do you?"

"Hmm?" I was hoping not to have this conversation . . . again.

"You don't believe that everything happens for a reason, do you?"

I sighed and decided to make the best of it. "I believe that *you* believe it."

"Jacob!" she scolded. "Why do you think things happen then? Stuff like this? Us being stranded on this island. God could have made sure that canoe stayed on the shore. But don't you think it drifted away for a reason?"

I pretended to contemplate her words in deep thought, but really I was trying to decide whether to cook up the last two hotdogs or save them in case we had to stay for another meal.

"Jake?"

"I'm thinking! I'm thinking!" I decided to save the hotdogs, then turned my attention to Anna, feeding into her obvious need for a deep discussion. "Okay, so if everything happens for a reason, why do kids die?"

Anna stopped, her eyes locked with mine. After a moment, she answered, "Do you believe death is a bad thing for a child?"

"Well, it can't be good."

"Don't you think heaven is a better place than here?"

"Than *here*?" I gave a sweep of my arm around the meadow. "This *is* heaven."

"Jake, be serious for a minute." Anna pressed her fingertips together as she thought. "Death is only sad for the people who are left behind. Those that go to heaven are in a better place."

"Okay, so if a kid dies and goes to heaven, don't you think he'd miss his mom and dad, and therefore be sad?"

"I think he still gets to see them everyday."

"And don't you think that would be kind of sad for the kid to be able to see his parents but not be able to receive any sort of love back from them?"

"But he does. I believe that while we sleep, we spend time with our loved ones in heaven."

I gave her a blank look as I wondered how on earth she came up with such a theory.

"Haven't you ever dreamed about your grandparents or anyone that has died?"

"Uh . . . no," I said, quite assuredly. "But you have, I take it?"

Anna smiled. "It was about a week after my cousin Grace was killed in a car accident. We were really close. Like sisters. We were only twelve when she died and I remember feeling like no one understood what I was going through. I just wanted to be alone so I could hold on to all of our memories and cry." Anna picked up a twig and broke pieces of it off as she continued. "So about a week after the funeral, I went to bed holding a picture of us in one hand and our 'best friends' necklace in the other. And that night I had the most vivid dream of her.

"We were sitting down by the river behind her house and skipping rocks like we used to always do.

We were both laughing, but then she got quiet and looked at me so seriously and said, 'Anna, please don't be sad that I went to heaven. I love it here. One day we'll be together again and we'll play jump rope like we used to.' I remember hugging her and feeling so happy for her. Then she said to me, 'Can you tell Mom that I've been sleeping in her bed every night and I want her sleep there too?'" Anna wiped a tear slipping down her cheek. "When I woke up I wondered if it was just a dream, but the next weekend when we were at Grace's house visiting my Aunt, I told her about my dream and told her what Grace had said, and my Aunt just started crying. Apparently she had been sleeping in Grace's bed since the night she died."

I reached over and caught another tear escaping Anna's eye. "Wow," was all I could say.

"So *that's* why I believe."

I gave Anna a minute to collect herself, then I quietly asked, "So why do you think Grace died?"

Anna stopped and looked up at me with serious eyes. "Grace died because some idiot had a couple of beer and thought it was okay to drive home from a party."

"Yeah, but do you think there was a reason for her death?"

"That was it. It was a man-made accident, Jake. I'm sure her death had a huge impact on that driver, who survived but has to live with what he's done for the rest of his life."

I nodded.

"Or maybe she was meant to do great things, and the Defiers just wanted to get rid of her."

I felt my eyebrows crinkle as I let that last theory settle.

"Anyway, don't know why I brought all that up." Anna laughed as she stood up and stretched. "It's starting to get dark. Do you think we should pitch the tent again?"

"Yeah, probably." I followed her to our gear and began unpacking the tent as I thought about Anna and her cousin Grace. How awful that must have been for her—to lose a cousin and a close friend like that. "Do you still dream about Grace?" I carefully asked.

She continued sliding the poles through the tent. "Every now and then. It's usually dreams of us playing jump rope, though." She laughed. "We used to have competitions to see who could jump the longest. She always won."

"Really? That surprises me," I teased.

"You can't win 'em all!"

"If you like, we could jump rope when we get back. I'm sure you'll beat me," I offered.

"Maybe I'll take you up on that sometime."

We finished pitching the tent and climbed inside. Anna curled up next to me and I don't think I had my sleeping bag zipped up before I fell asleep.

I WOKE UP to the feeling that I was being watched, and sure enough Anna was leaning over top of me with a silly grin on her face.

I tried to mask my morning breath as I said in my gruff morning voice, "What?"

"I've been watching you sleep for the last"—she checked her new watch proudly—"twenty minutes."

I struggled to sit up as I rubbed the sleep from my eyes. "You're a freak," I mumbled.

"*Me*? You're the one who sleep talks about baking apple pies!" Anna laughed as she struggled to roll her sleeping bag.

The memories of my latest dream came flooding back. I was in my grandmother's kitchen talking to her about Anna and our trip to Europe. We were baking apple pies like we always used to, and she was telling me about the new knitting club she joined. "With my grandmother."

Anna stopped and looked up at me. "Huh?"

"I was baking apple pies with my grandmother," I said, trying to recall more details from my nostalgic dream.

"The dead one?"

"Yeah," was all I could say. Maybe her theory was right. Maybe I had really just visited my grandmother. It did seem real. I shook my head to rid the confusing thoughts and finished packing.

"We should get down to the shore and start figuring

out how to make a raft or something," I said, unzipping the tent and heading out into the warm morning sun.

WE WERE ONLY at the shore for a few minutes, having just finished washing our faces and brushing our teeth, when I heard a low rumbling noise. "Do you hear that?" I asked.

"No," Anna answered, cocking her head toward the lake. The noise got louder.

"I think it's a motor." In the distance, at the mouth of the cove, a small white object came barrelling around the corner. "It's a boat!" I shouted.

Anna jumped up on the fallen tree and started waving her arms to the speedboat fast approaching. "We're over here!" she shouted.

"Anna, get down from there!" I warned, not yet convinced that our approaching visitors were harmless.

"They're waving back. I can see Rachel's hair blowing. It's them!" Anna hopped off the log and into my arms. "I love you so much, Jake! I had so much fun this weekend!"

I laughed. "Me too." Holding her tight, I enjoyed our last minute alone. "How's your head?" I asked, stroking it softly.

"It's completely fine, Jake. I had forgotten all about it. Don't worry about it." Anna pulled away and touched her finger to my lip. "Thank you so much for this weekend."

"Thank *you*." I looked up and saw the boat slowing down, only about twenty feet away now. Nick was driving with Noah beside him in the front. Rachel and Claudia were standing up behind them. Rachel was waving excitedly, but Claudia looked mad as hell.

"Get in!" Claudia scowled at me, then turned sweetly to Anna. "How are you? Are you okay?" She helped Anna into the boat.

"We're perfectly fine, Claudia. We had a great time." I caught Anna giving Claudia a look and guessed that she was also telling her something without words. Claudia clenched her jaw and forced a smile.

"Hi, Claudia," I said sweetly. "Miss me?"

Nick coughed to suppress his laughter. "Did she ever! She's been talking about you all weekend." He slapped my back as I took Noah's seat next to him. "Have a good trip, buddy?"

"Yeah, it was good. Sorry about having to skip out on you guys like that."

Noah squeezed my shoulder. "It was the only way, man. *Most* of us understand." He jerked his head back toward Claudia as Nick manoeuvred us away from the island.

"How'd you guys find us?" Anna asked.

"Well, we practically tore both your houses apart looking for clues," Claudia grumbled. "We figured out that you were going camping somewhere because Jake's camping gear was gone, but we had to interrogate both your families."

"What'd my dad say?" I asked as casually as I could.

"Your dad was a little weird, actually," Noah said. "He left the room while we were talking to Abby and came back a few minutes later suddenly remembering you telling him that you were thinking about going for a hike on the other side of the lake."

Wait a second! I didn't tell Dad anything like that! How did he know where we were? And was he somehow responsible for our canoe going missing?

"So we spent most of yesterday walking the perimeter of the lake looking for you guys," Nick added.

"But since that didn't work out," Noah said, "luckily Rachel had a vision last night that you were stranded on an island."

"Really?" I asked, quite impressed with Rachel's developing skill. That was Rachel's biggest obstacle throughout summer training. No matter how hard she tried, she couldn't control her prophetic visions. Not being able to use them when she needed them.

Rachel smiled proudly. "I know, right?" She sat down on the floor of the boat between Noah's legs. "So we checked out the topographic maps of the area and found this little hidden island. Then we borrowed a speedboat from a friend of your dad's and came to find you."

"And it's a good thing, too," Anna laughed, "because Jake was about to build us a raft!"

Everyone seemed to find humour in that but me.

"Geez, you would've sunk!" Noah teased.

"Hilarious." I shot a scowl to Anna then pulled her up front to sit on my lap.

"I'm just kidding, baby," she said with a smirk.

I wrapped my arms around her waist and held her tight as we headed home. In the speedboat, it took less than ten minutes to get back to Anna's dock. I climbed out after Nick, then helped Anna out. She was still smiling from ear to ear.

"I think I'm going to head home and have a shower," I announced.

"Sure. Claudia and I can go with Anna to her house," Rachel offered.

"That's okay, guys. I'm just going to have a shower and a nap. I'll be fine," Anna said, hauling her backpack over her shoulder.

"I've got nothing planned," said Noah. "I can park down the street and keep watch for a while."

Anna chewed on her lower lip as everyone argued over who was going to protect her next.

"Guys, she's fine. I'm just down the street if she needs anything," I said confidently, remembering Anna's new bracelet.

Five blank faces stared back at me. Then I caught Claudia's expression change to an understanding one as I tried unsuccessfully to keep the tracking bracelet out of my thoughts.

"Jake's right," Claudia began. "She'll be fine."

The remaining four disbelieving faces looked to Claudia then back to me. Claudia and I locked eyes and that's when I knew that *she* knew.

Thank you, I thought.

She winked.

Maybe this would be the beginning of a new camaraderie.

CHAPTER 9

IT WASN'T DIFFICULT to gauge Ms. Peters's mood when we walked into her office the next morning. Sitting at her desk, arms folded and jaw clenched, I instantly regretted leaving the island. Anna reached for my hand and stood close to my side as I secured the door behind us.

I pulled a chair out for Anna and carefully watched Ms. Peters as I took my place in the chair next to Anna. "Good morning," I said hesitantly.

Ms. Peters took a deep breath and then exhaled loudly as she stood up to pace the room. "You knew better," she said coolly.

"Ms. Peters," Anna began, "Jake took every necessary precaution. We were completely safe."

Ms. Peters pursed her lips and forced a smile. "Thank you, Anna. You may go to class now." She opened the office door and Anna shot me a look as she left quietly. When the door closed behind her, Ms.

Peters slowly turned her attention back to me—the real target. "What were you thinking, Jacob?"

I didn't know if this was one of those times where you just sit still and be quiet, waiting for the rest of the lecture, or if it was a legitimate question. I decided to answer anyway. I wasn't in the mood for another lecture.

Before I could answer, she asked again, "Jake? Talk to me! *What* were you *thinking*?"

"I was *thinking* that when Anna told me she sometimes wished she didn't have her gift, I had to do something about it." I folded my arms defensively.

Ms. Peters took a step backward. "She said that?" She looked personally hurt by that. I almost regretted telling her.

"Yeah, and I knew she needed this weekend." I stood up and walked to the window. "Ms. Peters, it's not something I would normally do. But I felt like we didn't have another choice."

She slowly nodded as she chewed on her lower lip.

"And look at her now," I said. "She's like a new person again. Like her old self."

"Her spirit is definitely stronger now." Ms. Peters nodded in agreement. Then she lowered her head to her folded hands. "Jake, just please don't do anything like that again unless you consult me first, okay? We can't afford to lose the both of you. Time is closing in on us, and we need to be ready. Together."

"What do you mean—time is closing in?"

The concern in Ms. Peters's eyes sent a chill down my spine. "Your powers are getting stronger, Jake. We all are." She walked to the window, keeping her back to me. "And so are they."

"The bad guys?" I clarified.

"Yes, the Defiers. There has been a great shift in their energy. Their plan is in motion, and they will attack when we least expect it. We must be ready."

I wasn't sure what to say next. Part of me wanted to shout, 'bring it on!' but the other part of me knew that Anna would be their first target. A miracle worker destroyed.

"I'm sorry, Jake," Ms. Peters said as she walked toward me and rested a firm hand on my shoulder. "Don't concern yourself with those matters yet. Just concentrate on your training and keeping Anna safe."

I nodded.

"Thank you. You can go to class now." She held the door open for me as I left. I didn't look back. I didn't want to see her eyes full of the fear that I knew was there.

ON MY WAY to the cafeteria for lunch, Claudia caught up with me in the hallway, her pom-poms dangling from her left hand.

"Jake!" she called as she took my arm and pulled me aside.

"What's up?"

She looked around and then pulled me down to her level. "I want to apologize for being so hard on you yesterday. . . . You know, about the runaway island bit?"

"Sure." I hadn't put much weight to Claudia's cold shoulder. I figured it was just a girl thing and she'd get over it.

"It's not that," she said, obviously reading my thoughts again.

"Okay?" I raised my eyebrows with an invitation for her to explain.

"So don't be mad at me for telling you this, alright?"

"No promises." She reads my damn thoughts, how could I promise not to be mad? I could promise to *pretend* not to be mad. "Just spit it out, Claudia."

"I thought you took Anna to the island to *be* with her," she blurted, holding a look on her face that pleaded my forgiveness.

"Seriously?" I suppressed a laugh.

"I know. It was horrible of me to think that of you. I guess I just figured you were like most other guys, and I know you've had thoughts about her, so I just assumed. I'm sorry."

"Wait. How do you know we didn't?" Had she been so bold to come out and ask Anna?

"No, I didn't ask her. Give me more credit than that!"

"Okay?" *Give me more, then.*

"I've been hearing the thoughts of all the girls in the school. Word travels fast that you're a gentleman," she whispered so low it was barely audible.

"Come again?"

"Apparently that's all the girls are talking about. How you wouldn't take Anna. Yes, you're the celebrity of Bedford High." She grinned with a roll of her eyes.

I chuckled as two girls from my science class walked by and whispered to each other. "Hi, Jake," one of them said. And I couldn't tell you which one, or what her name was for that matter.

"She thinks you're hot," Claudia divulged. "And the other one wishes her boyfriend was more like you."

I grinned, enjoying the extra attention, but I turned my focus back to Claudia. "Okay, so will you tell me something then?" I needed to know what she read from Anna's mind when we got on the speedboat yesterday morning. She had clenched her jaw and rolled her eyes.

Claudia took a deep breath and looked away. "You hurt her."

There it was. The horrible memory I was trying so hard to suppress. The image of Anna soaring through the air and crashing against the thick tree. I pinched my eyes closed as I tried to flush the images away. But they kept coming back. Haunting me.

"I'm sorry, Jake. It doesn't matter anymore. I was only upset because I had the wrong idea about you. I just figured you were some teenager who couldn't control himself. I didn't realize how much you actually sacrifice to keep her safe."

I barely heard her as she rambled. My thoughts were still in the woods on the island, now trying to heal Anna as I worked through the emotions overcoming me.

Claudia continued, "And then I found out about the bracelet you gave to her. Jake, I've been wrong about you. I am so sorry."

I leaned up against the wall and slid down until I was sitting on the floor with my head in my hands.

Claudia sat down beside me and put her arm around me. "Jake, listen to me. It's over now. It was not your fault. I'm sorry I even brought it up. But you asked."

I slowly lifted my head. "How did you get your gift?"

"What do you mean?" Her eyes darted back and forth between mine.

"I need your gift. I need to be able to feel good from evil." *If I had that gift, I wouldn't have hurt Anna.*

"The only person I know who might be able to help you is James Chisholm."

"The Head Counsellor?"

"Yeah. He's the only one I know with more than one gift, so he may be able to tell you how to earn another one. I don't know for sure, though."

I stood up and brushed my pants off. "Thanks, Claudia. Keep this between us, okay?"

"No problem . . . I think." She raised one eyebrow, which I ignored.

"I have to get to the cafeteria. Anna's waiting." I checked my phone's GPS and confirmed she was right where she was supposed to be.

Claudia followed me down the hallway. "By the way, I think her bracelet was a great idea. Makes her feel like she has a bit more freedom."

"Yeah. Another secret between us, okay?"

"Got it." Claudia hooked her arm in mine as we walked through the cafeteria together.

I CAUGHT MYSELF daydreaming in math, and unpleasantly surprised when I realized the class was only half over. I rotated my phone in my hands and decided to check up on Anna. The GPS told me she was sitting in biology class and her vitals were normal. Someone suddenly grabbed my arm and squeezed firmly.

"Hand over the electronics, Rovert." It was Mr. Meade, peering down at me over his giant nose. He reached for my phone with his other hand.

"Touch it and I'll break your fingers," I growled, slowly prying his hand off of my arm.

I heard a few gasps, one being Mr. Meade's. "What did you just say to me?"

"Let go of my phone . . . now." My tone was low and firm. I clenched my jaw and fought back the urge to throw him across the room. Perhaps my reaction would've been different with any other teacher, but this one really made my teeth grit.

Mr. Meade took a step back and flared his nostrils. The arrows in his eyes were aimed in my direction. Fortunately, an announcement over the PA system cut our exchange short.

"Would the following people please come to the office immediately. Nick Pulsifer, Claudia Henderson, Noah Morgan, Anna Taylor and Jake Rovert. Thank you."

A slight grin crept up one side of my mouth. I bit my lip as I watched Mr. Meade ball his fists. "Go . . . and don't come back!"

"Thank you, sir," I taunted as I gathered my things and walked out of the class, head held high.

I met up with Anna and Noah coming out of biology class.

"What do you think this is about?" Anna asked as soon as we were in the clear.

"I don't know," Noah answered. "But did you notice she didn't call Rachel? She must be with her. My guess is she's had a vision."

"Oooh, good call," Anna remarked.

We rounded the corner to the office and met Claudia and Nick coming from the opposite direction.

And, as guessed, Rachel was already sitting in Ms. Peters's office.

Ms. Peters ushered us in and quickly closed the door behind us. "Rachel's had a vision. We must act quickly."

Looking intently at Rachel, Claudia gasped. "Are you sure?" Why couldn't she just wait until the rest of us heard the news too? "Sorry," she followed up, looking at each of us in turn. "Sorry! Go ahead."

Ms. Peters already had a map laid out across her desk. She was leaned over, marking on the map with a pen. Deep in thought. Rachel stood by Anna and put her arm around her, which was strange. I felt my stomach tighten as my defences kicked in.

"There has been some governmental changes in Uganda recently," Ms. Peters began, watching Anna carefully. "Rachel has prophesized that the changes have stirred a lot of upset, and a nearby independent militant group is planning an attack on the city centre and will make their way throughout the country, killing anyone and everyone who gets in their way. This has the makings of a catastrophe similar to the Rwandan Genocide in 1994."

"That's terrible!" Anna gasped. "My parents are in Uganda. How will this affect them?"

Ms. Peters looked down at her map, pointing to the area circled in red pen. "Your parents are very influential people in Uganda, Anna. They help a great number of citizens and have accomplished many miracles." She swallowed before she finished, "The Defiers are planning an attack on your parents' compound."

Anna's face went pale. She slowly brought her hands to her chest as she shook her head back and forth. "No. No. No."

I reached for her, just in time to catch her limp body before it hit the floor.

CHAPTER 10

THE NEXT FEW hours felt like minutes as we raced to come up with a plan, which would see the six of us heading to Uganda to save Mr. and Mrs. Taylor. Although Ms. Peters was against the idea of letting Anna go with us, Anna would have none of it. She was going and there was no one going to stand in her way. No one wanted to address the idea that maybe it was Anna's parents the Defiers were after. . . . Or maybe it was Anna. Whatever the motive, they would need our help, and we all prayed that it would be enough.

WE TOOK SOME time to go home and pack and explain to our parents that we were heading on a trip to Africa. Nick and Claudia never had an issue with explaining things to their parents because both of their parents already knew about their gifts. Anna's parents already in Uganda, so she didn't need to tell them where she was going until she got there. Her Nanny was uneasy about it, but she made me promise to take good care of her. With Noah, he had so much free reign at his house that I honestly don't think his parents would even notice if he left for a week. My circumstance was a bit different. Mom thought it was amazing that we wanted to go on a "short-term mission trip," but it was Dad who had a dozen questions and seemed very uneasy about it. In the end, Mom and I won the argument, and within the hour, I was on my way.

WE LANDED IN Uganda twenty-four hours after leaving Halifax. It was early morning in Uganda and the sun was just starting to rise. Thankfully we were in first class for all three flights, so we were able to sleep.

Nick was nominated as driver of the rental car to Anna's parents' compound. Anna was secure between Noah and me in the backseat. She kept her long, beaded necklace in her hands the whole drive, holding it to her lips every once in awhile. I wondered what she was thinking and I often looked to Claudia for any clue. Claudia continuously wiped stray tears from her face, which I took as a sign she was feeling Anna's pain.

When we reached the compound, we were relieved to see that it was still intact. Concrete walls surrounded the small village, which was secured by large metal gates at the entrance. As we approached, two large, heavily-armed men—presumably the guards for the compound—walked slowly toward us.

Anna caught sight of her parents on the other side of the gate, playing a game of soccer with some local children.

"MOM! DAD!" she shouted, jumping out of the car and running to the gates. The guards gently held Anna back until her parents authorized us to come through.

"Anna!" Mrs. Taylor shouted as they embraced. "What are you doing here?"

"Mom, we have so much to talk about!" Anna turned to her father. "Daddy!"

"My little girl! Is everything okay?" He held her tightly, but with reservation.

The rest of us stood quietly in the background, waiting for our intro.

"Everything's fine, Daddy." Anna smiled. "These are my friends, Nick, Claudia, Noah and Rachel." She waited while everyone shook hands. Then she looked at me and beamed. "And you remember Jake."

"Jacob Rovert. You get taller every time I see you!" Mrs. Taylor laughed as she pulled me in for a hug.

"Mrs. Taylor, you get younger every time I see you," I mused.

"Oh, you're such a sweet thing." Mrs. Taylor blushed.

"Well, come in. Come in!" Mr. Taylor ushered us in through the gates. "Leave your car there. I'll have someone come get it for you."

PRIOR TO LEAVING for Uganda, it had been decided that Anna's parents did not need to know about the prophecy or the secret of our gifts. This was hard for Anna. Ms. Peters convinced her that it was in their best interests to know as little as possible. Their desire to protect their daughter would cloud their judgment and abilities to create their own miracles.

When we reached the Taylor's small concrete home, we were led in to sit around a large wooden table. Mrs. Taylor pulled out the family photo albums. Anna wasn't impressed with the array of embarrassing pictures, but the rest of us certainly got a laugh out of them.

"So Anna, why don't you tell your father and I why you are really here?" Mrs. Taylor closed the photo album and looked her daughter straight in the eye.

The rest of us looked at each other nervously. Would she tell them?

Claudia jumped in, "Flights were cheap."

Mr. Taylor shot her a disapproving look. "So you decided to skip school and hop on a plane to Uganda?"

"Daddy, I haven't seen you and Mom in six months! I missed you guys. Is that so hard to believe?" Anna sulked with her best display of big, sad eyes.

"It just happened to work out for all of us," Rachel added. "I had air miles that I had to use up by the end of the month, and I wanted Noah to come too."

Noah blushed. "And Anna would never go

anywhere without Jake," he teased.

This caught Mr. Taylor's attention. "Is that right, Anna?"

"It is," she said, reaching for my hand under the table. I gave it a squeeze to let her know we were in this together.

"Well, I am certainly glad you all came. It is so nice to have some company." Mrs. Taylor stood up with the photo albums held closely to her chest. "Now, who's hungry for some lunch?"

"We'll help you," Claudia stood up and pulled Rachel and Anna along into the kitchen.

Mr. Taylor glared at me from across the table. Smiling nervously, I wondered what he was thinking.

"Jake? I could use some help down at the river. Would you mind?" His eyes never left mine for one second.

"Sure. Yeah, no problem."

"We can help too," Noah offered.

"That's fine, Noah. Thank you. Jake and I can handle it."

I followed Mr. Taylor out of the room, looking back at Nick and Noah one last time with pleading eyes.

"Good luck," Nick mouthed.

THE WALK TO the river was uncomfortable to say the least. There was a good five foot distance between us as we made our way through the tiny village. I tried to make conversation, but Mr. Taylor didn't seem to have much to say in response.

When we reached the river, Mr. Taylor stood staring off in the distance, not even taking notice that I was still standing next to him.

He finally broke the silence by saying, "I see the way you look at her, Jake." He shoved his hands deep in his pockets and looked down at his feet. "And the way she looks at you."

Something bubbled up inside of me. I wanted to smile, but didn't dare.

"Jake, I need to know you're taking good care of my daughter." He swallowed hard and I noticed the water welling in his eyes.

"Mr. Taylor, I want to assure you that your daughter is completely safe with me." My mind flashed back to my moment of weakness on the island, and I felt a pang of guilt. "I . . . I promise you I will never let anything happen to her." *Again.*

Mr. Taylor pursed his lips in an effort to show his appreciation. "Thank you, Jake. I just can't be there with her all the time. We chose a life that brings us halfway across the world more than she deserves."

"She respects your work, sir. She understands why you need to be here." A tear slipped down his cheek.

"Do you love my daughter, Jake?"

"Of course, Mr. Taylor." I started, a bit too formal. The corner of my mouth turned up. "I love Anna. I love her so much, sir. I can't imagine living without her. I can't imagine waking up in a world without her by my side. She is everything to me, Mr. Taylor. Everything. There would be no world without her." I looked at the river, passing by slowly. "She is a rare and special girl."

By the time I had finished babbling, Mr. Taylor was smiling from ear to ear.

"That brings music to my ears, Jake!" He looked at me for the first time since we left the house. "That's how I've always felt about Anna's mother."

"We're very happy, sir."

"I always knew one day you two would wake up and finally see each other as more than just friends."

I chuckled, remembering our innocent friendship of the last few years.

"Jake? I don't know what stage you are in your relationship, but I'm asking you, as her father, to please respect her."

It took me a few seconds, but then I immediately knew what he was talking about. "Of course, sir. Of course. I . . . we . . . will be waiting until we're married, sir."

He exhaled large enough to sway the trees in the hot African sun. "Thank you, Jake." He grabbed a hold of me and pulled me in for a slightly awkward hug. "Thank you."

"It's no problem. It was a mutual decision, sir."

He let go of me and wiped his face dry, grinning

from ear to ear. "Well, that certainly does make a father happy to hear those words." Then he stopped suddenly and asked, "Does this mean you plan on marrying my daughter some day, Jacob?"

I swallowed hard. "Yes, sir, someday I hope your daughter will marry me."

"Well, Jake, someday I hope she will too. I would give my blessing for that marriage. I give my blessing, Jake." He slapped me so hard on the back that it sent me stumbling forward. "Sorry about that, lad. I'm just relieved to know my daughter is in good hands."

It was an uncomfortable conversation, but one that I was glad we had. We were now on another level, Mr. Taylor and me. But I also felt like I had a new level of responsibility. Not only protecting the girl I love, but also protecting this man's daughter. His shining star.

BACK AT THE house, lunch was ready and everyone was gathered in the sitting room, discussing the weather from what I could tell.

"You're just in time," Mrs. Taylor greeted us with a warm smile and a house smelling of homemade bread. Mr. Taylor followed her into the kitchen to get the table prepped.

Anna stood up and met me with a concerned look. She whispered, "I'm so sorry . . . for whatever he said."

"How do you know it was bad?" I whispered back.

"Nick told me he looked upset about something. Is

everything okay?"

I looked around the room at my friends, sitting quietly and watching my reactions closely.

"It's fine," Claudia announced. "We've got bigger problems right now. Let's go eat and we'll go for a walk after lunch to talk about things."

We waited for the others to leave the room.

Anna held onto my arm tightly. "You sure nothing's wrong?"

"Babe, trust me. Everything's fine. Male bonding stuff. It's all good." I kissed her worried forehead. "Did I miss anything here?"

"Nothing." Anna shrugged. "Just a lot of me worrying about you."

"I'm starved," I said, clutching my stomach for visual effect.

"Not a term they use lightly around here," Anna reminded me with a nudge.

"Right. I suppose not."

We wrapped our arms around each other and headed into the kitchen for a delicious, home-cooked African meal.

CHAPTER 11

IN THE EARLY hours of the morning, as the sun just started making an appearance over the horizon, the silence in our room was broken by a loud, horrifying cry. I sat straight up in bed and immediately looked to Rachel, who was white and frail looking, eyes wide and distant. Without moving her facial features, she slowly pulled her sheet up to her chin and rocked back and forth.

Noah carefully made his way to her side and put his arm around her rigid shoulders. The rest of us waited for her vision to end. Several slow, intense minutes past.

"Claudia?" I whispered. "Can you read her yet?"

"No," she whispered back. "She's not awake yet."

A few seconds later, Rachel's body jolted and her eyes pinched closed. "Today in the city centre. At high noon. At Nakasero Market. The market is full." Her voice was firm yet quiet. "There will be two people, both suicide bombers. They will start there and once they have completed their mission, a signal will be sent by their leader to the other bombers, staggered throughout the city, making their way to here." Rachel drew in a breath. "Their leader is on Kampala Road in the Diamond Trust Building, on the next street up from the market." Tears welled up and poured down her cheeks as she recalled her vision. "So many people will die. So many children."

No one said a word for several minutes. What were we supposed to do now?

"Well, we can't just sit here. We have to do *something!*" Anna cried as she stood up and began getting dressed, not caring who was in the room. Nick and I turned our heads away and I threw a pillow toward Noah to do the same.

"Okay, so we'll head into the city and then what?" Noah asked, still cradling Rachel's trembling body.

"I don't know," Anna began. "But we can't just sit here. I'll pray a miracle to spare our lives, and maybe we should split up and try to take down each bomber."

"But we don't know anything about them. How will we find them?" Noah asked.

"Got any better ideas?" Claudia argued.

"Guess not." Noah helped Rachel up and we all threw on some clothes.

Anna said, "We'll have to sneak out. Mom and Dad will want to come with us if they know where we're going. I'll leave a note."

"And hopefully we'll see them soon," Rachel added, with just a hint of uncertainty.

KAMPALA WAS ALREADY bustling with locals, children, tourists and vendors. We sat in front of a nearby restaurant and watched for anything out of the ordinary. The sun slowly made its way up in the sky. We only had half an hour left before the prophesized attack, but so far we hadn't had any luck. Suddenly, Nick stood up and his whole face cringed.

"They're coming. I can feel it," he said, slowly turning toward the street as a couple casually walked in our direction. Dressed in casual pants and matching blazers, had I not trusted Nick's ability to discern them, I would never have believed that these two regular, happy-looking people were about to voluntarily end their lives for a cause full of hate. *How does that make sense to them?*

"It's them," Claudia confirmed.

"What are they thinking?" I urged.

"That they are doing a great service to mankind." Claudia shook her head in disgust.

"Okay, I have an idea," Anna said, pulling us all in. "We need to split up and clear out the area. They're not scheduled to attack until high noon, right Rachel?"

"Right."

"Okay, so we have twenty-five minutes," Anna

announced. "We're too much of a target being together, so Nick and Claudia, why don't you two head into the market and start leading people out, telling them the market is closing because there's a lost child or something. I don't know. Make something up." She turned to Rachel. "Rachel and Noah, you need to clear out the office buildings. Get people moving out the back of the buildings."

"When will we meet up again?" Rachel asked before they headed out to fulfill their duties.

"Right here in twenty minutes. Jake and I will go find the police and take down these two before they get a chance to do anything."

"Sounds good."

"Good luck everyone. I love you guys." Anna grabbed my hand and we parted our friends.

As soon as we were submersed in the market, Anna twisted her hand free from mine and began running through the crowds.

"Anna? ANNA!" I yelled through the noise of the people, trying to keep my eyes on her pink t-shirt and bouncing ponytail. "ANNA! Where are you going?!"

She stopped in the middle of the market, and turning toward the well-dressed couple standing in the middle of the circle, she said with all the confidence in the world, "It's me you want. I can do miracles."

What the hell was she doing?! The couple exchanged a pleased expression and began casually walking toward her. She turned and ran, with the Defiers quickly following.

"ANNA!" I yelled after her as I ran to catch up, the couple only yards behind us as we pressed through the crowds. "What are you doing?"

"Leading them somewhere!" she panted as she weaved in and out of the crowd, apologizing to everyone in her way. "I'm so sorry, Jake! I have to do this!" She turned the corner and ran up the next street. Within seconds, we were sprinting up the steps of a building. Once inside, she stopped in the middle of the foyer, turned back toward the door and closed her eyes.

"What are you doing, Anna?" I pleaded, nearly in tears. "Please don't do this!"

"They want me, Jake." She wrapped her arms around me. "I won't let anything happen to you. I promise." She closed her eyes again and began muttering to herself.

"No, Anna! No! They'll blow us up!" I tried to pull her out of the building when the couple came running through the front doors, pleased that they had finally cornered us. Their eyes burned toward Anna, seeming not to notice me beside her at all.

"That's the point," she whispered back, squeezing tighter. "To blow us up."

Nothing was said by the couple before the man reached into his blazer. I closed my eyes, wrapped my arms around Anna and pressed my lips to her forehead.

That's all I could do. My heart was beating so fiercely that I could barely hear the commotion going on around us. I couldn't imagine living without Anna. How could she do this to me? My last notable thought before my world went dark was . . . *God, please don't let Anna die.*

THE AIR WAS thick with dust and smoke, making it difficult to breathe. Lying on my back, I focused on the breaths that I took and the burning sensation that each one caused. The sky seemed to get darker and darker until I couldn't see anything again. The pain was fading. I felt myself drift to a peaceful slumber. Then as if someone flicked on a flashlight in a dark room, a comforting bright light came toward me, almost enveloping me. The light took the pain away, if only for a minute. Perhaps staying in this light wouldn't be such a bad thing. But in the middle of the light, I saw a figure. A ribbon of beauty surrounding her. Anna? ANNA! What did this mean? Were we dead? Was Anna *dead*?! NO!

My body jolted as I fought against the soothing bright light. I had to get to Anna. I had to wake up out of this deep sleep and find her. There were voices all around me, and I struggled to make them out.

"His eyelids are moving."

"He's squeezing my hand."

"He can hear us now."

And then, "She's not going to make it."

Those were the words I needed to hear to shove me back into reality. The burning sensation in my lungs came back the minute I opened my eyes. Noah and Nick helped me sit up while Rachel held her sweater firmly on my throbbing side. It was dark between the tall brick walls on either side of us. No one dared speak. I followed Claudia's eyes to the ground and found Anna lying lifelessly at my side.

"Jake, I'm so sorry," Rachel finally said through tears.

"No!" I shook my head, refusing to believe anything they suggested.

Forgetting the pain shooting through my body, I picked Anna up and cradled her on my lap, her body limp. Claudia sat in front of us and carefully wiped the soot and blood from Anna's face.

"Baby, wake up." I pushed a strand of hair from her eyes. "Anna, wake up!" Leaning down, I kissed her neck, then chin, then lips. "Anna! Don't do this! ANNA! I need you!" I sobbed as I rocked her in my arms.

"Jake." Nick rested his hand on my shoulder, but didn't say anything else.

"I'm so sorry, Jake," Claudia said.

Rachel cried in Noah's arms.

"No," I said. "NO! She's *not* dead. She can't be. She wouldn't leave me like this."

I rested her body on the ground as I took a deep

breath and drew strength from somewhere deep inside, clearing my thoughts. A quick assessment of her body showed head trauma and several contusions over her body. Gently taking her face in my hands, I felt her cool lips against mine. "We can do this, babe," I whispered.

Several minutes passed as I leaned over her, repeatedly stroking her hair, kissing her face. Gradually the sound of everyone's voices dissipated and it was just the two of us. No one else. Just us. The coldness from her body seemed to melt as my hand continuously scanned her body. *God, please bring her back to me. She has so much more to give.* Finally, her breath hitched and became short and erratic, but present at least. Then her hand warmed in mine. Her chest began to rise and fall more consistently and her eyes flickered a few times before they opened and peered at me—so wide and innocent. The corner of her mouth twitched as a smile slowly spread across her face.

"I knew you could do it," she wheezed, followed by a small cough.

Thank you, God. "Don't *ever* do that to me again!" I warned, pulling her in to my chest. I wanted to push her away to let her know how angry I was. But more so, I never wanted to let her go again. I held her there for several minutes, not giving her the chance to pull away.

Gradually the others came back into focus and their quiet celebrations softened my mood. I gradually released Anna and assessed her body. Completely new.

A little blood-stained, but she could still win a beauty contest. Well, maybe. Would have to clean her up just a little.

Claudia smacked my arm and rolled her eyes. "*Anyway*. Anna, I'm so glad you're okay."

"Did it . . . did it work?" Anna looked to each of us for an answer to her cryptic question.

"We haven't heard of any other detonations. It definitely threw them off course," Nick updated. "And it's been almost twenty minutes."

"But . . . but is he dead?"

"Who?" Rachel looked as confused as I felt. What was she talking about? Maybe I hadn't healed her head properly, after all.

"The bombers?" Nick questioned.

Claudia let out a giggle. I assumed she was processing Anna's thoughts.

Anna looked to Claudia for the answer to her question. Soon all eyes were on Claudia who was smiling so proudly at Anna. Her eyes welled up as she answered, "You're a genius! The Diamond Trust Building. Their leader was in the Diamond Trust Building." She looked around at all of us. "She led them to the building so they would take out their own leader."

Anna's soft voice repeated, "Did it work?"

"I . . . I don't know. I assume so. The building was completely demolished. You two were blown right out into the street."

I shuddered at the image playing through my mind. The last thing I had remembered thinking was that, if we both died, they would have to bury me with my arms around Anna because I was not letting go of her.

Nick added, "Rachel and Noah carried you two off into the alleyway, and Claudia and I told the authorities that we overheard these bombers talking about there being more bombers a few blocks down and making their way to the compound."

Anna gasped. "Mom and Dad!" She grabbed my hand and made a dash for the road. "We have to go see if they're okay!"

We all followed, hoping and praying that Anna's plan had worked.

CHAPTER 12

GETTING BACK OUT of the city centre was not as easy as I had hoped. Anna sat next to me biting her nails off as Nick tried to manoeuvre us through the chaos. We slowly made our way through the streets, but just when we were almost out of the centre, we were stopped at a roadblock.

"You've got to be kidding me!" Anna shouted. I held onto her leg and rubbed her knee.

"What are they doing?" Noah asked as we watched them search the car in front of us.

"They're looking for more bombers," Claudia told us. "Nick, when they come to the window, ask them how many bombers they have caught so far."

"They're not going to tell us that, Claudia."

"Maybe not, but if they know, then I'll be able to know."

"Oh yeah. Sorry." Nick leaned over and greeted the officer at his door. "Afternoon, sir."

"Get out of your car. Put your hands on your head," his thick accent demanded.

We all did as we were ordered as three officers thoroughly searched us over. Then our car was checked from top to bottom.

"Sir, if you don't mind my asking, how many bombers have you caught?" Nick asked hesitantly.

The largest of the three officers turned and slowly walked back toward Nick, stopping within inches of his face. "Dat would be none of your damn business."

They stood toe to toe for a moment as Nick drew in a breath. Claudia pulled Nick back and said, "Thank you, sir. We'll be on our way so you can do your job. Sorry to be a bother."

Nick's knuckles were white on the steering wheel as we drove out of the city.

"Oh, relax, Nick. He was just doing his job," Claudia pointed out.

"It was his tone, and I'm sure his thoughts were arrogant too." Nick sighed. "I could've taken him in like three seconds."

Claudia kissed his cheek. "I know you could've, baby." Then she turned around and said, "So they've found three more bombers."

"Three?" Rachel said. "That's good. That's good. That's all there were in my vision."

"That's a relief," Noah said. "So does that mean they never got their signal to detonate?"

"Most likely." Claudia smiled and then looked at Anna, who was still biting her nails. "I'm sure your Mom and Dad are just fine, Anna."

THE GATES TO the compound were open when we returned. The guards were standing watch waiting to lead us to the Taylor's house.

"Anna!" Mrs. Taylor shouted as she ran toward the car, which was still in motion.

"Thank you, God," Anna whispered, wiping her tears. She leaned over and surprised me with a big kiss. "I love you, Jake!"

My heart skipped a beat, as it always seemed to when she said those words. All eyes were on Anna as I let her out of the car and watched her run into her parents' arms. "I love you too, Anna," I whispered back, although no one heard.

Rachel and Noah climbed out of the car and stood next to me as we watched Anna and her parents reunite. Nick and Claudia parked the car.

"Good job, Rachel," Noah said as he put his arm around her shoulders. "If it weren't for you, this would've turned out a lot differently today."

"Yeah, well done, Rach," I added.

A beeping sound came from Noah's cell phone deep in his pocket. He quickly reached in and silenced it.

"What was that?" Rachel asked nonchalantly as she casually flipped her hair over her shoulder.

"My phone," Noah mumbled.

The tension between the two of them was thick, although I had no idea what was going on.

"I know it was your phone, Noah. I'm not that stupid. What I meant was *who* was that?" There was no hint of indifference now.

"I don't know. It was a text." Noah kept his eyes straight forward and his hands in his pockets.

Rachel tried a different route. "Well, you should check it. It could've been your mom."

"Nah. She doesn't text. It's no big deal. There are bigger things going on right now."

Rachel stared at him with intense, fire burning eyes. "Give me your phone, Noah. Let me see who it was."

"No!" he retorted, finally challenging her obsessive-compulsive behaviour.

"It was *her*, wasn't it? It was Lexie." Her hands were tight on her hips and if looks could kill . . . well, I'd have my work cut out for me.

Noah sighed then jerked his phone out of his pocket and silently read the text. He added a smile as fuel to Rachel's fire, then said, "Yup. It was Lexie." Then put the phone back in his pocket and continued to look straight ahead with a smirk on his face.

Did Noah Morgan just stand up to Rachel Riley? Not that I blamed him, given all the rejections Rachel handed down to him on a regular basis. It was about time he gave up and moved on.

Rachel crossed her arms and pouted, and when she didn't get the sympathetic reaction that she was accustomed to, she walked toward the house on her own.

"Dude, what was that all about?" I asked as soon as she was gone.

Noah relaxed and we slowly walked toward the house. "I've been talking to Lexie. Rachel doesn't like it."

"You think?" I teased.

Noah laughed. "I'm just tired of her games, you know? One minute she's all cuddly and into me, and the next minute she won't let me touch her. It's just frustrating."

"When did Lexie come into the picture?"

"Up until a week ago, she's just been a good friend. But she's showing more interest, and I kind of like it." Noah pulled his phone out and read, "Miss you. Hope you're having fun. Looking forward to our date when you get back."

"Noah, I think it's great that you're moving on from Rachel, but do you think it's wise to get involved with an Ungifted? Your relationship could put her in danger. Remember my whole dilemma with Anna last year?" I carefully reminded.

"Oh yeah, but I don't plan on getting that involved with her. It's just for fun."

We reached the house and ended our conversation

as we walked into the sitting room where everyone was gathered.

"Jake!" Mrs. Taylor stood up and greeted me with a big hug. "Thank you for taking care of my daughter. Anna told me it was your quick thinking that kept you all out of harm's way today."

"Is that what she said?" I said with a sneer. "Well, I can assure you Mrs. Taylor, I will always do everything within my power to keep your daughter safe." I took a seat on the arm of Noah's chair. "It's your daughter's adventurous spirit that you have to be concerned about," I said with a bit of grit as I was not yet in the right frame of mind to forgive Anna for her careless act.

You could've heard a mouse scamper across the floor. I kept my eyes on Mrs. Taylor, but I could feel everyone staring at me.

Mr. Taylor finally broke the silence. "I know what you mean, Jake. She definitely has a mind of her own." He nodded as he smiled thoughtfully. "I'm just thankful no one was hurt. We were worried sick when we heard about the bombing."

I clenched my jaw as I watched Anna listening to her father, seemingly untouched.

"Nothing to worry about, Daddy. Jake made sure I was safe."

Mr. Taylor grinned as he stood up and slapped me hard on the back. "Good job, son." He continued to the kitchen. "Now, who's hungry? I know I am."

Claudia leaned over to Nick and whispered something before getting up and heading into the kitchen with Mrs. Taylor, Rachel and Anna.

"Jake," Nick said after the girls were gone. "You gotta go talk to her."

"Why? What's the point?" I rubbed my forehead with my hand.

"You're angry. You need to talk to her."

"I'm not ready." I shook my head.

"Listen, Jake. You're not the only one with issues. We all have problems going on right now." He looked to Noah and I caught his eyebrow raising. Noah snickered.

"Just go work it out."

"Fine," I gave in.

I WASN'T EXACTLY sure where I was going to take her. Maybe to the spot her father took me the day before. Or maybe not. That had a nervous feel to it and I was sick enough with the day's events still playing through my head. On a last minute decision, I led us outside the security gates and down the bank to the river. I figured a walk down the river would be refreshing and much needed.

"Slow down, Jake. Do you even know where you're going?" Anna called as she hurried to catch up.

"It doesn't matter. I just need to clear my head."

"You're not still upset with me, are you?" Her

words were like a slap in the face. Especially since I had been trying so hard all day to keep my emotions under control.

I stopped and slowly turned to her, my eyes blaring. "Are you serious?" Her face was blank. I decided this wasn't the venue to have the discussion considering the security guards were still in sight, so I took her hand and kept leading the way down to the river.

Several minutes passed of us trekking through the bush before Anna dared to speak again. "Jake, I don't think we should go too far off base. We don't know where we're going and I'm sure the rest of the group would not approve."

"Since when do you care about what they think?" I snapped.

"Since you're with me and I'm honestly scared," she said in a weak voice. It was enough to make my internal defences peak to another level. If Anna was scared, I was going to make damn sure nothing came close to us.

"I didn't mean to make you nervous. I just wanted to be alone," I gently explained. I spotted a large rock by the river about a few hundred feet ahead. "Just up there."

The rock was surrounded by thriving trees and bush. The river slowly passed by the base of the rock and the other side of the river was a wide plain with tall grass. I never imagined Africa to be so beautiful. Even in its dryness and stifling temperatures, the stillness and splotches of colour were beautiful.

I hoisted Anna up onto the boulder and then pulled myself up using the neighbouring tree as a support.

"Wow, it's so amazing!" Anna exclaimed as she shimmied over, clearing a place for me next to her. I kept a bit of distance between us, subtly letting her know I had still not completely forgiven her.

"What gives, Jake? Why are you so upset about this?"

"You could've died."

"So?"

I threw up my hands, so frustrated with her lack of concern for her own life. "What do you mean *so*? Anna, why are you so thick-headed about this? *You - could - have - died*! Doesn't that mean *anything* to you?" I finished with biting my teeth together in an effort not to keep ranting. I needed her to answer first.

"Of course it does, Jake. But only because I know how much it means to you. But if it weren't for you, then the answer is no. No, my own death does not concern me." Her eyes met mine and I wondered if she could see the hurt that I tried so hard to hide. "Jake, I know that I am living my purpose in life. My purpose is to use my gift to save people, and if I die doing that, then that is the best way to go."

Still clenching my jaw, I said, "Rachel saw your death. When the explosion happened, she had a vision."

"She should really hone up on her skills then, huh?"

"Anna, this is not funny. If I hadn't come around in time, you wouldn't be sitting here next to me right now. Heck, *I* wouldn't even be sitting here. If you weren't with me, I would die."

"Jake, don't talk like that." Anna folded her arms across her knees and stared ahead. "Babe, I really think you need to accept this. We have been given gifts that are so awesome and rare. Our purpose is to help mankind and that's what I was doing today. I knew you were going to be okay and I knew you were strong enough to heal me, even though that wasn't my concern."

A rare tingling sensation filled my nose and in reaction my eyes began to water. I quickly turned away in time to catch a few drops spilling over onto my cheeks.

"Are . . . are you okay, Jake?" her soft voice echoed in my ear.

Giving my eyes one last wipe before I turned back to her, I said, "Anna, I can't imagine living without you."

"I feel the same way." She smiled reassuringly.

"And I don't want to live without you anymore."

"What do you mean? You're not living without me." Her eyebrows puckered.

"I kind of am." I reached into my pocket and felt for

the smooth rock that I had kept with me ever since last year when we found it at the shore of the lake—rustic and dark on one side; perfectly smooth and white on the other. Anna had said that it reminded her of us. I wasn't sure if that was a good thing or a bad thing. But either way, I knew it was special enough to keep. It had become my good luck charm.

"What are you talking about, Jake? You've lost me."

I swallowed hard, although my mouth felt as dry as the air I was breathing. "Anna, the first time I met you, I knew you were special. The first time we kissed, I knew you were the other half to my whole. I know that we were made for each other and that one day we will be old together sitting on the back porch swing, watching our grandkids run around as we plan our next big adventure."

Anna caught a tear escaping from her eye. I could barely hear my words with the pounding of my heart resembling a herd of elephants.

"Anna?" I continued as I took her steady hands in my trembling ones. "Will you marry me?"

Had I caught her off guard? Or was she just trying to figure out a way to let me down easy? Either way, her delay felt like hours. My eyes locked on hers but I suddenly became very aware of our surroundings. The leaves rustling behind us sounded like they were mocking me. The river that trickled gently beside us began to sound like a sneering crowd. But oddly, I didn't care what the environment was saying to me, I only cared what Anna's next words were going to be.

"Jake, I . . . I . . ." she began, looking down at our hands.

My heart began to sink in anticipation, but I held a strong face. At the very least, she now knew how I felt.

"I would *love* to marry you!" She leaped into my arms as I waited for her follow-up "but." But it didn't come. The moisture returned to my mouth as a heavy weight lifted off my chest.

"So that's a yes?"

"Yes! Yes, of course!"

CHAPTER 13

SEVERAL MINUTES PASSED where we just held each other. A sense of completion and strength came over me. Like this new adventure was going to take us to unparalleled heights. We'd be an unbreakable force. I could feel it.

"I am so happy right now," Anna moaned, her voice vibrating against my chest.

"Me too." I kissed the top of her head. My smile was permanent. Then I remembered the rock deep in my pocket. When we were in Italy in the summer, I had it chiselled down into a ring with the intention of giving it to her on some special occasion. This was it.

I slowly pulled away from her and got down on one knee. Holding her hand in mine, I recited, "Anna Jane Taylor, ever since the first moment I met you, I knew you were special. Different from all the other girls. You were a keeper. I may not have known it then, but over the years it has become crystal clear to me that you are the woman I want to spend the rest of my life with." I took the ring from my pocket and held it up in the sunlight. "Will you marry me?"

Anna gasped. "It's so beautiful! And unique!" She studied it for a few seconds then looked up at me and said, "This is our rock!" Holding one hand over her mouth, she let me slide the ring onto her left hand. Then she cleared her throat and said in a proper English accent, "Why of course, Jacob Austin Rovert. It would be my distinct pleasure."

This would be a moment I would never forget. It was one of those occasions where every sight, sound and smell around us would be engrained in my memory forever.

"Jacob, is this really the rock from the lake?" She ran her fingers around the rim of polished black and sparkling white.

"Yeah. I brought it to a goldsmith in Italy and had them carve it into a ring. I know it's not a diamond or your typical engagement ring, but I will get you one of those too."

"No, no. This is perfect. I love it. I don't want a fancy ring. I want this. This means more to me than anything." She grabbed a hold of my face and pulled me in for a kiss. "This has been the perfect day!"

I chuckled to myself. Only Anna would say such a thing. We nearly got killed, but it was a perfect day in her eyes. Only Anna.

Anna nearly jumped up, stared straight ahead and gasped. "Jake! Do you see it? Can you see them?"

I followed her eyes to the field across the river and watched as a herd of giraffes slowly made their way into our view plain.

"They're beautiful," Anna whispered.

"There must be a dozen of them." I tried counting them, but all their spots blended in with each other.

"Oh, look, Jake! There's a smaller one over there. He's hiding behind his mother." Anna's eyes welled up as she watched the giraffe play alongside his mother. It was almost more fascinating watching her reactions than it was to watch the giraffes.

"Yeah, he's cute." I pulled her into me and wrapped my arms around her as we watched the herd make their way east, the littlest giraffe lagging behind. Anna nuzzled her head into my neck and sighed with a sound of content.

The tall brown grass near the herd swayed and rustled. But there was no wind. Something brown—a shade darker than the grass it was hiding in—caught my eye. A lioness! My eyes darted through the grass and I spotted two more crouching in the grass about a hundred feet from the herd and watching them carefully. And then another . . . and another. They were quietly and strategically setting themselves up in a perimeter around the back of the herd. The little giraffe was trailing further behind now and it became quite clear what was about to happen next. "Let's go," I said quickly, pulling Anna up to leave.

"Really? Already?" Anna's confused eyes bounced back and forth between mine.

I angled her away from the field and watched over her shoulder as one lioness leapt at the small giraffe, but was swiftly kicked away. I clutched Anna's face and held her lips to mine. She closed her eyes as she kissed back, but the foreign sound of the giraffe crying out had her pulling away within seconds.

"Baby, don't look," I warned, holding her cheek to mine.

She drew in a loud breath and exhaled, "Noooo."

Two more lions jumped at the giraffe—one from behind and the other clasping its powerful jaws around the giraffe's neck and quickly bringing him to the ground. Only one adult giraffe stayed long enough to witness the horrible scene. Her baby was gone. She quickly turned and followed the herd.

I swayed Anna in my arms until the giraffe stopped struggling and became still. "Shhh. Shhh. It's okay. It's part of life."

When the giraffes were gone and the lionesses were quietly feeding on the remains of the young, I scooped Anna up in my arms and sprinted home with her head buried in my neck, not giving much thought to anyone noticing my super-human speed. Once safely back in the compound, we walked the remaining few hundred feet to her parents' house.

"Thanks for keeping that image out of my head," she finally said.

"Sure."

"You're right, though. It is a part of life. His purpose was to feed the lions. As young as he was, he fulfilled his purpose. He is in Africa heaven now." She let out a satisfied sigh.

I knew what she was getting at. Back to that whole "purpose" conversation we were having earlier.

"Probably." I decided to let her have this one.

"YOU'RE BACK!" RACHEL shouted as we walked in the front door. Everyone was sitting in the common room sipping tea and snacking on pastries that made my mouth water.

Anna's smile lit up the room as we entered. It seemed to reflect off of every mirror in the room.

"So?" Rachel probed as she clapped her hands. "How was your walk?"

"It was nice." Anna smirked, wrapping her arms around my waist.

"Why are you glowing like that, Anna? What happened?" Mrs. Taylor set her tea down on the table and braced herself.

"Jake . . ." Anna started. "Jake and I . . ." She giggled and threw her hands over her mouth as she hopped up and down.

"Are engaged," I finished for her.

Anna threw her hand out and Rachel and Claudia hopped off the sofa to inspect the ring while Anna told them the story of how it originated. Nick and Noah both shook my hand with congratulations, and then gave Anna a big hug.

Finally, I looked up to the two people I worried most about. The others backed up and left Anna and I standing face to face with Mr. and Mrs. Taylor. Their serious faces watched us carefully. It was Mr. Taylor who spoke first.

"My boy!" he finally said as he held his hand out, but before I could give it a firm shake, he pulled me in for a hug and nearly knocked me to the ground. "She's in good hands with you, Jake!"

"My daughter's getting married!" Mrs. Taylor cried as tears ran down her face and onto Anna's shoulder.

We exchanged positions and I let Mrs. Taylor cry on my shoulder while Anna had a moment with her Dad, talking about how his little girl would always be *his* little girl.

"So," Rachel interrupted, "let's hear details!" She pulled Anna down on the couch next to her.

"So we went for a walk off the compound," Anna began. I nervously looked to Mr. Taylor who gave me a disapproving look. He definitely wasn't going to like the part of us being so close to lions then. "And we found this gorgeous spot by the river and we sat there and talked about the day and then Jake gets all romantic and sappy and tells me how he can't imagine life without me and then he just got down on one knee and asked me to marry him." Anna summed it up pretty nicely.

"Awww, that's so sweet," Claudia cooed.

"Oh! And we saw a herd of giraffes in the field across the river too," Anna added, deliberately and thankfully leaving out the part of the lion attack.

Claudia looked sharply at me, presumably having just heard my thoughts. "Tell me later," she mouthed. I nodded.

"Giraffes?" Rachel asked, scrunching her eyebrows. "Is that all?"

Anna looked to me for assistance.

"Uh, yes. Giraffes. Why?" I pried, shooting her a look. What was she a mind reader now too?

"I just . . . I just thought you might have seen some hippos or something. Aren't hippos big in this area?" She threw Mr. and Mrs. Taylor a smile, but I could tell there was something deeper going on.

"No, Rach. We didn't see any hippos." I studied her face, which was riveted with confusion. "Did you?"

"Did I see hippos?" She stared blankly at the coffee table. All eyes were on her. "Yeah."

"Okay, you've lost me!" Mr. Taylor laughed as he stood up. "That's a great story, though, and I wish I could stay to hear more. But if you'll excuse us, your mother and I have some chores to do around the compound."

"We'll be back for dinner." Mrs. Taylor kissed Anna on the forehead and we watched as they left through the front doors.

"I had a vision of hippos," Rachel finally said, answering our silent confusion.

"Like, in the field? With the giraffes?" Anna questioned.

"I didn't see the giraffes. Just a herd of hippos. Four of them. Drinking from the river. You were watching them." Rachel looked back and forth between Anna and me. "Is that right?"

I slowly shook my head. "No, not at all. There were about a dozen giraffes. They didn't come close to the river, though."

"And a lion?" Claudia prompted. I guess she wasn't going to forget about it.

"A few, actually," I corrected.

"They ate the baby giraffe," Anna added very nonchalantly.

"Gross," Noah grunted.

"Guys, this isn't about the lions or the giraffes," Nick added, turning our attention back to Rachel who was in a catalytic state staring at the coffee table with her mouth ajar. "Rachel's vision was warped."

"You know what?" Rachel snapped her head up and looked around at us with a weak attempt of a smile. "I'm sure it's just from the crazy day we had. I just need some sleep."

"Yeah, I'm sure that's all it is, Rach. Why don't you go lay down for a bit?" Anna suggested.

"I think I will." Rachel stood up and left for the back bedroom.

Noah followed. "Did you want some company?" he asked sympathetically.

Rachel stopped in mid-stride. "No. I just want to be alone."

Noah came back to the living room and slumped down on the couch. "Women," he grumbled.

"Oh, please!" Claudia narrowed her eyes in disgust. "Like you had nothing to do with her mood."

"What'd you say?" Noah quickly controlled his voice to a whisper as he sat up to challenge Claudia.

"Don't act all innocent, Noah. You know what you did!" Claudia squared off and the fight was on. I looked to Nick to see if he thought intervention might be necessary, but he just shrugged.

"Enlighten me, Claudia!" Noah stretched his arms behind his head, an inviting grin on his face.

And it was on.

"Who's Lexie, Noah?"

"A friend."

"You like her?"

"Yeah, she's cute."

"Did you ever think about how that makes Rachel

feel?"

"Every day."

"Then why—"

"Are you seriously suggesting, Claudia, that I should care about how my relationship status makes Rachel feel? Are you suggesting that I just wait for Rachel to make up her damn mind about whether or not she wants to be with me?" Noah pushed himself up off the couch and walked to the window. "She obviously doesn't feel the same way about me as I feel about her, so why bother anymore?" He clenched his jaw. "I'm moving on."

"Noah," Claudia began.

"Just mind your own business, Claudia. Stay out of my mind. . . . *Please*." And with that, Noah walked out the door, kicking the dirt as he went.

I kind of understood where he was coming from. Although I knew Claudia genuinely cared for the whole group, she sometimes goes about things the wrong way. If she thought she could help, she should've talked to him in private, at least.

"Yeah, I get it," Claudia answered my thoughts. Man, that could get annoying! She stormed off into the kitchen, Nick following closely behind.

Once the room was clear and we were alone, Anna sat on my lap and wrapped her arms around my neck. Kissing me softly, she said, "At least *we're* happy."

I chuckled. "Give me some sugar, baby." I flipped

her down on the couch and pressed my body into hers. Her warm hands found their way up my shirt and her fingernails tickled my spine as her tender lips discovered mine. Her soft moans kept my lips pressed to hers.

Suddenly the front door burst open and Noah stood in the doorway hunched over catching his breath. I reluctantly sat up, pulling Anna with me.

"What is it, Noah?" Anna asked, fixing her hair.

"Turn on the TV! I just heard two locals talking about the attack in Kampala. It's all over the news apparently."

Nick and Claudia joined us in the living room as Anna turned on the television and flipped through the stations until we found the local news.

The reporter stood in front of the remains of the Diamond Trust Building and reported the news that we had all been waiting to hear. "Today marks a momentous day in history for the people of Uganda. Earlier today, the local police received a tip regarding several suicide bombers strategically placed throughout Kampala. In a strange display of events, two of the suicide bombers detonated their bombs this afternoon inside the Diamond Trust Building where the group's leader was in hiding. It has just been confirmed that the body of their leader was found in the rubble and he has been declared dead. Police have not yet released the identities of those involved as they continue to investigate this incident. In any event, Uganda is celebrating the take down of a potentially major catastrophic event."

The cameras kept panning the rubble and dust that now covered the city centre. Flashbacks flooded my brain of Anna running through the crowds of people, and the bombers drawing closer and closer. My palms began sweating and my heart was racing, begging the images to be erased.

"Can you believe that?" Anna finally squealed, waking me from my horrible daydream. "We did it!" She jumped into my arms and I held her tight.

"That's awesome," Noah said, a little less enthusiastically. "Can we go home now?"

Nick laughed. "Yes, our work here is done."

CHAPTER 14

WE GOT UP early the next day, said our good-byes and headed off to the airport. Rachel had slept through the whole afternoon the day before, didn't even wake up for supper and then slept through the entire night. Needless to say, she was feeling extra bubbly in the morning. We were all going to feel the effects of that.

Noah had received two text messages since we got up at four a.m. until we left for the airport an hour later. I watched Rachel for any sign of jealousy, but she seemed to be okay with it.

"So when we get to the security line-ups, head to the third line-up. The second one breaks down shortly after we arrive. It'll cause a big delay," Rachel told us as we weaved through the busy halls.

As instructed, we made our way through the third line, holding our tickets in hand. I couldn't wait to be back in Canada. Mom was going to be thrilled to hear our big engagement news. Dad, on the other hand, would find some way to make me feel inadequate or immature. I shuddered at the thought of having to tell him.

Claudia led the way through the security check without a problem. Nick followed suit, but at Anna's turn, the light above the walk-through flickered then went out. The female guard stopped Anna and made her walk through it again . . . and again, but nothing happened.

"Must be broken," she muttered as she pulled Anna aside and commenced a physical search.

I glanced up at the number above our heads. Line three. I looked over at line-up two, and it was still fully operational. I cautiously looked at Rachel who had a desperate look of confusion on her face. She shook her head and whispered, "It was two. It was supposed to be number two. I'm sure of it."

Claudia and Nick watched with sympathy as the rest of us each took our turn for our physical. With the recent terrorist attack, they were being even more thorough, which made for some awkward touching. Finally we were through and on our way to our gate. What a relief.

The girls decided they wanted to sit together on the plane and discuss wedding plans. Anna and I both took the aisle seats so we could still be next to each other.

Once we were sitting comfortably in our seats, Claudia whispered to Rachel, "Don't worry yourself about it. We can talk to your mom when we get back. I'm sure there's an explanation."

"Yeah, sure," Rachel mumbled. "But let's not focus on that. Let's talk about Anna's wedding! Oh, I am so excited!" she squealed.

I tried to tune them out, but I was a tad bit nervous about what they were planning behind my back. Anna and I had already decided that it would be a small wedding. Nothing fancy. Just family and close friends.

"Have you put any thought into when you want to have the wedding?" Claudia asked.

"Yeah, actually," Anna answered. "Jake and I decided the twelfth of May."

"Really? What day does that fall on?" Rachel asked.

"I'm not really even sure, but it doesn't matter. That's the date we found out about my gift, thus the date we found out we could be together. It's an important date for us."

"Perfect!" Claudia exclaimed excitedly. "So we have a date and that gives us what? Like seven, eight months to pull this together?"

Anna laughed. "Yes, but I don't want a big, fancy wedding. Just something simple."

That's my girl. Tell them how it is.

Claudia and Rachel exchanged a look that I couldn't quite make out. But then they laughed, so I guessed they weren't buying what she was selling.

"Sorry, sweetheart. This will be the highlight of

your senior year. It's going to have to be big. Especially if I'm helping you plan it." Claudia pulled out a pink notepad and pen from her purse. "Okay, let's get started."

Anna turned and gave me an apologetic look. "S'okay, babe. Go have fun with it." I kissed her hand and turned away. I did not want to hear any further details.

"Dude, I can't believe you're actually getting married." Noah shook his head with what I interpreted as disbelief, although it could've been pity.

"Crazy, eh?" Still not sure what angle he was coming at me with.

"I think it's great," Nick added. "You two are a pretty good fit."

In an effort to get the focus off of me, I asked Noah, "So what's the deal with Lexie?"

Noah looked down at his cell phone in his hands. "Yeah, I think I'll give it a whirl."

"Is she gifted, or is this just a fling?" Nick asked, obviously making a point.

Noah cocked a smile. "Fling, I guess." He became serious again as his eyes flickered toward Rachel. "I don't know."

"I know it's none of Rachel's business, but has she said anything to you?" I carefully asked.

Noah squinted at the seat in front of him, as if trying to count threads. "Yesterday I asked her one last time if she saw her and I together." He bit his lip and his voice lowered to a near growl. "And she said 'never.'" He shrugged. "It's time to move on."

"Ouch," Nick said.

"Yup." Noah buried his phone in his pocket. "Lexie's a nice girl. It'll be a welcomed change."

"Well, good luck with that. If you want to do a double date, Anna and I would be up for that," I offered, hoping I wasn't lying.

"Thanks." Noah rested his head back and closed his eyes. "Now, if you don't mind, I need to get my beauty rest."

"Yes, you do," Nick teased.

I looked back to the girls who were still giggling and scrawling away on Claudia's notepad. Anna's excitement was spilling out through her giggles. She was completely turned toward Claudia and Rachel and her ponytail bobbed at each suggestion. Seeing her like this made everything simple and pure again. I felt bad for Noah, but honestly? I still couldn't have been happier.

WE HAD FOLLOWED the sunrise all the way home which was going to make for a very long day. After stopping at Anna's house to drop her bags, we headed to my house to share the big news. The outside light was still on, which was a clear sign that everyone was still in bed. We tiptoed into the house and headed into the living room to relax.

"I'm so glad to be home," Anna said with a yawn as she stretched out on the couch, laying her head on my lap.

I stroked her hair, watching the strands fall from my fingertips. Suppressing a yawn, I mumbled, "Me too."

Anna rolled over so she was facing me. "I love you."

I gently lifted her body enough so I could slide down on the couch next to her. Holding her warm body next to mine, my fingers stroked her face as we kissed.

She moaned, "I can't wait until we're married."

"You'll have to learn patience. You don't have a choice, my love," I teasingly reminded her.

Her teeth gripped my lower lip. "A little more than seven months to go."

"Yeah, how did all that wedding planning stuff go with Claudia and Rachel?" I hesitantly asked.

"Great, actually. It was a lot of fun. I've asked both of them to be bridesmaids. I hope you don't mind."

"Not at all. I was planning on asking Nick and Noah, so that'll work out."

"And the only other thing is a wedding song. I think Claudia's got the rest taken care of." Anna laughed.

"A wedding song? What were you thinking?"

"Uh-uh! No way! I made enough decisions! This one is all yours, baby. Let me know what you come up with, okay?"

I rolled my eyes. "Sure, sure. But, in the meantime,

if you have any suggestions, feel free to throw them out there."

Anna laid her head next to my chest and wrapped her arms around me. "Let's have a nap," she brilliantly suggested.

"Sounds good to me." And the last thing I remembered thinking about was our wedding day and the evening that followed. Sweet dreams.

A FEELING OF being watched suddenly came over me. I flipped my eyelids open and found Anna still sleeping in my arms. I breathed a sigh of contentment, but then nearly jumped off the couch when I noticed three bodies standing over us.

"Geez! You trying to give me a heart attack?" I quietly scolded Mom, Dad and Abby, who appeared amused at my reaction.

"Why are you back so soon? Or did you even end up going?" Mom whispered.

I decided avoidance was my best option. I firmly pinched Anna's side causing her to jump.

"What? What happened? Did it work? Are they dead?" Anna shouted as she sat straight up on the couch.

Mom and Abby exchanged a giggle. "Hi, Anna. Sorry if we startled you," Mom apologized.

Anna quickly realized where she was and looked to me for help.

"You must have been dreaming, baby. No one's dead here." I forced a chuckle.

"So why are you kids back so soon?" Mom asked again as she took a seat on the loveseat across from us.

"Oh, there's a lot going on in Uganda right now, and it wasn't really a good time to visit." I faked a yawn and put my arm around Anna's shoulder, pulling her back on the couch. "Besides, we'll see her parents next May."

"Oh, is that when they're coming back, Anna?" Dad asked.

"It is now," she answered with a giggle.

"We have some news, actually." I took Anna's hands and tried to keep a straight face. "We're getting married."

Silence. Anna's grip on my hand got tighter and tighter. Mom's mouth was ajar. Abby's smile was growing by the second. Dad . . . well, Dad looked disappointed.

Mom finally spoke, "Are you . . . are you pregnant?"

"No!" Anna shouted. "Heavens, no!"

A hefty sigh of relief breezed through the room. "Phew!" she exclaimed. "Well, this is big news, Jake! When did this happen?"

"A few years ago . . . down at the frog pond. She was the only girl I knew that had enough balls to kiss a frog. How could you not marry a girl like that?"

"You're going to be my sister!" Abby jumped up

and ran into Anna's arms.

"I know! I can't wait!" Anna echoed her excitement.

"Oh! Can I help with the wedding? Pretty please?" Abby begged.

"I was hoping you'd ask! It just so happens Jake and I will need a flower girl. Do you think we could count on you for that?"

"Definitely! And anything else you need!" Abby was even more excited than Claudia and Rachel. This was going to be one big girl-fest, I could tell.

"So,"—Dad's cold voice cut through the excitement—"married at the ripe old age of seventeen." His disapproving glare was no surprise.

"Eighteen, actually," I said. "I'll be eighteen by then."

Probably wasn't the smartest thing to do. If I've learned anything from my father over the years, it's that there are some people you just don't talk back to— whether correcting their mistakes, or otherwise. And he was one of them.

"I hope you have thought this through, Jacob. You have a great future in front of you. I'm sure you both do. I hope you stay focused on the things that are most important."

I felt Anna stiffen beside me, so I decided this was one of those times that needed intervention. "Actually, Dad, Anna *is* what's most important to me. We have thought a lot about this, and we've decided that we are ready for this commitment."

He nodded without saying another word. If he only knew that Anna and I already knew what our future held—a lifetime of healing and miracles.

"Well, this is fantastic news!" Mom interjected, standing up to congratulate us with one of her tight squeezes.

"Thank you, Mrs. Rovert. Jake and I are very excited."

"We've decided on May twelfth for a date, so that gives you girls lots of time to plan." I laughed, tussling Abby's hair. She was still bouncing with excitement.

Dad was sitting now in his usual position in the corner chair. Even though his reaction wasn't at all surprising, I had hoped for a little bit more . . . for Anna's sake.

CHAPTER 15

"ANOTHER JOB WELL done, gang!" Ms. Peters applauded as we gathered in her office the following morning. "You know there's a lot of talk about you six being the next Legend."

"*Us?*" Noah laughed.

"No, I'm quite serious, Noah. I talked to Mr. Chisholm after news spread of your achievements in Uganda, and he is very excited about this group's future."

"I agree," Claudia added assuredly. "I think this team is pretty darn impressive!"

"Well, we have a few kinks to work out," Rachel mumbled, "so we're really not quite ready to be dubbed the next *Legend*."

"You're only human, sweetheart. There may only be six of you, which is only half of the original Legend, but your powers are so great now. It's something I am so proud to be able to witness for myself." Ms. Peters took a sip from her coffee. "Oh! And I hear congratulations are in order!" She quickly set her coffee down and turned to Anna and me.

Anna squealed with delight, which woke us all up.

"Are you excited, Anna?" Ms. Peters laughed.

"Very!"

"Ms. Peters," Claudia began, "would you mind announcing their engagement on the morning announcements this morning?"

"What are you doing, Claudia?" I warned.

"It'll save you guys from having to tell everyone personally. Let them hear it straight from Ms. Peters."

"I don't know," I started.

Anna spoke up. "At least wait until recess so we have a chance to tell our close friends first."

"Sounds good," Ms. Peters said with a wink. "Now get to class or wherever you need to be. I've got a school to run."

IF IT HADN'T been for the GPS bracelet, I probably would've panicked a few times during the day. Anna showed up late to every one of our classes, I couldn't find her in the hallways anywhere, and she only found me halfway through lunch break.

"Where've you been all day?" I asked as we ate lunch in the cafeteria.

"Retelling our engagement story over and over and over again," she chimed.

"Oh, I see. How's that working out for you?"

She leaned into me and whispered, "I am the luckiest girl in the world."

Claudia appeared out of nowhere and leaned down between us. "That's what everyone else is thinking too."

"Of course they are," I teased as I straightened my shirt collar. "I'm a good catch."

Anna smacked my arm. "You should really be careful. You have a big game after school."

"So?"

"So you don't want to let your head get too big or it might get mistaken for the net." She snagged one of my carrots and broke it with her teeth.

We engaged in an instigated stare down. The corners of her mouth twitched and I couldn't hold mine back. We both laughed as I stole a kiss from her.

"You guys are so cute!" Lexie said, bringing us back into a room full of people and conversations.

Lexie was sitting comfortably next to Noah, while Rachel sat a few chairs down.

"So," Lexie said, "Noah said you two would be up for a double date this weekend?"

My sandwich got stuck in my throat as I tried hard to swallow. I coughed a few times before I was able to move it safely to my stomach. By this time, Anna was pinching me under the table.

"A double date?" Anna said sweetly, her eyes

flickering in Rachel's direction. Thankfully, Rachel was engaged in conversation and not paying attention to ours.

"Yeah, sure," Noah added. "We were thinking about maybe going rock climbing."

I still wasn't sure how comfortable Anna felt about it, so I decided to answer with, "That sounds like a lot of fun. Let us check to make sure we don't have any family commitments first. . . . You know, with the engagement and all, we might have some dinner or something."

"Oh, yeah. Of course." Lexie smiled. "And if it doesn't work out this weekend, maybe next weekend."

"Sounds great," Anna said, looking toward Rachel again. This time, Rachel glanced in our direction. She looked disappointed. Was it because of Anna's impending betrayal, or something else? Rachel got up to leave the table and Anna quickly followed.

Noah and I locked eyes for a split second. Long enough to communicate that something wasn't right with Rachel, but then he rolled his eyes and put his arm around Lexie. It was a safe assumption that whatever was bothering Rachel was none of Noah's concern anymore. I couldn't decide whether that was a good thing or not.

THE RUGBY GAME started right after school. In the huddle before the first half, Nick pulled the team in and reviewed our plays, then added, "Guys, watch out for numbers twenty-seven and forty-five. They're the Larsen brothers and they're always trying to pull tricks to take down our strongest players. Last year they broke Kyle Manson's femur and put Jared Smith in a coma with another dirty stunt."

"What should we do?" Noah asked.

"Just watch out for them. There's not much else we're *allowed* to do."

It wasn't long into the game when one of our teammates scored, igniting the Larsen brothers' lust for revenge, as predicted. Claudia and the cheer squad did their part to excite the crowd, while Rachel and Anna sat huddled together in the middle of the first bleacher. Anna looked comfortable, content, and safe, so I tried to focus more on the game than her safety.

I took a quick pass from one of our guys and kicked it, as far as I *humanly* could, to my teammate down field. Scotty caught the ball and began running with it. He didn't make it far before the Larsen brothers came at him from both sides. And just as expected, the crunch of their bodies echoed across the field.

Noah, Nick and I ran to Scotty. Noah threw one of the brothers aside and I knelt down beside Scotty, who was unconscious.

"Don't heal him yet," Nick quietly warned. "Let them take him off in the stretcher first."

"Why? Wouldn't it be better if I healed him now? It

wouldn't be as obvious," I countered.

"We need a medic over here!" Nick shouted to the sidelines. Then he turned to me and said, very seriously, "This way you have reason to do what you're about to do."

"Which is?"

"Bring justice." Nick clenched his jaw and glared at one of the brothers who was walking off the field with a big grin on his face.

Noah didn't need any convincing to follow through with our new plan to bring these guys to their knees. We shadowed the brothers and waited patiently for our opportunity. Then it came. The ball spiralled through the air and twenty-seven ran to catch it. Just before the ball reached his hand, Noah shot out of nowhere and checked into him, sending him at least ten feet down the field. Now it was my turn. His brother ran down the field to his rescue, and as he neared my position, I clotheslined him into the ground. Both brothers were lying still on the ground now. Plan executed.

The whistle blew and we headed back toward our bench while the Larsen brothers were assisted back to theirs. The darkness in their eyes promised revenge.

"Let's have it," Noah taunted as he jerked his head back.

"Jake? Everything okay?"

I turned to find Anna standing behind our bench. "S'fine, babe." I leaned over and kissed her forehead.

"You're sweaty." She grinned as she wiped her forehead.

"It's turning you on, isn't it?"

She pulled my jersey in and pushed her lips into mine. "Win this one for me?"

"It's yours." I winked, kissed her once more then turned back to my team. My eyes rested on the opposing team and I caught the Larsen brothers watching Anna walk back to her seat next to Rachel. A growl formed in the pit of my stomach.

We won the game thirty-five to fifteen. It would've been a closer game, but I couldn't risk losing after promising Anna it was hers. The cheerleaders celebrated with their cheers while Anna and Rachel ran over to join our celebration.

"Great game, guys!" Rachel said. Turning to Noah, she added awkwardly, "You played really well."

"Thanks." Noah smiled.

But then Lexie skipped over and threw her arms, adorned with pom-poms and all, around Noah's neck. "Great job, superstar!"

Noah quickly refocused his attention to Lexie and spun her around. "Thanks to the cheerleaders!"

Rachel watched for a second then shook her head and walked away.

"I'm going to catch up with Rachel. I'll see you soon?" Anna said, backing away.

"Yeah, I'll be there soon." I blew her a kiss, then a

"be careful."

It wasn't three minutes into celebrating when a shiver went up my spine. Something wasn't right. I did a three-sixty and found Nick cocking his head to the side, as if trying to decipher something. My eyes scanned the area and found the Larsen brothers striding across the field toward Rachel and Anna.

"What are they doing?" I said to Nick as we watched them approach the girls.

Claudia quickly threw down her pom-poms and jogged over to Anna's side. She put her hands on her hips and it was pretty clear that she was telling them to get lost. Rachel's finger went up in the air and she started aggressively pointing at one of them. Telling him off maybe? And that's when forty-five grabbed Rachel's finger and shoved it to the side.

Before Nick and I could even move, Noah was across the field. It didn't take long for us to catch up, although Noah had already thrown forty-five into the bleachers. Rachel's mouth was wide open.

"You okay?" Noah asked Rachel.

"Uh, yeah . . . yeah, I'm good. Thank . . . thank you," she stammered.

The other brother greeted us with a wide grin. Not one bit intimidated, so it seemed. He looked at me and with a nod toward Anna, he said, "This your girl?"

Anna was frozen in place and her eyes were wide with fear. The guy quickly snagged her and held her in front of him, caressing her waist with his hands.

"Mmmmm, she's nice and warm," he taunted, pulling her a few steps back.

"Jake?" Anna's voice finally croaked. "Don't fall for it."

My eyes didn't leave his for one second. Not even to figure out what Anna was talking about. My heart was beating at an uncontrollable speed. My hands were balled into tight, iron-clad fists. His blood was about to be mine.

Just as I was about to pounce, with a plan to heal Anna as I ripped apart this guy from behind her, I felt vice grips lock me into place. It was Noah and Nick, struggling with all their strength to restrain me.

"GET OFF ME!" I growled, eyes still locked on his.

"Let the girls take care of him," Nick said in his alarmingly calm voice.

Some might have thought it was amusing to watch Claudia and Rachel pound a two hundred and fifty pound athlete into the ground, but the only thing on my mind was Anna. I held her shaking body in my arms, while Nick and Noah still held me back.

"Jake, I'm fine. I'm fine," Anna kept repeating.

"I wanted to kill him." My voice was so hoarse and cold.

"I know. That's why he did it. Someone must have put him up to this. Someone who knows about us." Anna brought my face to hers. "Baby, you have to be careful. You are going to be tempted like this, but it is so easy for you to lose your gift. Please don't be careless."

I clenched my teeth together in an effort not to argue. At that time, there was nothing you could say to me that would convince me that this guy's death was not required.

"Oh, crap!" Anna whispered.

"What is it?"

"Mr. Meade. He's watching us. He may have seen the whole thing."

"So? Don't you think he'd understand?"

"Depends on what he saw, I guess. Two puny girls beating up a rugby player? Did he see you guys sprinting at lightning speeds across the field? Noah throwing that guy into the bleachers?"

"It's okay," Rachel joined in. "He'll take it to mom and that'll be the end of it."

Noah touched Rachel's arm. "Good job on that guy. Didn't know you had it in you."

Rachel looked at him coolly. "Lexie's waiting for you. You'll have some explaining to do."

What was she doing? I definitely did *not* understand girls! One minute she's all upset, the next minute she's nearly shoving him into Lexie's arms.

CHAPTER 16

ALTHOUGH ANNA TRIED, she couldn't come up with a viable reason to skip out on our double date with Noah and Lexie. We arrived at Beyond Gravity, the indoor climbing gym, a few minutes early so we were all ready to climb by the time Noah and Lexie showed up.

"We're here!" Lexie skipped over to Anna. "I am so excited! I've never been rock climbing before. Have you?"

I quickly glanced at Anna who looked reluctant to be having this conversation. "Uh… yeah. Yeah, we love rock climbing. Right, Jake?"

"Yup," I said, not having anything else to add.

Lexie giggled and nudged into Noah. "I guess you're going to have to spot me in case I fall."

Noah looked down at her and smirked. "Sounds good."

"Why don't you guys go get suited up, and we'll meet you over by the North wall?" I suggested.

"Cool," Lexie piped. "Come on, Noah!"

We watched as they walked away, Lexie's arms tightly woven around Noah's waist.

"He doesn't seem that into her, does he?" Anna whispered.

"He just likes the attention."

"Do you think they'll last?"

"Not long," I answered. "Did you tell Rachel where we were going tonight?"

"No." Anna hung her head. "I felt too guilty. I just avoided her all day. I'm such a bad friend."

"Not at all, Anna. Technically Noah and Rachel were never together, and she made it clear that she didn't want to be with him, so Lexie's fair game."

Anna looked up at me with confused wrinkles across her forehead. "How'd you come up with that? About her having made it clear that she didn't want to be with him. Who said that?"

I wasn't sure the direction of this, but I somehow felt like I was in trouble for something. "I . . . uh . . . Noah said it?"

"Noah said she didn't want to be with him?"

"Yes . . . I think?" I stammered. "That's how he took it, anyway."

"That's not true at all!" she defended. "Rachel loves Noah."

"What?!" I *definitely* didn't understand women. "What the hell is her problem then?"

"She . . . she . . . she's afraid to lose him!" she blurted. "Ryan promised to make her miserable and to kill anyone who gets in the way of that."

"What?!" I repeated. I mean, I knew Rachel's ex-boyfriend had some serious psychological issues, but this was just overboard. "How do you know this?"

"She told me and Claudia. He sent her a text while we were in Europe this summer. You have to keep this to yourself, Jake. Rachel doesn't want Noah to do anything stupid. She doesn't want him to get hurt. Or worse."

"So she's just going to let Ryan rule her life from an empty threat?"

"What if it's not empty, Jake?" Anna looked away and hesitated before continuing, "She would rather watch him be with someone else than live a life without him at all."

"Noah should know this," I protested. To know that the same guy that kidnapped Anna and nearly killed her last year was still having an impact on our circle of friends, really got under my skin. I was mad, to say the least. Fuming.

"Jake, relax. Rachel is trying to figure out a plan to get rid of him, but she needs time."

I grabbed my hair with my hands. "This is insane. Why didn't you tell me? What if he decides to go after you again? I don't like this one bit. Noah should know about this!"

"NO! You can't tell him, Jake. I promised Rachel I wouldn't say anything to you, but it's been killing me. Please, please, don't say anything."

"You're asking a lot, Anna."

"I know, baby. I know. But Rachel thinks if she gives him some time, Ryan will get over this." I could hear the hesitation in her voice, which made me extremely uncomfortable, but before I could ask any more questions, Noah and Lexie were on their way over to us.

"This conversation isn't over," I mumbled as I greeted Noah and Lexie with a nod. "Let's climb."

WE SPENT OVER an hour climbing, and Lexie was just as clumsy as she eluded to be. She enjoyed Noah catching her as she "accidentally" fell every single time. Finally, Noah suggested that we go to the Coffee House before calling it a night.

Small talk with Lexie was a lot like pulling a hangnail—a bit of a struggle at first but once you found a topic that she was interested in, it was painful to listen to her go on and on.

"So when's your next game, anyway?" Anna asked, clearly not actually interested, but just fishing for a new topic.

"Next Friday, I think," Noah answered.

"That last game was pretty intense!" Lexie said. "That was really sweet of Noah to stick up for you like that, Anna. He's like your big brother."

"Stick up for me?" Anna asked. Noah got a few degrees more uncomfortable.

"Yeah, when that guy like grabbed your arm?"

"Oh, no, that was Rachel." She immediately stopped when she realized that this wasn't just a misinterpretation of the story, but a deliberate cover-up from Noah.

"Oh," Lexie said quickly. "I didn't hear it that way."

"Was it Rachel?" Noah said. "I didn't know for sure. Doesn't really matter. Those guys were completely out of line."

"Don't remind me," I grumbled, feeling my fists ball up.

"It's over with." Anna squeezed my knee gently.

The sound of my cell phone ringing startled me. I was thankful to have the interruption, until I looked at the call display and realized it was Rachel. Anyone but Rachel. I handed the phone to Anna since that's who she was likely looking for anyway.

Anna looked at the display and smiled nervously. "Excuse me," she politely said as she turned sideways and answered the call. "Hi!" She sounded perky, yet full of remorse. "We're, uh, at the Coffee House. What are you up to?" She started playing with a strand of hair. "Who? Oh, um, just Jake and Noah . . . and Lexie." She took a deep breath. "It's okay. It's fine. We're just leaving now anyway. I'll call you when I get home? . . .

Okay, bye."

She handed the phone back to me and I noticed the colour had drained from her face. "You okay?"

"Not really," she whispered. "Can we go now?"

"Sure, babe."

"Was that Rachel?" Lexie asked, appearing somewhat amused.

"Yes," Anna answered matter-of-factly.

Lexie smirked. Noah stiffened.

"Is everything okay?" Noah asked as he took a swig of his coffee.

"Yeah. Yeah, I think so. I didn't really get a chance to talk to her. I'll call her back when I get home." Anna stood up and took her coat from the back of the chair.

"Did she sound okay?" Noah asked. It was odd for him to show so much interest in front of Lexie, but he did look concerned.

Anna wouldn't look him in the eye. "I really don't know. I didn't really talk to her."

I stood up and helped Anna with her coat. "We're going to head out now. That was fun, guys."

"Yeah, that was so much fun!" Lexie replied. "We should do this again next weekend."

I waited for a response from Anna, but a few awkward seconds passed, so I answered, "We'll see." I turned to Noah. "You up for hitting some balls tomorrow?"

"Yeah, sure."

"Cool. I'll call you in the morning."

Noah nodded. "Later."

The walk to the car was quiet, but as soon as we were in and the doors were closed, Anna started. "Can you believe her? Acting like she's all concerned about Rachel when she doesn't give a damn about her feelings. She is *so* not right for Noah!"

"Okay, more importantly," I cut in, "what is this crap about Ryan and Rachel? Have they been talking? What exactly did he say? What did Rachel say to you?"

"Rachel just said that he texted her back in July with all this stuff about getting his revenge on her for hurting him and that as soon as she moves on to someone else, he'll be there waiting in the shadows, waiting for his revenge. It was something dark and creepy like that."

"Did she text him back?" My hands tightened around the steering wheel.

"Not that I know of. She was pretty upset about it. She made Claudia and I promise not to tell you and Nick. I feel so sick for betraying her." Anna wrapped her arms around her waist.

"You didn't betray her, Anna. She's in over her head here if she thinks she can get rid of him on her own. We're going to need to come up with a plan together."

"She's really just hoping he'll forget about her and move on. She thinks he just needs time."

I sighed. I couldn't think of a better solution. "You'll

let me know if he sends her another message?"

"As long as you promise not to tell Noah." Her hopeful eyes caught mine and I couldn't look away for a few seconds. How could I let her down after she trusted me like this?

"I wish you wouldn't put that on me. Noah is my best friend. I don't get why she feels it's best that he doesn't know. He would definitely *want* to know why she's been rejecting him all this time."

"Jake, you know Noah better than anyone else. If Noah found out that the only thing standing between him and Rachel was Ryan's threat, he would take care of it on his own. Ryan's got a strong group behind him. Rachel doesn't think we can take them."

I took a bit of offence to that. "I beg to differ."

"Not with her visions being as screwed up as they are. She's unpredictable right now."

"Yeah. Has she figured out why she's having messed up visions?"

"Not yet. She sees James Chisholm sometime next week, so she's hoping for an answer then."

I nodded. "Anna, please no more secrets?"

She reached for my hand and gave it a squeeze. "Promise."

WE PULLED INTO Anna's driveway just after ten o'clock. The lights were all out so we quietly crept up to the front door.

"Did you want me to stay, or are you okay?" I asked.

"I should really call Rachel back. I'll see you tomorrow though."

"Sounds good." I leaned in for a kiss.

"Oh, wait!" Anna pulled back and stuck her finger in the air. "I won't see you tomorrow until later, actually. Claudia and Rachel are taking me dress shopping." She giggled as she recalled her plans.

"Dress shopping!" I exclaimed. "Sounds like fun. How long do you think you'll be? Where are you going? What time will you be back?"

Anna laughed. "Babe, I know it's hard for you to let me go do these things on my own, but really, I'm in good hands with Claudia and Rachel."

I looked down at her tracking bracelet, snuggly wrapped around her delicate wrist. "I know. It's just hardwired in me now to worry about you all the time. I'm marrying a miracle worker. The rest of my life will be dedicated to protecting you." I smirked as she rolled her eyes.

"And the rest of my life will be dedicated to teaching you how to relax." She wrapped her arms around my neck and I pulled her in close. "What happens when we have kids? Are you going to be as protective of them too? You won't have any time to save the world."

I pulled her warm body as close as possible and

held it there. "You feel so good." I pressed my lips to hers and felt all the stress of the evening evaporate.

"I can't wait to be yours," Anna whispered.

"You're already mine." I picked her up and spun her around. Anna squealed. "And don't you forget it, woman!"

"You're so bad." Anna swatted my arm. "I should go call Rachel back. She probably wanted to confirm tomorrow."

"Right. So have fun tomorrow." I let her hand go as she walked inside. "Remember—simple!"

"Claudia wants big and beautiful. You want sweet and simple. Should be interesting to see what I walk down the aisle in!" Her devious smile spread across her face.

"Call me when you get home."

She nodded. "G'night, babe."

One more kiss and next thing I knew she was in her house, locked away safe and sound. I turned on the personal tracking device and headed home, thinking of my wife-to-be.

CHAPTER 17

EVEN AT THE early hour of eight o'clock on a Saturday morning, it was invigorating being out on a field of green and swinging at balls as hard as I could. Nick believed that it was never too early to play golf. I guess that's why we always got stuck with the sunrise tee-off times. This time *I* booked the tee-off time, so we got to sleep in an extra two hours.

Noah's game was off. Five holes in and he was still losing an average of three balls per hole. After Noah's horrible tee-off on the sixth, Nick dropped his clubs and sat down on the grass. "Wake me up when he hits one anywhere near the green."

Noah's knuckles glowed white around his driver. He flexed his jawbone as he drew in a breath and swung again. This time, the ball went about fifty yards *past* the green.

"What the hell was that?" Nick said. "What's going on with you? You suck today!"

I shot Nick a warning look and pulled Noah's driver from his grip. "Let's just play best ball. Everyone has an off day once in awhile."

Noah picked up his golf bag and started walking down the fairway without saying a word.

"What's going on, Noah? Talk to us," Nick urged. I really wished he'd just give it up. I knew Noah well enough to know he wasn't going to take much more before he'd blow up.

Noah shrugged.

"How was your date last night?"

"Fine." Okay, this was good. Progress. A word was better than silence.

"How's Lexie? You like her?"

"She's okay. Why are you asking about Lexie? Do you honestly think my game has anything to do with her?" Noah asked through clenched teeth.

"No, not at all. I'm just curious if Lexie's replaced Rachel yet."

Okay, that did it. Noah hurled his clubs down the fairway and spun around. "Why does everyone have to keep talking about Rachel? Rachel this! Rachel that! What does it even matter what I think or *did* think about Rachel? Who cares! It's in the past!"

There was a sharp coolness in Noah's eyes. A look that reflected pain. I wanted to tell him the reason behind Rachel's behaviour. That she actually isn't being selfish or cruel. She is doing this *because* she loves him. I bit my lip and looked away from his hurting eyes.

"I didn't mean anything by it, man. I didn't realize it was still a sensitive subject for you." Nick kept walking. "Lexie's cute. She seems nice."

"Yeah, she'll do," Noah mumbled as he followed.

IT WASN'T UNTIL the fourteenth hole when my cell phone rang. It was Anna. My heart started beating faster, wondering if something was wrong. Were they in trouble? Did they need me? *I knew I shouldn't have left her!*

"Are you okay?" I asked immediately.

"Relax, we're fine. Where are you guys?"

"On the fourteenth hole at Glen Arbour. How are you girls making out? Keeping it simple, I presume." Fat chance of that, but thought I should throw that reminder out there.

"Uh, yeah, sure. Keeping it simple." Claudia and Rachel could be heard laughing in the background.

I rolled my eyes. "Okay, whatever. I guess you only get married once. Right?"

"That's the plan, anyway." Anna giggled. "Anyway, we were just calling to see if you guys wanted to meet us at Boston Pizza for lunch?"

"Sounds good to me. I'll check with the guys." I nodded to Nick and Noah. "You guys up for lunch with the girls?"

"Sure," Nick answered.

"Yeah, why not," Noah added without looking in my direction.

"We're in. We'll meet you there at twelve thirty?"

"Can't wait!" Anna kissed the phone then said good-bye. Even her radioactive kisses were sweet.

The phone wasn't in my pocket for two seconds when Noah casually asked, "Where's lunch?"

"Boston Pizza," I answered.

"Who's all going?"

"Just Claudia, Rachel and Anna." I fought back the smile forming. Noah struggled with his too, as he kept his eye on the fairway.

And that was all he needed to bring up his game. It went from his worst game of the season to his best. Just like that. All he needed was a bit of inspiration.

THE GIRLS WERE waiting in the round booth when we arrived. Claudia had her familiar pink notebook laid out in front of her and the three of them were leaning over it, quietly discussing.

"Quick! Put it away! The guys are here!" I teased as I slid in next to Anna.

Claudia flipped the book closed and held it against her chest as Rachel hopped out of the booth to let Nick in to sit next to his girlfriend.

Noah sat down next to me, across the table from Rachel.

"I don't bite, Noah," Rachel said as she patted the

seat next to her. "There's more room over here."

Noah hesitated before answering, "It's okay. Jake's warmer."

Awkward silence. Rachel's eyes spelled the definition of hurt. If this had happened yesterday I would've thought she deserved it, but today I felt sorry for her. Knowing her motive now.

Claudia took in a quick breath and glared at me. Nuts. I forgot about Claudia's mind reading! I wasn't supposed to know about Rachel. *I didn't tell him . . . yet*, I thought to her.

Claudia cleared her throat. "So the girls and I were just going through the wedding checklist," she began, "and it *appears* you've been left with the important task of choosing your wedding song."

It was pretty clear she wasn't confident in my song choosing capabilities.

Nick laughed. "Who, Jake? That should be interesting."

I joined in. "I was thinking maybe *Run this Town*. What do you think about that, Claudia? Who's gonna run this town tonight? The wife or the husband?"

Anna giggled, but straightened up when she caught Claudia's serious expression. "I'm sure Jake will put a lot of thought into the song and will choose one appropriately," she said with a grin.

"Mmmmm," Claudia mused. "Anyway, just let me know as soon as you pick one. I'll take care of making sure we have it."

"Yes, ma'am."

"Oh! And you two need to pick a honeymoon destination. I'm not involved in that one, but really you should get on that one soon. You might be able to get an early booking discount or something."

"You mean you're going to let us go on a honeymoon by ourselves?" I said sarcastically, but yet serious. I never thought a honeymoon with just the two of us would be an option.

"Mmmm," Claudia started, "good point. We'll have to talk to Ms. Peters about that one. It would probably be too dangerous, really."

"No!" Anna said, throwing her napkin on the table. "I draw the line there! We've been more than responsible with everything. We've proven we can take care of things on our own and I will *not* be dragging our four best friends along on our honeymoon with us. It's not happening!" Anna finished with a firm look and then carefully picked up her napkin to re-fold it. "Sorry. I just wanted to get that out there."

Noah was the first to laugh. "Well, I guess it's settled then. Anna gets what Anna wants!"

"What's *that* supposed to mean?"

Uh-oh.

"Now, now, children!" Nick interrupted. "But seriously though, I really don't see the harm in letting them take a honeymoon on their own. As long as we know where they are going and that sort of stuff—"

"You can't know where we're going, you idiot!" Anna was still on fire.

"She's right," Rachel added. "Anyone could read our minds about where they are. It'll have to be kept secret."

It was silent for a moment while everyone thought that one through. Then I said, "Even from us."

"But how?" Anna said. "How do we keep it a secret from ourselves?"

"I guess we'll have to figure out how to book a destination without knowing where we're going until we get to the airport. Sounds silly, but I can't think of another way to keep us from thinking about it," I said, trying to weigh our options.

"Yeah, that's probably the only way," Rachel added.

"I don't like it," Claudia protested. "Not one bit." She bit her lower lip. "But it does seem like the only way."

"Yeah, so Anna and I will get on that one. I honestly never put much thought into our honeymoon before now," I admitted.

"Yeah, right!" Nick laughed.

Thankfully, the waitress interrupted us. She took our orders then went away. Probably wondering what our secretive conversations were about.

I turned my attention back to Anna. "So how did the dress shopping go today?"

Anna beamed. "Fanifi—"

"Shhh!" Claudia cut her off. "He needs to know nothing except where to be and what time."

You're a freak, I thought. A sharp pointed heel dug into my shin under the table. I bit my lip and forced a friendly smile.

"*Anyway.*" Anna rolled her eyes. "How was your game?"

"Great!" Nick answered. "Noah ended up beating us."

"Really?" Rachel asked surprised.

"Why is that so hard to believe?" Noah asked defensively.

"I . . . I . . . I guess I thought you'd have a bad game." She stared at her napkin in front of her.

Claudia studied Rachel's face then asked, "Did you really win, Noah?"

"Yes!" Noah said, annoyed. "I mean, the first of the game I sucked, but I did much better on the back nine."

Rachel shook her head slowly. "I don't get it."

"Rachel saw that you started the game out well, but then you did horribly on the last few holes. You ended up losing," Claudia filled us in.

"Thanks, Rach." Noah smiled.

"It just . . . it just doesn't make any sense!"

"Did you go see Mr. Chisholm yet?" I asked.

"I did. I saw him last night. He told me to be strong and brave and not to be afraid or discouraged. Then he said he'll always be there for me if I ever need anything."

"What does that even mean?" Nick asked.

"I don't know," Rachel answered. "I mean, it's nice to know he's got my back, but it's not really helping me with my gift."

Noah cleared his throat. "I think what he's trying to say is that Rachel is worrying about something beyond her control. Her gift has been warped until she can figure out how to trust herself and her own strength."

Everyone sat quietly, starring at Noah. He shrugged. "There's your translation."

"Rach?" Nick turned to Rachel. "Anything you want to talk about?"

Rachel shot a quick look to Claudia and Anna. "It's nothing I can't deal with on my own. I don't need the rest of you worrying about it too."

"Is there . . . is there anything I can do to help?" Noah asked quietly.

"No!" Rachel said sharply. "Just let me work this one out on my own, please."

CHAPTER 18

I HAD JUST finished getting dressed for church when Dad opened my bedroom door. He stood there for an awkward moment, then came in and sat on my bed.

"What's up?" I asked, slightly confused.

"So you're pretty serious about getting married to Anna, I guess." Although it wasn't really a question, I felt I should answer.

"Yes, Dad." I turned back to my closet and pretended to look for something so he didn't catch me rolling my eyes.

"Jake, I just . . . I just think you're too young. You both have so much growing up to do." Dad stood up and walked to the window.

"Okay, Dad? You *have* to give it up. We're both adults and can make our own decisions."

"I'd hardly call you adults. You're seventeen, Jake!"

"Exactly! We're seventeen! I'll be eighteen soon and Anna will be eighteen soon after the wedding." I closed my closet door and took a deep breath. "Dad, we love each other. I know she's the only one I will ever want to be with. She's everything to me and I couldn't imagine life without her. I want to do this, Dad."

He stared at his feet on the carpet. "I guess there's no convincing you otherwise then, is there?"

"Nope." I held my ground against him. First time ever.

"Okay, then." He nodded and headed for the door. "Oh, by the way, your mother isn't feeling well. She's staying home from church today and I'd like you to stay home too. Help her out with Abby."

"Me? Why? Can't you?" Pushing my luck slightly, but I was already dressed and ready to go and Anna would be waiting for me to pick her up soon.

"No, I can't," Dad answered firmly. "I have some errands to run. She's quite sick, Jake. She'll need you there to grab her a cold facecloth and to keep Abby out of her hair. I'll be back in an hour or so."

"Can't you do your errands later?" I protested.

Dad's face turned cold. "You'll do as I say, Jake." And he walked out of the room, closing the door behind him.

Man! Impossible! I kicked my hamper and watched it topple over and the clothes sprawl over the floor. "I can't *stand* him sometimes!" I muttered under my breath. Definitely not loud enough for him to hear, though. Definitely not.

I picked up the phone and called Anna. "Hey, babe," I said when she answered the phone.

"Hi! You leaving now?" She still sounded sexy. Even on a Sunday morning.

"Actually, I can't take you today. I'm sorry. Mom's sick so I have to stay home and take care of her." I gritted my teeth as I thought about Dad running his insignificant errands and leaving me home to take care of Mom.

"Oh, that's too bad. Is she okay?"

"I'm sure she's fine. Probably just the flu or something." I was still bitter. "Anyway, have fun and call me when you get home."

"Sure. Kisses."

"You too." I hung up the phone and sat down on my bed. Taking a deep breath, I decided to make the best of it. I programmed Anna's route into my cell phone and made sure the alerts were set, then I stuck my phone deep in my pocket and headed down the hall to check on Mom.

She was bundled up in about five blankets and a box of tissues was half-emptied beside her on the bed. Abby sat by the fireplace at the other end of Mom's bed reading books.

"What are you doing?" I said with a laugh.

"Reading to Mom," she defended with a sneer.

"Mom? You awake?" I whispered as I carefully sat on the edge of her bed and felt her forehead.

"Uh," she groaned.

"It's okay. Get some sleep. Let me know if you need anything." I turned to Abby. "Psst! Come on. Let Mom rest."

I led Abby down the hall into her room and sat on her floor next to her dollhouse.

Abby's face lit up. "Are you going to play Barbies with me?" She jumped on the floor beside me and handed her Ken doll to me.

I drew strength from within and reluctantly took the doll from her hands. "Sure am," I said with an exaggerated smile.

We played with her Barbies for an extremely long twenty-six minutes. I kept checking my watch and couldn't believe how slow time was passing. Finally I tucked Ken into bed and said, "Ken's going to sleep now. We'll play later when he wakes up."

Abby rolled her eyes but then laid Barbie down next to Ken and tucked her in too. "Jake?"

"Yeah?" I stood up, stretched, then sat on the end of her bed.

"When you and Anna get married, will you still live here?" She hopped up on her bed and lay down, holding her pillow to her chest.

"Hmmm, that's a good question, Abs. I guess we haven't talked about it too much, but I suspect we'll end up getting our own place."

Abby looked disappointed. "But how are you going

to buy your own house? You're both in school."

I guess I had never thought about how best to explain how we came up with the money to buy our own house. Maybe a lottery? Or an inheritance from Anna's grandparents?

"You're right, Abby. I don't really know. How would you feel about us living here for a bit? Until we can afford our own place?"

Abby's eyes lit up. "Yes! Please do that! I'd love to have a sister!"

The truth was I'd prefer to live in a cardboard box on the side of the road than under the same roof as Dad. I knew he wasn't about to make married life very easy for me. I didn't get it, though. He and Mom had a great relationship. So it seemed.

"Jake, you promise you'll stay here?"

"Sure, kid. For a little while, okay?" I tussled her hair.

"Cool," she said. "But when you *do* get your own house, what kind of house do you think you'll buy?"

"Hmmm," I said as I stroked my chin. "I guess I never thought about it before. Anna likes old Victorian houses, and I think I'd be okay with that. A fixer-upper, maybe? Something close to you, of course, but with a big property for privacy." I started picturing all the state-of-the-art security equipment I would have throughout the property.

"That sounds nice. Make sure it has a bedroom for

me though, okay?"

"I'm sure there will be a whole west wing with your name on it!" I teased.

A high-pitch beeping sounded and my pants began vibrating. It took me a few seconds to realize what it was. . . . My phone! I snatched it from my pocket and my eyes scanned the screen to figure out what was happening.

"What on *earth* . . ." Abby began.

"Shh!" I scolded. The map showed Anna's location being at the church, but the screen was flashing red. Her vitals showed a quickened heartbeat and when I pressed the "diagnosis" button, a proper English voice spoke to me: "Subject is in danger. Oxygen is minimal. Heartbeat is high."

I quickly punched in my code to access the video on Anna's bracelet. Although the visibility wasn't good enough to see anything, I could hear screaming and crying. My heart was racing too fast. I couldn't figure out what to do next.

"Jake?" Abby's voice interrupted my scattered, panicked thoughts. "If you need to go, I'll take care of Mom."

That was it—the push I needed to get me functioning again. I needed to find Anna. Figure out what was going on.

"Thank you, Abby!" I ran out of her room and down the stairs. Within minutes, I was speeding down the road toward the church.

Mindlessly, my fingers dialed Noah's number. "Noah!" I shouted when he answered. "Anna's in trouble. Something's going on at the church. Can you grab the others and get over there now?"

"Yeah, sure. What's happening?" Noah asked.

"I don't know! Just get over there now!" I ended the call and found myself pulling into the church parking lot.

My breath got stuck in my chest as I surveyed the scene—flames were shooting out of the windows, and smoke was billowing high into the sky! How did this happen? How did it get so advanced? Why weren't the fire trucks there already?

I jumped out of the car before it was completely stopped. Some people were gathered at the side of the building, but according to my GPS, Anna was still inside, so I didn't stop to ask any questions.

Anna and I always sat on the right hand side of the balcony, so I ran to the set of doors that were closest to the balcony stairs. Closest to her. When I reached the doors, I pulled on them, but they didn't open. I squinted through the doors and through the thick smoke, I could see bodies lying on the floor by the doors. They were locked in! They couldn't get out! I took a deep breath and punched my fist into the door as hard as I could. The glass shattered. I quickly broke the rest of the glass out of the frame, climbed through and began pulling bodies out as I came across them. This was going to take me forever, and I needed to get to Anna. Then I had an idea. . . .

I leaned down and healed two otherwise healthy-looking guys and when they opened their eyes, I ordered them to help take the other bodies out of the lobbies and hallways. Then I ran back into the burning building and up the stairs. With my face buried in my arm, it was a struggle to keep from tripping over all the bodies.

"ANNA!" I called through the thick smoke. "ANNA!!"

I checked my phone again and zoomed in on her location. According to this, she was only a few feet from me. I reached around for her and called her name again. But nothing. I had no choice. I was getting weak from the smoke and I couldn't handle another minute in the building. I grabbed three bodies that were within a few feet of me and carried them out, down the stairs and broke through a window, landing on the soft grass outside.

My eyes adjusted and I searched the bodies around me. None of them Anna!

"NO!" I cried as I jumped up and ran back toward the burning building.

"JAKE!" I heard someone scream from across the parking lot. It was Rachel. "Jake, where is she?"

I didn't answer. I just turned and ran back into the

building. I heard the others catching up behind me as I entered the building. I ran back up to the balcony. "ANNA! ANNA, ANSWER ME!" *God, please! Don't take her from me!*

Someone coughed weakly. I crouched down on the floor and crawled around, feeling my way. Then my hand touched familiar warmth—Anna's hand! I jumped up, threw her over my shoulder and ran back down the stairwell, grabbing anyone that I could on my way. Just as we were at the bottom of the staircase and only a few feet from the door, I heard something behind me, like heavy footsteps coming down the staircase. Turning around, I caught sight of the dark silhouette of a man standing in the middle of the staircase with a mask over his face, protecting him from the thick smoke that was killing everyone else. With no time to waste, I continued down the hall and out the broken window.

Back outside, I collapsed on the ground with the four other bodies that I had just pulled from the building. I found Anna and pulled her into me. Her face and arms were covered in burns. Her dress was charcoaled and clung to her skin. *Heal her body,* I thought. *Heal her now! Make her whole. Make her new. This I pray, I beg of you!*

I coughed and a ball of smoke escaped my lungs. Then I heard and saw the sweetest sound and sight from beside me—a cough and another cloud of smoke. "Anna!" I cried as I held her tightly. The burns gradually disappeared from her face and arms as I rocked her in my arms.

"Jake!" Noah called as he ran to our side. "Thank God! Anna, are you okay?"

"Yeah, I'm good," Anna said, her head still buried in my chest.

"Where are the others?" I asked.

"They're coming over now. The firefighters and paramedics are here now, so they're not letting us back in. They're already suspicious, so Nick thought it was best we stay out."

"And just watch innocent people die?" Anna argued as she struggled to sit up.

"What else can we do?" Nick said.

Anna pulled me over to a firefighter who was giving a policeman an update of the situation.

"I don't get it. All of the doors in the building were chained and padlocked from the inside . . . except the lower level door. And that's the door that the kids escaped from," the firefighter said as he scratched his head.

Anna grabbed the arm of the firefighter. "Are the kids okay?" she asked.

"Miraculously, yes."

And it was that response that assured me that Anna had something, if not everything, to do with their survival.

Claudia pulled us back into a huddle. "Okay, guys,

we have to figure this out. Nick and I will wander around trying to find some clues as to who could have done this. Noah and Rachel, you guys go see if there's anything you can help the firefighters with. Maybe they could use your strength for something. Jake, you need to get to work healing some of these people. Anna can go with you," Claudia finished.

We separated and as I headed toward a group of lifeless bodies, I spotted a familiar blue BMW out of the corner of my eye. I squinted to get an ID on the driver who seemed to be in a hurry to get out of the parking lot. I regretted it the moment I saw him. . . . Dad!

CHAPTER 19

WE WORKED HARD for the next two hours, fixing, healing and helping in any way we could. Exhausted and covered with soot, we decided to leave when the fire was finally out. I was glad to have the distraction of the chaos around me to keep my mind off of my dad and why he would be at the church. I concluded that he was probably on his way home from running errands and stopped in at the church to see what the commotion was about. I was sure I would get the full story when I got home.

After getting her a change of clothes, I brought Anna back home with me, mainly because I wasn't prepared to let her out of my sight for another minute. When she and Abby were deep into playing a board game, I hurried upstairs to check on Mom.

"Oh, Jake! Are you okay? I heard about what happened at the church! Is Anna okay? Where is she?" Mom hurled her half dozen questions at me as soon as I opened her bedroom door. She was propped up in her bed with the telephone next to her.

"You look horrible," I revealed. "No offence." I sat down on the edge of her bed, hesitant to breathe the germ-filled air. "We're fine. Anna was trapped in the building, but I managed to find her when I got there. She's downstairs now with Abby."

"Oh, thank God!" Mom cried, pulling me in. "Your father told me about the fire when he got home. Then Abby told me you had gone to the church to find Anna. I was so worried."

"Dad's home?" I looked around the room.

"He's in the shower."

I noticed the pile of his clothes by the hamper. I casually walked over and looked down at them for some sign of something. The smell of smoke hit my nostrils.

"What are you doing, Jake?" Mom asked suspiciously as she leaned closer.

"Was Dad at the church?" My heart began to race.

"No, I don't think so. He just said he drove in and around the parking lot when he was on his way home. He saw the fire trucks and wanted to know what had happened."

I guess it was believable. I didn't actually see him out of the car. What was I thinking, anyway? This was my *father*! Of course he wasn't to blame for the fire! I shook my head and then tried to laugh it off.

The shower shut off and a few seconds later the bathroom door opened.

"Geez, Jake! What are you doing in here?" Dad held the towel around his waist.

"Sorry, Dad. I was just talking to Mom about the fire."

"Yeah, that's pretty awful." He walked past me and over to Mom. Bending down, he planted a soft kiss on her forehead. "I'm so thankful you weren't there," he whispered.

Mom reached for his hand. "Me too." Their hands touched and Mom gasped. "Geez, David! What happened to your hand? Is that a burn?"

Dad pulled his hand away. "Oh, that. Yeah, it is, actually. Stupid me—I touched the burner on the stove this morning." He walked over to his closet and opened the door.

My eyes were fixated on the fresh burn on the top of Dad's hand near his thumb. Something inside of me wanted to blame him for this tragedy. For almost killing Anna. I knew he didn't want us together. Maybe this was his sick and twisted way of making sure it didn't happen. But something else inside of me begged for the evidence not to be there. He was my father. The man who taught me how to catch a ball. How to ride a bike. Build a fort.

My mind was racing, coming up with argument after argument for both sides. I wanted to flush it out of my memory and not believe anything, but my instincts were there to protect Anna. . . . Anna! She was still waiting in the living room . . . unprotected.

"I gotta go!" I declared. "Anna's downstairs waiting."

Dad quickly stepped out from his closet. "She is?" he asked, seemingly alarmed. "Is she . . . is she okay?"

"Yes, Dad. She's fine," I answered indifferently.

"That's fantastic news," he said with a smile that I could only interpret as fake. He turned his attention to Mom. "Joanna, we should try to reach someone—the pastor, secretary, or anyone—and see if there's anything we can do."

I left the room at that exit point. Still unsure how to take everything, but deciding to let the authorities deal with it. I would stay on my guard, but I wasn't about to be the one to take my Dad down, even if he was a criminal.

A WEEK PASSED without another incident or sign of motive from Dad. I decided to let it go when I heard that the police had a lead on some twisted teenagers.

Anna was waiting on her front step when I pulled in to pick her up for school on Tuesday morning. She was dressed in my favourite jeans and pink cardigan. Her hair bounced around her shoulders as she skipped down her walk.

"Hey, cutie!" I greeted as she plunked herself into

the car.

We met in the middle and exchanged a sweet morning kiss—the fuel that would keep me going through until recess.

I paused and assessed her guilt-ridden face. "What did you do?" I accused, instantly assuming she went overboard again on wedding arrangements.

"Nothing!" she defended with a scowl.

"Well, then, how about telling me what you're hiding?"

Anna looked away as I pulled out of her driveway. "Why can't I keep anything from you?" she mumbled.

"Why would you want to?" I drove slowly, keeping one eye on Anna and the other on the road.

"I'm trying to be a good friend too. Not just a good girlfriend."

"Fiancée," I casually corrected. When it didn't seem to make a difference, I added, "Anna, you're a fantastic friend. We've gone through this. You should be sharing everything with me. Not just because you're my fiancée, but for your protection."

She nodded slowly.

"So please tell me what's going on."

Anna took a deep breath. "Rachel doesn't know that you know anything. Claudia does, but she's not going to tell Rachel because it would upset her."

"Okay. Makes sense." I wasn't comfortable with all the secrecy surrounding such an important issue, but

I'd have to hear her out before I made any judgments.

"She got a voicemail from Ryan." She fiddled with the tassels on her scarf. "Apparently he knows that she had lunch with "some guy" on Saturday. He made another threat. Said he'll be watching her and when he figures out who her boyfriend is, he'll be taking care of business." Anna shuddered.

"Who does this freak think he is?" The anger brewed inside of me. My fingers gripped the steering wheel tightly.

"Slow down, Jake!" Anna yelled, breaking my concentration.

I pressed the breaks and calmed myself before pulling into the school parking lot.

"Rachel's thankful now that Noah didn't sit next to her at Boston Pizza. Otherwise, Ryan would've gone after him already. She was sitting next to Nick, but so was Claudia, so Ryan's probably trying to figure out who's who. You know?"

"Yeah, good thing. So what's she going to do now?" It was hard to bite my tongue on this one. Leaving such a thing in the hands of Rachel, Claudia and Anna wasn't something I'd call brilliant.

"She's got a plan, I guess," Anna said quietly. "Just please don't say anything to Noah. Rachel has to keep her distance from him . . . and Nick."

"Why can't she just go to the police? She could give them the text and the voice mail message."

"She doesn't want to get them involved yet. She said there isn't enough proof to get him put away. It would just piss him off even more."

I nodded. "Anna, we should really take care of this together. All of us."

"I know, Jake. I've tried convincing her of that, but she is adamant that it won't work."

My car door suddenly opened and Noah was leaning over top of me. "What's up, guys?"

"Noah, you scared me half to death!" Anna shouted, clutching her chest.

Noah laughed. "I was going to do it to *your* door, but I knew you'd kill me."

"You're damn right I would!" Anna laughed as she got out of the car. "Have you seen Rachel yet?" she asked casually.

"Not yet." Noah backed up to let me out of the car. I shoved him against the car next to us.

"So I'm thinking about asking Rachel to the prom this year. What do you guys think?" Noah asked, shoving his hands deep into his pockets as we walked toward the school.

Anna choked on her coffee. We watched as she coughed for a few seconds and regained her composure. "Sorry!" she finally said. "What . . . what did you say?" So fake.

I laughed and rolled my eyes. "What about Lexie?"

"She's yesterday's news. Rachel and I have been

talking on the phone lately. Things have been going well, so I thought maybe I'd ask her and see what she thinks." Noah threw his arm around Anna as we walked into school.

"Why do you need to ask her now? Why not wait until we get closer to prom?" Anna suggested.

"I thought about that, but there are a dozen other guys bound to ask her, and if I wait too long, it might be too late." Noah held the door open for us. "What do you think she'll say? Has she talked to you lately?"

Anna was struggling with getting her words out. Her lips were moving, but nothing was coming out.

"Dude, let Anna talk to her and feel her out first. I'd hate to see you get rejected again."

Noah nodded. "Yeah, good point. Me too. Plus, I wouldn't want Lexie to hear that I asked Rachel if she's going to say no, anyway."

"True," Anna finally said. "So you ended things with Lexie?"

"Well, not really, I guess. She's always just been a filler. Someone to pass the time with," Noah said.

Anna shook her head. "Boys!"

Noah caught sight of something and perked up. "I'll see you guys in a bit." He headed outside to greet Rachel coming up the walkway.

"Poor guy," Anna whispered.

I took Anna's hand and kissed it. "Don't worry about Noah. He's tough." I led her down the hall and groaned as I caught sight of Mr. Meade and Claudia heading our way, deep in conversation.

"This guy grates my nerves," I groaned as they came closer. Claudia had her arm hooked into Mr. Meade's and she was laughing at something that couldn't possibly be amusing.

"He can't be *that* bad," Anna whispered as she greeted them with a smile. "Claudia doesn't seem put off by him."

"Mr. Rovert!" Mr. Meade's voice reminded me of glass shattering over concrete. He smiled at Anna. "Ms. Taylor, how are you, dear?"

Anna beamed. "I'm good. How are you?"

Claudia interjected, "Listen, I have to go, but I'll catch up with you two later. Good-bye, Mr. Meade. It was nice chatting with you!" She skipped off down the hall and out of sight.

"I hear congratulations are in order!" Mr. Meade said as he held out his hand in front of me.

I stared at it for a second, but a nudge from Anna prompted me to extend mine in response. "Thank you."

"When's the big day?" he asked Anna.

"May twelfth," she said excitedly. I loved watching her talk about the wedding. So carefree and happy.

"Great time of year!" Mr. Meade said. "My wife and I were married in May. Late May."

"I didn't realize you were married," I said as politely as I could muster.

Mr. Meade laughed. "I bet you're thinking who would marry a grumpy old man like me, right?"

"Well, I wasn't thinking *old*," I said, half-teasingly.

"What is your wife's name?" Anna asked.

"Margaret," he answered proudly. "She's a travel agent."

"Oh, a travel agent! We need one of those!" Anna clapped her hands together in excitement. "We have to book our honeymoon." She grinned widely.

"That's right, you'll need a honeymoon, won't you?" Mr. Meade laughed. "Where are you going?"

"We're not sure yet," I answered honestly. *Nor will we know until we get there.*

Mr. Meade reached into his coat pocket and pulled out his wallet. "Here," he said handing a business card to Anna, "this is Margaret's card. Give her a call and she'll be happy to help you arrange your honeymoon."

"Oh, thank you, Mr. Meade!" Anna studied the card carefully. "Margaret Mullaly? Did she not take your last name?" Uh-oh. The age-old debate about last names.

"She didn't, actually. Margaret's a very head-strong, independent woman. She felt like it was taking away part of her identity or something. I got used to it." He looked back and forth between the two of us. "What about you?"

Anna wrapped her arms around me and patted my chest. "I'll be taking Jake's last name. It's important to him." Phew! I did not want to have that argument later.

"Proper thing." Mr. Meade smiled.

"Thank you so much for this," Anna said as she held the business card to her chest.

"Yes, thank you," I echoed.

"No, problem. You kids enjoy the wedding planning. It'll be over before you know it." He smiled again before he walked off down the hall. Then he turned and said in his familiar cold voice, "Rovert! Don't be late for class!"

I waited until he was out of earshot. "That guy has more than one personality. That's for damn sure!"

Anna giggled. "Yes, but we are one step closer to finishing our checklist!" She waved the card in front of my face.

"You mean Claudia's checklist," I reminded her as we headed down the hall to our first class—math with Mr. Meade. And I was late.

CHAPTER 20

AN OTHERWISE QUIET cafeteria was interrupted by Noah slamming his fist down on the table as he sat down.

"I don't get her!" he snapped.

Anna gently kicked me under the table. "Who?" she asked, although she very well knew the answer.

His hard eyes looked up from the table. His voice was almost cold. "Rachel." He dropped his head on the table and sighed. "One minute she's acting like she actually cares about me. The next minute she's acting like she doesn't even know me. I just . . . I just don't understand her at all."

"Oh, Noah," Anna soothed as she reached for his arm. "Give her some time."

"I've given her time. I'm just so sick of this back and forth crap. It's so frustrating. So defeating."

I wasn't sure what angle to come at him with. On the one hand, I wanted to encourage him to give her time, knowing that she would eventually have the nerve to tell him about Ryan. But on the other hand, if Ryan was serious with his threat, I didn't want Noah getting blindsided, either.

"Let the bitch go," I finally said. Anna's sharp fingernails in my side caused me to immediately regret saying it.

Noah looked at me, puzzled. "You're right, Jake. You've always been straight up and honest with me. Thanks." He straightened up and took a breath.

A wave of guilt washed over me. Could he see it written all over my face? Before I had a chance to say anything, Rachel walked into the cafeteria. Anna waved her over.

"Speak of the devil," Noah said as he whipped out an apple from his backpack and took a bite.

"Hi, guys!" Rachel chirped as she pulled up a chair and sat down next to me. "What's the gossip?" She looked back and forth between Noah, Anna and me, then said, "Who died?"

Then I had an idea. Whether good or bad, I wasn't sure yet, but I had to do something. "We were just talking about graduation, and the prom. You planning on going?"

Noah's eyes were burning a hole in my face, followed by Anna's fingernails digging into my leg.

Rachel looked confused. "What's that, like eight months away? Why are you talking about it already?"

"I don't know. I guess it's that time of year where you pick your date for the prom." I cleared my throat, then continued, "Noah was thinking about asking Lexie."

Rachel stiffened. "Lexie?" She shot Noah a look. "Why so soon? Why don't you wait? I mean, I think it's great that you're going to ask her. She'll be thrilled. But why don't you wait just a few more weeks?"

Noah looked confused. "Why?"

They exchanged a long, intense look and then Rachel's phone started beeping. She quickly looked down and read a text on her screen, then put it away and said firmly, "You should definitely ask her, though."

I scoffed. "Who's texting you?"

This time subtlety wasn't Anna's intention. She slapped my arm. "It's none of your business, Jake!"

Rachel laughed and looked down. "It's okay, Anna." She smoothed her hair over her shoulder and then confirmed, "An old friend."

"Well, it's been nice chatting with you guys." Noah stood up to leave. "I've got to go find Lexie. Maybe I'll ask her to the prom now since there's no one else I'd rather take." Ouch.

"Yes, you should do that. Before someone else snatches her up." Rachel gritted her teeth.

Noah walked away and Rachel kept a composed look on her face as she gripped the phone tightly between her hands.

"Rach?" I said as I stood up and placed a hand on her shoulder. "Deal with whatever it is you have to deal with and get over it. We need you back."

"I'm working on it," she groaned.

"Babe, I'm going to the washroom. You girls okay here?"

"We're good. Go cause problems somewhere else," Anna said, glaring at me, but then softened her hard mouth and smiled slightly.

ON FRIDAY AFTER school, I dropped Anna off at her house and then headed home to finish up my homework for the weekend. When I walked into the house, Dad was sitting at the table having a coffee.

"Hey, Dad." I threw my bookbag on the empty seat next to him and went into the kitchen to grab a snack.

"How are things, Jake?" Dad stroked his chin as he often did when he had something important to say.

"Things are great," I answered hesitantly. Where was he going with this?

"Have you made any more wedding plans yet?" He took a long sip from his mug.

"Sure."

"I was thinking it must be pretty expensive planning a wedding. Your mother and I were talking and we were thinking that if you postponed the wedding for one more year, just a year, we would have enough money saved up to pay the costs for you."

This was a new angle. Hoping that if we postponed the wedding, then maybe I would have a chance to change my mind. I wondered if he really thought that I was that delusional?

"That's nice of you to offer, Dad, but we're going to be okay. Anna's parents are taking care of most of it." It wasn't completely untrue. They *thought* they were paying for most of it, but they were a little naïve when it came to understanding the value of a lot of the things Claudia was putting into the wedding.

Dad put his mug down on the table and twisted it in his hands. "Jake, please reconsider this wedding. You're so young, and you're not even done school, and you—"

"Dad, drop it!" I shouted, raising my voice louder than I had ever dared toward my father. "Anna and I are getting married and there's nothing you can say or do to change that! And if you want to be invited to the wedding, I suggest you stop trying to talk me out of it!"

He watched me closely for a long, drawn out ten seconds. Then the corner of his mouth twitched and a grin spread across his face. "Okay, then. I'll drop it."

"Thanks," I grumbled as I grabbed my bookbag and headed up the stairs, counting down the days until I was free to leave.

Yes, he was my father, but there was still something about him that I couldn't trust. Although I couldn't pinpoint it. His evasiveness? The way he is always in my business for no good reason? Now more than ever, I wished I had the gift of Discernment. Not only would the gift have been useful on the island, so that I didn't harm Anna, but I could also use the gift now to distinguish Dad's intentions. Were they out of genuine concern? Or was it an evil purpose?

I decided to call James Chisholm. Maybe a visit with him could lead me in the right direction to getting this other gift, if it was even possible.

When I got to my room, I looked up James's phone number. I dialed quickly and held my breath as the phone rang.

"It's about time you called, Jacob," was how he answered the phone.

"Okay, that was creepy," I said after a few seconds.

"Caller ID." He laughed. "You'd like to come have a visit, am I right?"

"Yes, sir." I gripped the phone tighter, wondering if he already knew what I wanted.

"I've been looking forward to it. How would you like to come over now?" James offered.

"Now?" I did a mental scan of my schedule. It was Friday night so Anna and I had plans to watch a movie, but nothing she wouldn't forgive me for canceling. "Now is good."

James gave me directions to his house and I hung up feeling much better.

I called Anna. "Hey, babe," I said when she answered.

"Miss me already?" she teased in her sweet, sexy phone voice.

"How did you know?" I tried to keep my mind off of holding her warm body next to mine. "Actually, I'm not going to make it over tonight. I'm going to talk to James about a few things. Is that cool with you?"

"Oh, sure. Is everything okay?" she pried cautiously.

"Everything's good. I just want to ask him a few things about my gift and such." I swallowed the nervous lump forming in my throat. "I'll see you tomorrow?"

"Don't forget the girls and I are going shopping tomorrow during your rugby practise."

"Oh, right. I would've forgotten about that. Thanks for reminding me," I said reluctantly. Was it ever going to get easier letting her go off without me?

"That's what I'm here for."

"Okay, so I'll see you around lunchtime tomorrow. Be careful, Anna."

"I will, baby. I love you."

"I love you more." I hung up the phone before giving her a chance to counter.

THE LONG, DARK road was lined with thick trees and overgrown shrubs. It was not at all what I pictured for

James. I was imagining more of an urban setting, but this had me second-guessing my GPS.

Finally, my GPS instructed me to turn right in two hundred feet. When I looked to the right, the tall stone columns threw me off. A large iron gate with James's initials blocked the golden coloured driveway, but as I approached, they slowly opened. Immaculate gardens lit up by Victorian-style street lamps bordered the circular driveway. My nerves subsided as I slowly drove up one length of the driveway and parked at the top of the arch, taking in my surroundings. I got out of the car, and stared at the palatial building in front of me—a gorgeous mansion with turrets and large, beautiful windows that overlooked the gardens. This was definitely not what I had pictured for James Chisholm. In front of me now was a drawbridge, which led over a moat that ran along the perimeter of the building. The bridge led me through a stone archway and into an open courtyard.

"Come in, Jacob!" James greeted me from across the courtyard with open arms. He was standing in front of a set of large, ornately carved wooden doors. "It's so nice to have you here."

I struggled to formulate any coherent words. "Good," I said, and then realized it didn't make any sense.

"Welcome to my little piece of paradise," he exclaimed.

"Uh-huh?"

James laughed and pulled me by the arm into the main house, three times as high as my house and twice as long. It was pristine white with white leather furniture, white accents and white walls. Surprisingly though, it was very comfortable and warm.

"Now, Jake, I don't want to keep you too long, I know it was a long drive for you to get here and a long drive home, so why don't you sit down and tell me what's on your mind." James held out a glass of water.

"Thank you," I said, gratefully taking the water. "Mr. Chisholm, I've come to ask for advice."

"You've come for a few reasons, haven't you, Jake? Tell me what is the most important to you right now. Let's start with that." James sat down in a chair across from me and I suddenly felt very at ease. Like I was talking to a lifelong friend.

"Okay, so I need to know how I can get another gift," I blurted.

"You don't like the one you have?"

"No, it's not that at all. I *love* my gift. It's great. Really. I just . . . I just—"

"You just want more power," he finished for me.

"If you put it that way, it sounds pretty selfish." I scratched my head, wondering how I could re-phrase it.

"Isn't it?"

I didn't care for the way this conversation was going. "But that's not the reason I want Discernment. I feel like if I had it, I would be a better healer. I could rely on my own senses."

"If you had it, you wouldn't have hurt Anna." Again, finishing my thoughts.

"And that." I pushed the memory back in my head again, repressing it where it belonged.

"But you were able to heal her. You can't be perfect, you know."

"But you are," I pointed out, somewhat childishly.

He just laughed and shook his head. "Okay, let me put it this way. If you want two gifts, Jacob, you must prove that you can handle it. Many people can't even handle one gift, and they end up losing it because of that. To have two gifts, Jacob, would put a lot of responsibility on you."

"How so? How do people lose their gifts? I don't understand that part."

"Your gifts are to be used for good. If you begin using your gift for selfish reasons, or misusing your gift in any way, it will be taken away just as fast as it was given to you."

I nodded slowly. "So how would having Discernment and Healing be a greater responsibility than just having one?"

"Imagine you're about to heal someone who has been in a serious car accident, and as you are about to heal him, you suddenly discern that he is a very evil person. Do you heal him? Or does your disgust for him get in the way?"

"Interesting," I said, considering what I might do. Of course I tried to think that I would heal him anyway because I knew James could read my thoughts, but what if I could mind read too? What if I knew he was a serial killer?

"You see what I mean, Jake? You would have to prove your strength before you could earn another gift such as Discernment." James was speaking softly, but his words still hurt. I so badly wanted to walk out of that house—or mansion—with a gift that could answer my questions about my father. But it was evident now that it wasn't going to happen.

"James? Do you know anything about my father?"

James hesitated and I caught a glimmer of regret in his eyes. He turned away and looked out the window before answering. "Jacob, honour your father and your mother. It is the law."

"But—"

"It is the law, Jacob," James interrupted. "No matter what the circumstances. Good or evil. Known or unknown. It is the law."

CHAPTER 21

THE FIELD WAS wet from last night's rain, but it still felt good to get outside and get dirty. I had a bit of aggression to work off from my earlier chat with James Chisholm. My mind was working overtime to figure out how I could earn the gift. How I could prove I was strong enough to handle both gifts.

Nick blew the whistle for a ten minute break, which was a welcomed change to the intense drills he was putting us through. Noah and I headed back toward the bench as Nick jogged over to us.

"What's with the Hitler approach on practise today?" Noah said as he threw the ball at Nick.

"Gotta get you girls in shape for the big game next week," Nick teased.

We sat down on the bench as the assistant coach came over to us. "Jake, your bag's been making all sorts of beeping noises. Probably a watch alarm or something."

My breathing ceased and I lost my heart somewhere in my stomach.

"What is it?" Nick urged, catching the expression on my face.

"My . . . my phone." I grabbed my bag and began rummaging through it until I found my phone, which was flashing red. The alarm sounded again.

"What the hell is that?" Noah said, leaning over my shoulder to get a better look.

"She's in trouble!" The three of us were across the field and in the school parking lot before anyone could ask any more questions.

I jumped in the driver's seat and didn't check to see if Nick and Noah were safely in before I tore out of the parking lot, following the GPS to somewhere downtown.

"Jake! Where are we going? What's going on? What *is* that thing?" Noah shouted from the backseat.

"It's a GPS locating device I have on Anna. It's connected to her bracelet. It tells me everything about her. Where she is, her vitals, if she's in trouble. And she is. She's downtown somewhere near the dockyards by the looks of it." My heart was still racing and I was quite surprised I could even speak. "Not even close to the shopping mall!" I growled.

"That explains why you've been letting her out of your sight. We all thought you were becoming human again. Apparently not. Does Anna know about this?"

Noah asked irritatingly.

"Not yet, but she'll soon find out. Nick, use your phone to call the police and tell them to meet us downtown at the abandoned warehouse on Bloor Street."

"Sure." Nick made the call as we weaved in and out of traffic. Then I remembered that I could listen in on the audio. I keyed in my code and turned up the volume. We all listened with horror.

"Please don't do this!" Anna's faint voice begged. There was a lot of scratching noise, and I envisioned someone gripping her by the wrist. Tears stung my eyes and I could hardly see anything but red. "Please don't kill her. I'll do whatever you want, just please don't hurt Rachel."

Nick gasped and my eyes flickered to the rear view mirror where I saw Noah's eyes turn black as night.

"Give me that!" Noah demanded as he reached over the seat and ripped the phone from my hand. He held it closer as he listened.

"Anna?" It was Claudia's voice. "Can't you do something? He's going to kill her. You need to do something, Anna!"

"We're . . . we're tied up, Claudia. I . . . I can't concentrate. I'm so scared. I need Jake! I knew this was a bad idea. Jake tried to warn me. He told me we should've told Noah. This wouldn't have happened if Noah knew. He would never have let this happen to her." Anna's trembling voice was all I needed to break every traffic rule and speed limit sign. I used mind movement to push cars out of intersections, which I had never done before. I wasn't even aware of my powers to this degree until now.

"Jake, what the hell is Anna talking about!" Noah shouted as more of a demand than a question.

"Ryan," Nick answered. "Ryan was threatening her life, and yours, if she got close to you. That's why she's been a bitch. She's been trying to protect you."

"Why didn't you tell me!" Again, not really a question.

"I just found out this morning. Claudia told me before they left for shopping. She said Rachel was dealing with it and for us not to worry. If I knew that this was going to happen, I would never have let them out on their own without us."

"Jake?" Noah asked again, trying to sound calmer.

"It's true." I completely regretted promising not to tell. This was obviously something I did not expect or want to happen.

Noah punched the roof of the car. "Why wouldn't she have told me?! I could've taken care of him before this happened!" he shouted as he gripped his hair.

"She thought she was protecting you. She loves you, man." I said, not caring about any secrets anymore.

I heard Noah sniff and I looked in the mirror and caught him wiping his cheek. "Jake, get us there now!"

he growled between gritted teeth.

The GPS took us to the front of an abandoned warehouse. I slammed the car into park and we all jumped out.

"This way," I whispered as I motioned for them to follow me around the side of the building. We found an old door that was left slightly open. I peered in and saw that it led to a hallway, so we slipped in, letting our eyes adjust to the darkness as we swiftly walked down the hall. We reached another doorway and I slowly peeked around the corner.

Rachel was up against the wall on the far side of the room and Ryan was pressed up against her, slowly undressing her at gunpoint.

"Please, Ryan, don't do this!" Rachel cried weakly.

That was all Noah needed to push me aside with more force than I could resist. I took a deep breath and watched as Noah took in the same sight that I saw just a few seconds before. I knew it was the best way to get his adrenaline going, so Nick and I didn't hold him back.

Noah let out a loud growl as he flew across the room, closing the gap between him and Ryan. Ryan turned and pointed the gun toward him so I pulled my strength up and used mind movement to throw Ryan back. It was enough to catch him off guard and let Noah jump in to do the rest. I knew Noah had enough anger in him to finish Ryan off if he had to. I just hoped he had enough strength to resist.

I searched the room for Anna and Claudia and found them tied up to a wooden beam with two of Ryan's friends guarding them.

"Jake!" Anna shouted as Nick and I sprinted toward them.

The two guys squared off and met us with full force. While Nick went after the smaller guy with the gun, I didn't hesitate to take on the bigger guy with the knife. He swung at me, and I ducked, grabbed his wrist with my right hand and pushed him down with my left, twisting his arm until he let go of the knife. His leg came around and swiped at mine, sending me down. He dove for his knife, but I used my mind to push it further away, then grabbed him by his shoulder, twisted his arm behind his back and pulled hard until he begged for forgiveness.

The sirens were getting louder. I looked to Nick who had just finished off with the guy he was fighting, and Noah who was trying hard not to finish off Ryan.

"Noah!" Nick yelled as he threw one last punch to knock out his challenger. "He's done."

Ryan was beaten pretty badly, but still conscious—he had put up a good fight. Noah had taken his share of punches too, by the look of him. The police busted into the room and commanded everyone to put their hands up. Noah punched Ryan one last time before surrendering his attention back to Rachel.

About a half dozen uniformed officers entered the building and surrounded Ryan and his friends. Nick and I quickly untied Anna and Claudia. Anna fell limp in my arms.

"I'm so sorry, Jake. You were right. I should've listened to you. I'm so sorry," Anna sobbed in my arms.

My adrenaline was racing through my veins and I wanted to throw someone through a wall, but I was just so happy that she was okay. "Did they hurt you? Did they touch you? Are you okay?" All the questions I wanted answers to, but I knew the wrong answer could easily send me over the edge.

"We're fine," Claudia interjected. I wondered if she was afraid that Anna was going to tell me something that she knew I couldn't handle hearing.

"Rachel!" Anna shouted as she broke free from my hold and ran across the room to her friend. Rachel was sitting on the floor, rocking back and forth in Noah's arms. Whimpering like a cold and abandoned puppy.

Noah wasn't talking. He looked relieved that Rachel was okay, but on the other hand he looked angrier than I had ever seen him. When Rachel finally looked up and dried her eyes, Noah said, "Why? Why would you keep this from me?"

Rachel flung her arms around Noah's neck. "I'm so scared of losing you!"

"Rachel, I'm not going anywhere, but I can't help you unless you let me." He lifted her chin up. "Please let me."

They exchanged a moment where it felt a little awkward to watch them, but then Rachel slowly leaned in and kissed him, almost shyly. Then her eyes closed and she kissed him again. Noah was motionless, eyes closed and seemingly enjoying Rachel's lips on his.

"Noah, I'm so sorry," she finally said. "I . . . I love you."

The smile on Noah's face was another of his emotions I hadn't seen in a long time. He lifted her from the floor and spun her around. "Rachel Riley, will you go to the prom with me?"

She laughed and wrapped her arms tightly around his neck. "I will! I definitely will!"

THE DRIVE HOME was intensely emotional. Rachel sat in the back on Noah's lap, kissing him over and over and over—making up for lost time. Claudia sat in the middle of the backseat next to Nick and silently cried in his arms. And Anna sat up front with me, where I could keep one eye on her at all times. Her frequent glimpses to the backseat demonstrated how overly happy she was that Noah and Rachel were finally together.

"So here's a question," Anna said softly as she ran her hand through the back of my hair. "How did you know where we were and that we were in trouble?"

Before I could come up with a believable excuse, Nick answered, "We tracked you guys using that nifty little tracking device in your bracelet there."

Anna's eyes darted down at her bracelet and then to me. "What is he talking about, Jake?"

I took a deep breath and pushed my head back into my headrest. "Babe, don't be mad."

"I don't like when you start explanations that way," Anna reminded me.

"I can track you with your bracelet. That's how I knew you were in trouble today. That's how I knew about the fire at the church. That's why I've been letting you do things on your own without me." I held my breath and flinched, expecting a physical reaction.

"I see," she said as she ran her fingers over her bracelet. "So it wasn't so much a gesture of thoughtfulness, but more so because you still needed to have some sort of control over my every move?"

"I beg your pardon?" I asked, slightly taken aback with the tone she was using.

"I thought you were loosening the reigns a little! I thought you were trusting me more! But you weren't! You were trusting this *bracelet*!" She took her bracelet off and waved it at me in disgust.

I sighed, but then I remembered the ordeal we just went through. "Wait a second! You should be *thanking* me! If it weren't for me and my over-protectiveness, you three would be dead right now! Actually, *you* probably would've been dead last Sunday in the fire. So don't go blaming me for being too protective, when this *bracelet* saved your life more than once!"

Noah and Rachel weren't kissing anymore. Claudia had stopped crying. And Anna only paused for a few seconds before clasping the bracelet back onto her wrist. "Good point."

CHAPTER 22

EVERYONE CAME BACK to my place afterward. Rachel curled up on the couch with her head on Noah's lap, while Nick sat in the chair with Claudia perched on the arm, and Anna and I settled in on the loveseat.

"I am so glad that is over with," Rachel sighed as Noah stroked her hair.

"Mmmm," Claudia agreed. "I have to admit I was pretty scared there for a bit."

Nick clenched his jaw as he stared straight ahead.

"But the second I saw you"—she stroked Nick's face—"I knew everything would be okay."

Nick nodded but didn't say anything. Claudia slid down on his lap and pulled his arms around her.

"So how are we gonna make sure this shit never happens again?" Noah said.

"I think we should make a pact right now that there are no more secrets," Anna suggested, looking to each of us for consensus.

"Sounds good to me," I agreed, and I convinced myself that my father's potential guilt was not worthy of sharing.

"We're in," Nick said, holding Claudia tighter.

"Yup, me too." Noah looked down at Rachel still curled up on his lap. "Rachel?"

"What if it's better that no one knows?" Rachel was obviously contemplating a scenario.

Noah didn't have any of it, though. "It's *never* better that no one knows. Look at today for example. You thought you were protecting me, but look where it got the three of you." He paused to let it sink in before continuing, "Rachel, I'm a big boy and I can take care of myself. If you would've told us what was going on, we could've figured out a plan together, one that didn't involve having you raped or killed."

Rachel shuddered.

"I'm sorry," Noah quickly added.

"No, you're right. No more secrets. I'm in."

We sat in silence for a minute until we heard the front door opening and my Dad announcing his presence.

"Hey, Dad! We're in here," I called.

Dad came down the hall and stopped when he saw everyone. He kept his distance, which I thought was odd. He was always trying to fit in with the younger crowd so I expected him to sit down next to Noah and start talking about rugby or something.

I caught Claudia's confused expression as she looked over at me then back to my father. Then she stood up and said, "I've heard so much about you, Mr. Rovert. It's a pleasure to meet you. I'm Claudia." She took a few steps toward him with her arm extended, and he backed up in response.

"Oh, you don't want to shake my hand," Dad laughed as he held up his hands. "I think I'm coming down with a cold or something." He forced a cough and then nodded politely. "Nice to meet you too, Claudia. I hope you don't mind, I've some work to do upstairs, so I'll catch you kids later." He quickly headed back down the hallway.

"What's up with your dad?" Noah asked, obviously catching the mysteriousness of his actions.

"I don't know," I answered honestly, wondering if he really was sick, or whether he knew about Claudia's mind reading. He must be sick. That would make sense. Mom was just sick. I shook it out of my head.

"Okay, so here's a question," Rachel said as a welcomed change to the subject. "Are you still with Lexie?" She sat up next to Noah and watched him as he answered.

"Oh yeah, I kind of forgot about her." He laughed, showing little concern.

"So what does that mean?" Her face was a bit distorted as she tried to keep it free from emotion.

"Hmm, yeah," Noah began, "I guess I have a

decision to make here." He stroked his chin with his thumb and forefinger.

There was a few seconds of silence and it almost hurt to see Rachel's face twisted the way it was as she waited for more words to come out of his mouth.

"Noah," Claudia said with a grin as she shook her head, "tell her what you're thinking and stop being a jerk!"

Noah pulled Rachel onto his lap and squeezed her tightly until she coughed. "I guess I choose you."

"Noah!" Claudia warned.

Noah sighed and rolled his eyes at Claudia. "Okay, so it's always been you. Since the first day you walked into the school last year. There's never been a day that has passed that it hasn't been all about you. Lexie was just a filler. Someone to take my mind off of you. And of course I plan on calling her tonight to let her know that it's over."

Rachel smiled and ran her fingers through his hair. "And for me, it's always been about you. Just so you know." She kissed him on the forehead. "Oh, but you're not planning on telling her about *us*, are you?"

"Are you nuts? Lexie's got a mean streak in her. I am *not* doing anything to set her off on you, my pretty princess."

"Pretty princess," Rachel smiled as she held her head high. "I like the sounds of that. But also, so you know? I can take Lexie."

"I'm sure you could," Noah said, "but I would rather not have to test that theory."

THE WEEKEND PASSED too quickly, and on Monday, Noah, Rachel, Anna and I were tossing around a football on the field during lunch hour to pass the time.

Something caught Noah's attention just as Rachel tossed the ball in his direction and the ball hit him in the chest.

"What was that?" Rachel teased as she ran over to snag the ball from the ground.

Noah's eyes stayed focused on something, or someone, across the field. It was Lexie, standing at the edge of the field with her arms crossed, and two of her friends flanking her on either side.

"Let's get out of here," Noah said as he started walking away.

"Noah, it's fine," Rachel reassured him. "Trust me, I've seen what happens."

"Yeah, and the success rate of your visions hasn't been that high lately, so forgive me for wanting to trust my instincts on this one."

"What's going on?" Anna asked, heading to Rachel's side with a protective flare about her.

"Oh, nothing. Lexie thinks I'm the reason why Noah broke up with her over the weekend. So she's going to confront me about it." Rachel was very matter-of-fact and didn't seem concerned at all.

"Rach, please?" Noah begged, pulling her arm gently.

Rachel didn't answer him. She just stared at Lexie and watched as she and her friends approached us.

Noah threw his arms up and groaned, "Impossible."

"Hi, Anna. Jake." Lexie nodded as she approached.

"Hi, Lexie." Rachel smiled.

"Don't pretend we're friends, Rachel."

"I wasn't." Their eyes were still locked as if no one else mattered.

"Lexie," Noah began, "what are you doing here?"

Without taking her eyes off of Rachel, Lexie responded, "Clearing something up." She forced a smile and continued, "Tell me something, Rachel. What part did *you* play in our break up?"

"Lexie, please—" Noah started.

"It's okay, Noah." Rachel put up her hand to silence him. "Lexie deserves the truth."

"This should be good," Lexie said to her friends.

"Lexie, I'm sorry that things worked out the way they did for you. I really am. I'm sorry that I ever gave Noah to you for that short period of time. I made a big mistake. I should never have let him go."

Lexie seemed a little caught off guard by that answer. "You *let* him go?"

"Sure. We've always been right for each other. Always been sort of together in our own way." She threw a wink in Noah's direction. "I'm just sorry you got caught in the middle of it."

The lava that was Lexie's anger was about to erupt. Her eyes were narrowed, her teeth were clenched, and her fist tightened. I was about to intervene when I saw a glimmer of excitement in Rachel's eye. That's when I knew that *she* knew it was coming too.

"You bit—" Lexie swung at Rachel, but Rachel was already out of the way. She grabbed Lexie's fist with her right hand and shoved her to the ground with her left.

"I saw that one coming," Rachel said with a grin. "Do you want help up, Lex?"

I tried to suppress my laughter as Lexie's friends helped her up and they all pranced off, huffing and puffing.

"Oh ye of little faith," Rachel said to us after they were gone.

Noah pulled her in and held her firmly. "You're so hot when you're feisty." He kissed her then pulled away. "But don't do that again."

WE HAD A routine meeting with Ms. Peters after lunch where we received the same lecture about holding back secrets. She wasn't happy with Rachel for keeping Ryan's threats from the group. Once she was done lecturing everyone, she cleared her throat and sat down in her chair.

"I also want to talk to you guys about your gifts and

ensuring that you don't lose them," she said as she took a sip of her water. "I'm a little concerned about your gift, Rachel."

"My gift? Mom, I'm sure it's okay now. I had a proper vision just this morning. I'm sure the stresses about Ryan's threats, and then the stress of Noah being with Lexie, were the reasons for my visions being all screwed up."

"I'm sure that had a lot to do with it, Rachel, and I'm glad you had a proper vision this morning. My concern now is your focus. My dear, love is a very powerful thing. It *will* cloud your visions in the initial stages." Ms. Peters sighed. "Perhaps we should all be on the look-out a little bit more. Rachel's visions should be accurate now, but she may not see everything she would normally see."

"What should we do?" I asked.

"There's nothing we can do, Jake. It's a natural part of life for prophets."

"So what can the rest of us do to ensure we don't lose our gifts?" Nick asked.

"Stay focused on the reason you all have your gifts in the first place—to help others. We're not here to judge people. We're not here for ourselves. We're not here to play God. We're here to help. To fight evil."

We all nodded.

"Good. Now, just remember, Noah and Rachel, you will be more of a threat to the Defiers now because you are both powerful Gifted Ones. You'll be weak for the next few months until you're out of your honeymoon stage, so until then, you must stay on your guard."

"Okay," Noah said, putting his arm around Rachel and kissing the side of her head.

"I have a question," I interrupted. "How does that affect me and Anna? You said that when powerful Gifted Ones get together, they are more of a threat? What does that mean for us when we get married?"

The lump in Ms. Peters's throat became noticeable as she swallowed. She pressed her fingertips together and looked out the window. "It's a real concern, Jake. We're working on it."

Nothing else was said as she waved for us to leave her office. Anna tucked herself close beside me and I held her tight to my side until I had to let her go in Noah's care for biology class.

"Take care of her," I whispered as Noah followed her into the classroom. A sick feeling plagued my body. What did Ms. Peters mean by that? Why hadn't anyone talked to us about it? What were we getting ourselves into?

CHAPTER 23

THE WEEKS FLEW by without drama or emergencies. Before we knew it, spring was here and we were welcoming a week-long break from school. Noah and Rachel were still on cloud nine, never to be seen without each other. Unfortunately, Ms. Peters was right about Rachel's visions being clouded. She was only having visions during her sleep and couldn't remember half of them when she woke up. One dream, in particular, scared her, but when she tried to recall it, she couldn't remember any of the details.

The rest of us began relying on our own dreams and intuitions. I kept having that horrible headless horse nightmare where the angel in the middle of the field was calling for help and the black headless horse galloped across the field and swallowed her whole. It didn't make any sense so it wasn't important enough to tell the group about, plus I had been having this nightmare for over a year now, so it was almost a regular part of sleeping. I was sure they'd just tease me about it anyway.

As I laced up my skates in Anna's backyard, I remembered back to the first time she and I skated on the lake together. We were out in the middle of the lake for hours. Not a care in the world. Not one inkling of fear that we could fall through the ice. Completely invincible. And now, three years later, when I looked at the ice, all I saw was potential for her to get hurt. How was it that I could go from not caring what happened to us, to feeling nauseous at the idea of something happening to her?

"What are you worrying yourself about now?" Anna said as she sat down on the log beside me with her skates in hand.

"Hey, babe." I greeted her with a kiss. Watermelon lips. "I was thinking, how about we skip this skating stuff and head back to my house. We haven't had much alone time lately, and I've been craving watermelon lately."

She looked intrigued as she pulled me closer by my hood strings. "I would *love* to, Jake, but I . . . I . . ." and she mumbled something that I couldn't make out.

"Huh?" I moaned as I kissed her neck while unbuttoning her coat. I lifted her onto my lap and we fell back into the snow. I pulled her face into mine and kissed until she drew away and sat up.

"I *said*, I invited the others over for a skate, so we

can't right now. Sorry!" Her please-don't-be-mad-at-me look was still sexy with the glow of the sunset behind her.

"Are you kidding me?" I groaned, sitting up beside her.

"I'm sorry, Jake. I feel like I haven't spent much time with Rachel and Claudia lately and with the wedding coming up, I really wanted to have some fun with them."

"Is the wedding stressing you out?"

"Not really. It's just I feel like everything's always about the wedding and I want to make sure we're all still friends by the end of it." She laughed as she returned her attention to her skates.

Was she having second thoughts? Maybe the wedding was stressing her out because she wasn't sure she was making the right decision. "Tell me something and be honest, okay?"

"Sure. What is it?"

"Do you still feel confident that we should be getting married?"

"Of course I do! One hundred percent. Not a single doubt in my mind. Jake, you are my best friend. You are the only one who truly gets me. And you *still* make my heart race when you come around. I mean, sure one day that will probably get old, but I know one thing will never change—I will always want to spend the rest of my life with you by my side."

My heart kind of tickled. "Good. That's good to hear," I said. "I'm glad you're so confident about it."

"Of course I am. You're the one for me. When you know, you just know."

I nodded as I finished lacing up my skate. *When you know, you just know.* Her words repeated in my head. I was thrilled Anna was so sure about the wedding because it made it more real for me. I heard it was common for guys to get cold feet, although I'm sure their reasons were different than mine. I knew Anna and I were meant to be together forever, but I was so damn scared to lose her in the process of forever.

"Party's here!" Noah called from the bottom of the driveway as he and Rachel made their way through the snow toward us.

Anna jumped up. "Yaye! I'm so glad you guys could come!"

I couldn't help but disagree with her on that one. My preference would have been to be snuggled up by a cozy fire at my empty house right now.

"I brought hot chocolate!" Rachel called back as she held up a thermos.

"Fantastic!" I tried my hand at enthusiasm. I hope it didn't come off too sarcastic. Anna hit me. I guess it did. "We'll meet you guys on the ice," I said as Noah and Rachel took our places on the log.

Claudia and Nick arrived next. Anna and I skated around, and I watched as she practised her twirls and fancy little tricks.

We spent over an hour on the ice and it really wasn't that bad once we got on and started playing around with hockey sticks and pucks. My attention slowly shifted from Anna to the game as Nick, Noah and I tried to keep each other away from the puck.

Suddenly my instincts heightened and my head whipped around toward the girls. Anna was skating fast, and then she whipped around backwards and jumped in the air, twirling once before she landed. Unfortunately, her landing wasn't as graceful. Her feet slipped out from underneath her and she crashed hard on her back, her head bouncing off the ice.

Everyone dropped what they were doing and skated to Anna's side. I pushed my way through and knelt down beside her. She was now face down with her hands held tightly to the back of her head. The blood was trickling through her fingers.

"Anna! Are you okay?" I shouted as I tried to remove her fingers.

"Ouch!" she moaned. "Don't touch me."

"Move your hands. I want to take a look. I'll fix you," I pleaded, trying to move her fingers again.

She refused and gradually sat up. "That hurt," she said with a tiny chuckle.

"Your twirl was awesome, though!" Rachel praised.

"It was, wasn't it? I've never done one before. That felt amazing!" Anna laughed.

"Well, that's fantastic!" I scowled. "Now move your stubborn hands and let me fix your head. You're bleeding."

Anna glared at me. "Don't touch me, Jake. Let me be normal for once. Let my body figure out how to heal itself. I'm not dying, alright?"

"Okay." I raised my hands and backed away. "Let me know when the pain gets too much and you want me to intervene, okay?"

"It won't happen," she said with fire in her eyes. And that's when I knew that she wasn't going to whisper one word of pain about her head to me for the rest of the night, no matter how much it hurt.

"You're so stubborn." I reached down and helped her up. Noah took her other side and we skated off the ice.

"I guess the party's over." I tried to sound disappointed.

"Are you going to take her to the hospital?" Rachel asked.

"No." I winked at her. "She'll be fine. She's staying at my house tonight and I'll keep a close eye on her." Full well knowing that I intended on healing her one way or another.

Claudia shook her head. "You're *both* stubborn."

BACK AT MY house, I wrapped some ice in a tea towel and told Anna to hold it on her head. That was about the extent of what she'd let me do for her. She got comfortable on the sofa and I turned the fireplace on.

"You okay? Does it hurt?" I asked, knowing she wouldn't actually tell me if it did.

"Yeah, I'm good." She rolled over on her side and a groan slipped from her lips. She winced but caught herself and smiled innocently.

The front door suddenly opened and someone ran into the house.

"Hello!" I shouted as I jogged to the entryway. It was Dad. "What are you doing home? Isn't your flight in like a half an hour?"

Dad was out of breath but managed to catch it long enough to answer. "Your mother forgot her passport on the table." He ran into the kitchen and grabbed some documents off the counter. "Hi, Anna!" he called over his shoulder.

"Hi, David!" Anna called back.

"See you next week!" he shouted as he headed back to the door.

"Have a good trip, Dad."

"Hey!" Dad stopped and turned around quickly. "Did you two figure out yet where you're going for your honeymoon?"

I laughed. "That was random. Uh, yes and no, actually. We left it up to the travel agent. We didn't want to know where we're going, nor did we want anyone else to know, so we gave her a list of places that we were interested in, and she booked it for us. We won't know until we're on the plane."

"All we know is that it's going to be someplace warm," Anna added.

"Hmm," Dad said. "Why would you do it that way?"

"We want it to be a surprise. We figured it was more exciting that way." I watched his confused expression fade.

"Interesting. Well, you guys have fun this week. Bye, Anna!"

"Bye, David! Have fun!" Anna called from the living room.

I headed back into the living room, returning my attention to the wounded. "How are you feeling now?" I asked as I sat down and pulled her feet up on my lap.

"Jake, I bumped my head. I'll be fine." Anna rolled her eyes. "So your dad seems pretty interested in our wedding plans. He must've finally accepted the fact that we're getting married."

"Yeah, must've," I mumbled. "He's been strange lately. It's almost like he doesn't want us to get married but he's pretending he does. I don't get it."

Anna sat up and looked at me. "I don't get why he doesn't want us to get married. Do you think he thinks we're making the wrong decision?"

"I don't know what's going through his head." I fought back the urge to tell her about all of my suspicions with Dad. Would she think I was crazy?

"Jake, how do *you* feel about us getting married? You asked me earlier if I had any doubts, but how about you?"

The only thing in this world that I wanted more than to be married to Anna was to keep her safe. And now, with the uncertainty of the threat that our marriage would cause, was I ready to put my greatest fear out there in exchange for wedding vows? And if not, what would that mean to Anna? She would be devastated. I couldn't do that to her. She would think I was being irrational.

"What do you think Ms. Peters meant when she said that our marriage was a real concern?" I asked, avoiding the question slightly.

Anna's eyes began to well up and the tip of her nose reddened.

"Anna, I love you more than anything, and I would give up anything and everything just to make you happy and keep you safe. I want to be married to you, I really do. I'm just a little concerned over Ms. Peters's comment. I've been thinking a lot about it and I can't get it out of my mind." I reached over and caught a tear that slipped down her cheek.

"I think what she meant was that once we're married, we pose more of a threat because we're a unified force and much stronger. So maybe she was a little concerned about the target that would be put on our backs." Anna shrugged. "Sure it's concerning to a certain degree, but I think we pose a threat regardless, and I'd rather be stronger and united if someone, or something, comes after us."

Someone or something. We're always going to be in danger, regardless. So if we're together, then at least we're stronger. The Defiers won't want us to be married because we'll be stronger.

"You're right. You're completely right," I said, and then watched the familiar grin creep back on her face.

"So," Anna began as she pulled me down on top of her, "have you picked a song for our first dance as husband and wife yet?" Her fingernails lightly tickled my scalp as she ran her hands through my hair.

"Do I have to answer that today?" I moaned, trying to avoid disappointing her.

"I guess you can have a few more days. But seriously, Jake, put some thought into it."

I silenced her with a kiss and pressed my body into hers. A lustful sigh escaped her lips as I smoothed her hair from her face. Then she winced and her hand went to the back of her head, reminding me that she was still hurting. I pulled her up to a sitting position and pressed my lips firmly into hers as I held her face to mine. My breath quickened as my temperature rose. I slid one hand around to her back and pulled her onto my lap. Her lips trailed down my chin, down my neck and slowly made their way back up. Resisting all the hormones raging in my body, I pulled her close and just held her against me. "You are incredible," I whispered.

Her chest rose and fell with each heavy breath. Then she pulled away and touched the back of her head. Her eyes narrowed as she turned them to me. "Did you just heal me?" she accused.

"It wasn't fair, Anna. Every time you kiss me, you make me whole. It's only fair that I repay the favour."

"Smooth, Jake." She snuggled back in. "I guess I should thank you. It was really starting to throb."

"You're welcome." I kissed her fingers and pulled her down next to me on the couch. Sleeping next to Anna was the best way to spend a few dark hours.

CHAPTER 24

WEEKS PASSED AND before I knew it, the wedding was only a couple of days away. I found myself pacing the kitchen floor as Nick and Noah watched the hockey game on the big screen in my living room.

"Are the nachos ready yet, Jake?" Noah called over his shoulder.

"Crap! I forgot!" I whipped open the oven door and rescued the nachos. "They're good."

Nick laughed. "How'd you forget? Isn't that what you're in the kitchen for? Watching the nachos?"

"Jake's love sick," Noah laughed.

"You're one to talk!" I called back. "How many minutes have you been away from each other now, lover boy?"

"Shut-up!" Noah said, hurling a pillow into the kitchen.

Nick laughed. "No, but seriously, what's it been? Like forty-eight minutes? You must be getting pretty antsy to get back to her, huh?"

"It's been fifty-four minutes, actually," Noah played along, "and yes, I might just go take a walk over to Anna's house and see how they're making out without us."

"Don't bother. We can just check in on them through Anna's bracelet," I laughed.

"Yeah, I gotta get me one of those." Noah came into the kitchen and helped put the nachos on a plate. "So your big day is coming up. How does it feel to know the exact date that your life is over?"

I shook my head. So typical of Noah. "Are you saying you wouldn't marry Rachel if she asked you tomorrow?"

"You're damn straight I wouldn't! Why mess with a good thing?"

"Yeah, right!" Nick laughed. "If that's what Rachel wanted, that's what Rachel would get. You're so whipped it isn't funny!"

Thankfully the phone rang and interrupted our pathetic conversation.

"Hey, babe," I answered.

"How are you boys doing? Staying out of trouble?" she teased with just a touch of seriousness. I couldn't blame her.

"Yeah, we're good. Watching the game and eating nachos. Being typical guys."

"That's what I'm afraid of," she said. "Anyway,

Claudia has just asked me if you picked out our song yet. What should I tell her?"

I held my breath and searched my head for a song. "I don't know, babe. I am thinking about it, but there just isn't a song that says it all. I want it to be perfect, just like you."

Nick and Noah laughed hysterically from the living room. I shot them a warning glare and raised my fist.

"Awww, that's sweet honey, but Claudia says get it to her by tomorrow or she's picking the song for us." I could hear the annoyed tone in her voice. Was she annoyed with me for not having picked a song yet, or with Claudia for pressuring me about it? Probably me.

"Okay. I'll talk it over with the guys tonight and have a song for her tomorrow."

"Thanks, babe. I love you."

Nick and Noah were staring at me, waiting for another opportunity to break up in hysterics. "Same," I said.

As she hung up the phone, I heard her giggle and say something like, "They're trying to be all tough over there."

"Dude, are you *sure* you want to get married? I mean you only have two more days to back out before you're stuck with her for the rest of your life." Noah offered his usual style of support.

"Lay off of him, Noah," Nick said. "I'm sure he's thought it all through." Thanks, Nick.

"I have no doubt in my mind that I want to be with Anna for the rest of my life," I started, taking a breath before I decided to share my feelings. "My concern is putting her in danger, you know? Apparently, once we're married we'll be a stronger team which means we'll be susceptible to more danger."

Noah stared blankly before concluding, "You're getting cold feet."

I shook my head and pinched my eyes closed. "It's not that, Noah."

"No, I get it," Nick said. "It's a legitimate concern, but I guess you have to be sure that you're up for both challenges. Marriage *and* being on guard twenty-four seven."

"Yeah, because once you get married, there is no turning back," Noah added.

Sometimes I wondered if he was really the best choice for my Best Man.

LATER IN THE evening, I found myself sitting out on the back deck counting stars and contemplating marriage and destruction. Two things that, in normal circumstances, you shouldn't have to consider in the same context, but our lives weren't normal.

The patio door slid open behind me and I prayed it wasn't Noah. His advice wasn't what I needed to hear at that moment.

"You okay, Jake?" It was Abby, sliding a chair up

next to mine. I was relieved.

"Hey, Abs." I shot her a smile as she sat down next to me. "I'm good. Just thinking."

"About your wedding?"

"Yeah, I guess." I had been out there so long I couldn't remember what I came out for in the first place.

"Well, if it means anything, I think it's awesome that you and Anna are getting married. It's definitely the right thing to do."

"How do you know?" I asked, cocking my head slightly as I looked at her wise little face.

"Are you having doubts?" she countered.

"Not really. I mean I *know* I love her and I *know* I want to marry her, it's just I can't explain why. I feel like there are so many variables involved and I'm kind of scared of making the wrong decision." I looked at her inviting face and realized that, even though she couldn't have possibly understood, she really had a way of looking like she did. "Anyway, I guess I'm just looking for that sign, you know?"

"Are you wishing you would've waited another five years?"

Was I? Would another five years make everything easier? No. Waiting five years, or ten years or twenty years wouldn't keep Anna any safer. I shrugged.

Abby grinned and reached out to touch my hand. "When you know, you just know."

I looked at her strangely for a minute. Her words sounded so familiar and they hit hard as I thought about them. *When you know, you just know.* Strangely familiar. They repeated in my head until I heard Anna's voice saying those exact words weeks ago at the lake when we went skating. We had been talking about getting married and I asked her how she knew it was the right thing to do. And she had said, "When you know, you just know."

"You know what, Abby? You are completely right. I *do* know she's the right one for me and I *do* know that I want to marry her, so I'm going to stop worrying about what *could* be and start concentrating on what *will* be."

"Glad I could be of help." She hopped up from her chair and wrapped her tiny arms around me tightly.

"How is it you are so much older than you are? You are the oldest ten-year-old I know."

"Eleven, actually," she politely corrected. "I had a birthday while you were in Europe this summer. Remember?"

"Geez, that's right! Sorry I missed your birthday, Abby. Are you still wearing that necklace I sent home for you?" It was a locket that Anna and I spent a whole day in Paris shopping for. It had to be the perfect one — in a shape of a butterfly — since I felt overly guilty for missing her birthday.

Abby dug down her shirt and pulled out the gold chain with the butterfly locket dangling from the bottom. "I wear it everyday, so my big brother is always with me." She opened the locket to reveal the picture of the two of us, taken on her tenth birthday the year before.

"I'm glad you like it." I smiled as she tucked the locket back down close to her heart.

"Well, I should go. Maybe I'll go clean the kitchen or something." She giggled as she headed back inside.

"Thanks again, Abby."

"For?"

"You know. Helping me realize that this *is* the right thing to do."

"Like I said, when you know, you just know."

Her words kept repeating in my head until I heard music to go along with them. I gasped. "Abby! You helped find our song!"

"What are you talking about?" Had I just grown three heads? Because that's how she was looking at me.

"That's a song! *When You Know*! It's perfect, Abby! Thank you!" I leaped from my chair and headed for the phone.

I dialed Anna's number as fast as my fingers would move, not paying any mind to the time of day.

"Is everything okay?" Anna answered, panicked.

I quickly checked the time and realized it was well into the middle of the night. What on earth was Abby doing up so late?

"I'm so sorry, babe! I didn't realize what time it

was."

"What's wrong?" she repeated, still groggy.

"Nothing. I just wanted to let you know I found a song for us." I thought it was still pretty good news, but the silence that followed suggested that Anna didn't share my enthusiasm.

"Seriously? *That's* what you called at three o'clock in the morning for? To tell me you found us a song?" Yeah, that pretty much solidified my assumption.

"Like I said, I didn't realize it was so late. I'm sorry."

Anna let out a little huff of air. "It's okay. I was just dreaming about you anyway, so it's nice to hear your voice."

"Dreaming of me, you say. Do tell."

Anna ignored me. "Are the guys still up too? What are you guys doing?" she asked through a yawn.

I looked in the living room and saw Nick and Noah passed out on the couches. All the lights were out and I just realized how quiet the house was. "No, apparently they're sleeping." Again, I wondered what Abby was doing up so late. "You should get back to sleep, I'll talk to you in the morning. Two more sleeps."

Anna let out a faint squeal. "I know. I'm so excited."

"G'night, babe."

"Sweet dreams."

I hung up the phone and took the stairs two at a time. The upstairs hallway was dark and there was no sign of light coming from Abby's room. I slipped into her room and found her sleeping soundly, snoring and all, tucked under her covers.

"Abby?" I whispered as I knelt down beside her bed.

Snore.

"Well, thanks for sleep walking . . . and talking." I smiled and quietly shut her door behind me.

CHAPTER 25

I COULDN'T REMEMBER a time when I was ever as nervous as I was today. I paced the large, cold room in the back of the church, barely taking notice of Noah and Nick sitting on the couch, twiddling their thumbs.

"It's four o'clock already. When are they supposed to get here?" Noah whined as he checked his watch for the tenth time in five minutes.

"They'll be fashionably late," Nick laughed. "Claudia style."

"Noah, why don't you call Rachel and make sure they're on their way," I urged, regretting my promise to Anna to keep my phone (thus tracking device) at home today.

"Jake, relax." Nick put a hand on my shoulder. "She'll be here."

The door opened and the pastor entered the room with a comforting smile on his face. "Jacob! Well, at least one of you is here," he teased, although I didn't find it funny at all. He cleared his throat and took a more serious approach. "We're ready for you three to go stand up front and wait for the bride."

I took a deep breath and wiped the palms of my hands on my pants. My heart was beating heavier although my breath seemed to slow. Each time my chest emptied, I had to remind myself to breathe in. I wondered if my face had any colour. My hands were cold and clammy and my head was becoming lighter.

"I need to sit down for a minute," I blurted as I grabbed the nearest chair to me.

"Okay, I'll give you a moment," the pastor announced, then he turned to Nick and said, "Bring him out in two minutes or less. She should be here soon."

I waited until the door closed behind him and then I pinched my eyes closed. "What if she doesn't come? I don't like this. I knew I should never have agreed to leave my phone behind."

"Relax, dude," Noah said. His first encouraging words of the week. "Rachel and Claudia are with her. They're fine."

I squeezed my hands, trying to bring the feeling back into them. Then I remembered the rings. "Noah, do you have the rings?"

"What rings?" he asked with a blank face. Right before I puked, he added, "Just kidding. Yeah, I got 'em."

Nick smacked the back of Noah's head. "Lay off, Noah. He can't handle any of your jokes right now."

"Dude, I can't believe in like one hour you'll be a married man," Noah said.

"Yeah, we should get him out there before Anna shows up and thinks he backed out." Nick looked to Noah. "Lift him on three. One . . . two . . ."

I rolled my eyes and stood up. "I'm capable." I took another deep breath and followed the guys out of the room, down the hall and to our designated places on the front podium. My heart was still racing, even more so now that I could see the church full of our friends and family. Mom and Dad sat in the front row where Mom was smiling and waving. Dad seemed to be forcing a smile, but then he gave a thumbs up, and for some strange reason, that made things a little easier.

A change in music turned my attention to the back of the room. The ushers slowly opened the doors to reveal Abby standing front and center in a frilly white gown and holding a basket of flower petals in front of her. Her face beamed with excitement and her curls bounced as she walked down the aisle. I was instantly proud of her. As she came closer and all eyes were on her, the butterflies in my stomach began playing tag again causing me to feel nauseous. I focused on my breathing and the idea that Anna must be in the hallway outside of those doors. They wouldn't have started the wedding without her. . . . Right?

Next came Claudia wearing a strapless turquoise dress that puffed out just above her knees. She never took her eyes off of Nick as she walked down the aisle and took her place across from us on the stage.

When Rachel made an appearance in the doorway, Noah gasped. Her hair was pulled up in a funky style on top with pieces hanging down and a big bow on the side. Her dress was different from Claudia's, but still the same colour. It was a straight, slimming dress that just touched to the floor.

Then, another change in music made my heart begin beating erratically as the pianist played the traditional Wedding March song. Anna, on the arm of her proud father, entered the doorway and stood for a moment while I caught my breath.

Breathtakingly beautiful. A long, silky gown hugged her perfectly sculpted body and flared out at the bottom with layers of lace that reminded me of icing on a birthday cake. The veil was just as striking with a thick edging of lace that weighed it down and kept it in place over her face. I was amazed that I could take notice of all the detail in her dress, but I owed it to the fact that I couldn't yet see her face, concealed under the veil.

The moment her father lifted the veil and kissed her on the cheek, the game of butterfly tag ceased and I suddenly felt warm and reassured. Her angelic eyes caught mine and I abruptly became aware of the gap between my lips. Mesmerized by her beauty, I never once took my eyes off of her throughout the whole ceremony. Not wanting to miss one second of her every move. As I said "I do," an amazing feeling of completion came over me. Completion of one chapter of our lives and the beginning of an adventure into another.

I kissed the bride. My bride. Anna.

As MUCH AS I appreciated the wedding ceremony, I was relieved when it came to an end and we headed back to Anna's house for a small reception with family and friends. It was about the only thing that was simple. Neither of us wanted a dance party so Claudia compromised with a backyard party at Anna's parents' house.

"Introducing Mr. and Mrs. Rovert!" Mr. Taylor announced loudly as we came through the front door. Anna threw her arms around my neck and kissed me with flare and drama.

"Save it for the honeymoon!" Noah shouted over a sandwich platter.

"This *is* our honeymoon!" Anna reminded him.

"So, Jake," Dad spoke up, "have you found out where you're going yet for your honeymoon?"

"You don't know where you're going?" Mrs. Taylor asked.

"No! I mean . . . yes, of course! Well . . ." Anna

began. She stopped, smiled while she composed herself, and then went on, "We wanted it to be a surprise, so we asked our travel agent to book a destination for us. We'll figure it out when we pick up our tickets at the airport tomorrow."

"Well, isn't that a sweet idea," Mrs. Taylor approved. "Who did you use for a travel agent? Your Aunt Dorinda?"

"Oh, no we didn't. I forgot she was a travel agent. We used a really nice woman from Maritime Travel. Margaret Mullaly.

I noticed Dad taking out a pen and paper and quickly jotting something down, but before I could investigate, the music began to play and Anna grabbed my arm, pulling me into the living room, to dance to our first song.

"The song is perfect," she whispered as we slowly held each other and rotated through the room with the music. "I can't believe you picked this out all by yourself."

My eyes searched the room until they found Abby. "I had a little help," I divulged, throwing a wink in Abby's direction.

As the music played, filling the air with words of promise and purpose, we held each other tightly. Securely. Protectively. Everything was perfect. We were married, surrounded by friends and family. No other cares in the world. Right now, anyway.

The last few notes of the song played and we slowed to a stop. I held Anna's head close to my chest and ignored the fact that dozens of people were watching us.

"Well, I'm too excited to wait any longer," Mom announced, breaking me from my revelry. "Can we give the kids their gift now?"

Mrs. Taylor shared in her excitement. "Now is probably as good a time as any." She looked to Dad and Mr. Taylor. "Are you both ready?"

How many people had a part in this wedding gift? What could it possibly be?

Mr. Taylor and Dad left the room and returned a minute later with a large gift-wrapped box.

"Jake and Anna, this is from your parents," Dad said as he and Mr. Taylor handed the box to us.

Anna giggled with excitement as I set the box on the floor. It was long and not very thick, so it had my curiosity. Anna ripped off the paper as I watched Mom, Dad, Mrs. Taylor and Mr. Taylor huddle together with anticipation.

"Your fathers made it!" Mrs. Taylor burst out as Anna slowly lifted up the top of the box to reveal a gorgeous, hand-carved, dark wooden "Welcome Home" sign.

Anna gasped, "It's beautiful! Daddy, did you really help make this?"

"Well," Mr. Taylor chuckled, "It was mostly David,

but I did have a hand in working with some of his tools."

After we admired the sign for a minute, Mom quietly said, "Now turn it over."

It took the two of us to turn the large sign over without hitting anyone or anything. Directly in the centre of the back of the sign, there was a small compartment sealed by a door. Anna lifted the latch and pulled out a silver key that was hiding in the compartment. She turned it in her hands for a moment and then looked up. "What's this for?"

"Your new house!" Mom and Mrs. Taylor both exclaimed in unison.

What??

"We bought you a house! As your wedding gift!" Mrs. Taylor squealed.

I had never seen Anna more lost for words. She stared at the key, then at our parents, then back at the key.

"Thank you," I finally said. "Thank you *so* much!" Words really couldn't express our appreciation, so I thought that was a good place to start. I didn't care if the house was a run-down shack in the middle of nowhere—Anna and I were going to have our own place.

I suddenly remembered my promise to Abby about Anna and me living with her. I looked up and searched the crowd for her and found her standing next to Mom.

My heart crumbled a little when I realized how she must have been feeling.

"Abby helped pick out the house," Dad said, probably noticing the wordless exchange between Abby and me.

"She did?" I asked, my eyebrows reacting to my confusion.

"I did," Abby said proudly. "That's why I asked you all those questions before about what kind of house you'd want to buy if you could. I was being a Secret Agent."

"So you didn't really want me to live with you forever?" I asked, instantly relieved, but slightly offended.

"Are you kidding? I get to be an only child! This is gonna be awesome!" She laughed. "But I *do* still expect a room in your new house for when I want to have sleepovers with my new sister."

Anna ran over and hugged Abby, lifting her off the ground and twirling her in the air. "You're such a special girl, Abby!" They both shared a teary-eyed moment while I took my turn examining our new house key.

"What do you say we go check out your new pad?" Noah suggested, bringing us all back to the realization that there were more of us in the room.

"Let's pack up the food and bring it over to the new house," Mom said, gathering some of the trays.

"Everyone is welcome to come!"

THE DRIVE TO our new house wasn't as long as I had hoped. We drove out of our subdivision, which was a relief, but only a few minutes down the road took us to a quieter street, with older homes set back off the road. We drove to the end of the road and then turned down an almost hidden driveway, overgrown with bushes. A half dozen three-tiered lampposts lined the driveway, leading us to the prize at the end—a beautiful old Victorian home with large bay windows on either side of the front entrance and a wrap around porch complete with an old, rickety porch swing.

Anna was squeezing my hand, tighter and tighter, as we neared the house, and I knew the exact second that she caught sight of the house because the circulation in my hand was instantly cut off and her nails dug deep into my palm.

"IT'S GORGEOUS!" she cried. "Are you guys kidding us? Is this really ours?"

"It's all yours, darling!" Mr. Taylor said from the passenger seat in front. "Now don't get too excited before you see the inside. It's a bit of a fixer upper, but you're definitely able to live in it. You'll just want to put your own finishing touches on it."

Dad stopped the car and we all piled out. Nick, Noah, Rachel and Claudia were behind us and just as astonished as we were, by the looks on their faces.

My heart was racing, but my mouth was dry. I was nervous—but mostly excited—to see the inside of the house that Anna had already dubbed our "Piece of Heaven."

CHAPTER 26

AN OLD STONE walkway meandered through aspiring gardens, leading us from the driveway to the front porch.

"This is going to be so beautiful once we dig out all the weeds," Anna exclaimed.

"I'll help," Rachel added. "I love gardening."

"Me too," Claudia added.

Anna and I made our way up the few steps onto the porch while the others waited on the walkway. The thick, wooden front door was carved similar to the "Welcome Home" sign. I slid the key into the lock and held it there for a few seconds. Anna put her hand over mine, and together we turned the key slowly until we heard the click. This was our house. Just ours. We were about to walk into our own home. Anna gently pushed the door open. Then I turned to her and swept her off of her feet.

"My dearest wife," I dramatized, "welcome to our

new home." I carried her over the threshold, Anna giggling in my arms, and kissed her softly before letting her back down on her own feet. Then we explored our new home together.

The foyer was large with an ornately carved staircase on the left leading up to a balcony that overlooked the foyer. An arched entry on our left, at the base of the staircase, led to a parlour room, which was complete with a large fireplace and thick crown moulding and a large chandelier hanging from the plaster medallion in the centre of the ceiling.

Anna slowly walked around the room with her mouth opened slightly. Then she closed her eyes and held her hands to her chest. "This is perfect."

There was nothing more pleasing to me than to watch Anna at that very moment—enjoying every detail of our new home.

I took Anna's hand and led her back through the foyer and into the room across the hall. It was a mirror image of the room that we were just in. I guessed it was meant to be the living room. We made our way down the hall and into a large country kitchen with a hearth room to the left that overlooked the backyard. Patio doors at the side of the hearth room led to the wrap around deck. To the right of the kitchen was a dining nook, perfect for morning breakfasts.

Anna's favourite feature was another staircase in the hearth room that led upstairs. She said it made more sense to have the stairs come into your main living area instead of the front entrance. I also liked the idea of how this provided a second escape route in case of an emergency.

We took the front entry staircase and followed it up to the second level. There were six closed doors throughout the hallway. The first two, at the top of the balcony, were matching bedrooms, connected by a door between the two and both with beautiful views of the backyard. I couldn't help but notice that the first one was pink and the second one was blue. I wondered if Anna noticed and took any meaning to that.

Continuing to the right was another door, across the hall from the twin bedrooms, which overlooked the front yard. We walked in and this time we both gasped in unison.

The room was lined with dark mahogany bookcases from floor to ceiling. A rich, wooden desk sat in the middle of the room.

"Wow," I said, running my hand along the large desk and picturing myself spending hours in that room tracking down Defiers and solving mysteries.

"I've always wanted a library," Anna disclosed. "Just like this." She walked over to the window and looked out over the front yard. I joined her at the window and wrapped my arms around her tightly. This was our home. Ours.

Anna turned her head up and kissed my cheek.

Then she pulled away and began to walk toward the bookcase. "Hmmm," Anna said as she reached out to touch a book sitting on the shelf, which happened to be the *only* book on the shelf, actually. "I wonder . . ." She pulled on the book but it didn't move. Then she held onto the top corner of the book and tilted it toward her. Something unlatched. "A secret doorway!" she exclaimed.

"No way!" I shouted with excitement as I hurried over to help her push the large bookcase into the unknown space.

The small room, which was no larger than a small bedroom, was windowless and empty. Not much of an attraction, but the idea of having our own secret room was exciting enough.

"This could be where we hide all of our important documents and pictures of our trips and stuff. You know, so the kids don't find them." Anna giggled.

"Good thinking."

We left the room and I closed the bookcase behind us, knowing everyone else would be walking through our house in a few minutes and I didn't want them finding out about our secret. I found a few other books in the desk drawers and put them on the shelves too, concealing the lone book.

Continuing to the door at the end of the east wing, we came across a bedroom slightly larger than the first two.

"This will be Abby's bedroom," Anna decided without hesitation.

"She'll love it," I agreed.

"We'll have to paint it purple, though. This green just won't do. And maybe a horse mural or something on this wall." She ran her fingers over the bare wall.

I smiled. "Any plans for the smaller bedrooms?"

She turned and gave me a devious look. "Well, since you asked," she said excitedly, "I was thinking that we should keep them pink and blue and maybe add some cute animal murals or something. . . . You know . . . for the future."

A strange bubbly feeling started growing in my chest, giving the illusion of excitement, which I thought was odd at the mention of children. "That sounds good," I conceded. "Eventually."

We left Abby's room and walked back down the hall, passing the staircase, and found another door on the right next to the pink room. It led to a good size bathroom with a claw foot tub and older fixtures.

"This will have to be upgraded," said Anna, "but it's really cute. I love it."

The last door at the end of the hallway led to our master bedroom. It spanned from the front of the house to the back of the house and had big bay windows at each end. Other than the kitchen table set and an old wooden picnic table in the middle of the hearth room, our bedroom was the only other room in the house that was furnished. Somewhat. My queen-sized bed was strategically placed between the two side windows, with nightstands on either side.

Anna stopped in the doorway and covered her mouth with her hands as she scanned the room. "Our very own bedroom, Jake," she finally said.

Her smile faded slowly as she walked to the back window and sat down on the window seat. She wiped a stray tear from her cheek.

"What's wrong?" I asked, sitting across from her on the seat.

"Nothing," she laughed. "Absolutely nothing."

My eyebrows creased. "Then . . . why are you crying?"

She looked at me and shook her head slowly. "I don't know. Overwhelmed, I guess. I just love it all. It's perfect."

I reached over and held her hand with mine.

"So the bed . . ." Anna said. "We get to sleep here tonight . . . together . . . alone." She looked at me mischievously. I laughed and then swept her up in my arms and carried her over to the bed. She let out a shriek as I tossed her on the bed.

"Mrs. Rovert, I am the happiest guy in the world right now," I declared.

"And I am the happiest girl." She pulled me down on top of her and we kissed. "BUT, we have guests outside waiting for a tour."

I sunk back on my pillow. "I forgot about them," I groaned. Then I pushed myself off the bed, pulling Anna along with me. "Come on, wife."

Anna rolled her eyes before following me out of the room and down the stairs to our waiting guests.

I whipped open the door and shouted, "It's awesome!"

"We love it!" Anna added, running to our parents with her arms wide open. "Thank you! Thank you! Thank you!"

Rachel stepped up onto the porch. "Can we see now?" she begged.

"Yes, of course! Come on in!" Anna exclaimed, holding the door open for everyone.

We gave the tour with Anna adding little things that she loved and things that she'd love to do, like painting, refinishing the fireplaces, updating the fixtures and more. The second time through I was able to appreciate the house even more as I wasn't as fixated on Anna's reactions.

Abby loved her new bedroom and was very excited about staying with us. We had to let her down easily about not being able to stay with us the first night, but promised her that as soon as we got back from our honeymoon, we would have our first sleepover.

RACHEL AND NOAH were the last to leave shortly after midnight. We walked them to the door and felt very proud as we closed the door and bolted it tight behind them.

"I'm exhausted," Anna said as she collapsed in my arms. "That was a long day."

"Why don't you head upstairs and get into bed. I'll clean up a bit down here first and shut the lights off, then I'll be up." I kissed her on the forehead and watched her as she headed upstairs on her own. A sense of nervousness came over me as I suddenly realized we were alone.

A few minutes later I was on my way up to our bedroom. The door was closed and there didn't appear to be any light coming from the room. I figured she had fallen asleep before she was even under the covers. I smiled at the thought of her sleeping in her wedding dress.

I slowly turned the knob and quietly opened the door and that's when I noticed the two candles flickering on our nightstands and rose petals thrown over the bed. Anna was standing off to the side with a glass of champagne in each hand and wearing the prettiest pink silk I had ever seen.

"Did you need help with your tux, Mr. Rovert?" she asked, slowly walking toward me.

"That won't be necessary," I said and whipped off my jacket and loosened my tie. I slid my hands around her silky back and pulled her into me, smelling her sweet lavender skin.

She set the glasses down on the nightstand then wrapped her hands under my suspenders, slowing pulling them down over my shoulders. Her eyes flickered to my chest as her fingers unbuttoned my shirt. After three buttons, I pulled it off over my head and let it fall to the floor. Then I lifted her up and laid her on the bed of roses. Her hair rested wildly amongst the petals and her skin glowed in the candlelight. I took a few seconds to commit the image to memory, having never seen her look more beautiful in my life.

I ran my fingers up her silky arms and held her warm hands above her head, slowly kissing her and pressing my body into hers. My heart was beating wildly causing my breath to become heavy and my movements to more rapid. Moans erupted from her lips as she lifted her chest into mine causing a surge of excitement and fury like I never imagined. I needed her. She completed me.

I backed up for a moment, pacing my breathing and trying to prolong the magic of this moment, but not taking my eyes from hers for one second.

"Come back," she whispered as she pulled down the covers and slipped in. I followed, pulling her on top of me and feeling her slowly slide her body down onto mine. Her warm legs wrapped around mine. I held her close, kissing her neck and breathing heavily down her back. Our movements were as one as her hair dangled and tickled my face. Her lips pressed to mine and I held her face as we kissed—passionately at first, but as a sense of completion came over me, I wrapped my arms around her and squeezed, and our lips slowed. A final sigh escaped her lips and she laid silently on my chest. I inhaled her scent and ran my hand over her smooth back, revelling in the fact that we now belonged to each other.

A few minutes passed without any words or movements. Then Anna sighed and ran her fingers up and down my chest. "I love you."

"I love you more," I whispered, believing it with all of my heart.

"Not even possible," she countered, and the tone that she used was the one she gave when she believed something with all of *her* heart.

"We'll agree to disagree on this one." I kissed her forehead before falling asleep for the first time with my new wife cuddled up beside me.

CHAPTER 27

FOUR A.M. CAME too early. When the alarm went off, I actually considered shutting it off and skipping our honeymoon altogether. That wouldn't have gone over so well with Anna though, so I decided I should roll out of bed. Then I remembered where I was—in our new house with Anna. By ourselves.

I flicked on the lamp and focused my eyes to where Anna was sleeping next to me. But she wasn't there. Her side of the bed was made and there was no sign of her.

"Anna?" I called into the large empty room.

"I'm in the bathroom."

I stumbled out of our bedroom and into the bathroom. She was fixing her hair in the mirror, completely dressed and ready to go.

"Come on, sleepy head. We have a honeymoon to go on!" She skipped into my arms and kissed me. "Ew. Oh. Um . . . you should brush your teeth first, though."

"Get used to it, my love," I teased as I tried not to breathe anymore.

"Just kidding." She laughed as she skipped out of the bathroom. "Our luggage is already in the car. I'll go make us some shakes. Hurry up!"

The transition to the shower was made easy by the already warm water. I would've liked for the shower to have been longer, but Anna came in a few minutes later announcing that the shakes were made and we had to go, so I climbed out of the shower and brushed my teeth . . . twice.

WE KNEW WE were flying with Delta Airlines, but still had no idea where we were going. When we got to the ticket clerk at the front of the line, she took our names and information and then handed us two tickets. "Enjoy your honeymoon," she said pleasantly.

Anna opened them up immediately. "St. Lucia!" she squealed.

"Shh!" I scolded, looking around to ensure no one heard.

"Oops! Sorry!" She threw her hand over her mouth, but then began to giggle. "I'm so excited! St. Lucia looks so beautiful. I want to hike the Piton Mountains. They're like a World Heritage Site. Two volcanic peaks jetting out from the ocean's edge. Oh, Jake, I can't wait!"

"I agree. St. Lucia will be beautiful. A great spot for

our honeymoon. Now, can we not talk about it until we get on the plane, please? I really don't want anyone overhearing us. Okay?"

"Oh, Jake! You're too paranoid. This is our honeymoon." She pulled on my arm and forced me to stop and face her. "Let's relax a little, okay?" Her eyes pleaded for my agreement.

"Okay," I sighed. "I'll relax. But first let's get on the plane."

THE FLIGHT WASN'T as long as I had expected. I guess when you're comparing it to a flight to Uganda, anything would seem short. It was mid-afternoon when we landed. Our hotel was another two hours away, and well worth the extra drive.

Nestled between the Piton Mountains, the turquoise Caribbean Sea and a thick, lustrous rainforest, our resort was an architectural masterpiece. Everywhere we looked there was something else to point to and marvel over. The stone façade was massive yet delicate at the same time, mixing well with the hardwood accents.

I stopped to look at Anna who was skipping back and forth between the gardens and the fountains. Suddenly the most beautiful thing in the whole country was Anna. Everything else just faded away and all I saw was her smooth blonde hair bouncing off the back of her bright pink tank top which met with her stark white tennis skirt that covered her silky, tanned legs.

My wife.

Our room was even more breathtaking. With only three walls surrounding us, the fourth wall was completely open to the rest of the world. To the left, our very own private pool lapped quietly along the edge of our room—seemingly endless, giving the illusion of being able to swim off the edge. To the right, plush furniture was thoughtfully placed to enjoy the amazing views of the Pitons and the sparkling Caribbean Sea below and beyond. Along this side of the room, a four-foot glass wall was all that separated us from nature.

"This is . . . this is gorgeous," Anna whispered as she slowly walked the perimeter of the room, her fingers grazing the stone walls before she came to the glass barrier. My breath hitched.

"It is," I agreed, trying to ignore the voice inside of me that whispered the dangers of having our room open to the outdoors. "Do you think there's some sort of metal gate system or something that closes off here at night?" I asked casually.

Anna skipped across the room and leaped onto the plush bed. "Probably not. But they do have this netting that goes around the bed to keep the bugs out." She pulled the curtains closed around the bed then peeked her head out. "Come here, lover boy!"

I forced a chuckle, my eyes staying on the vast openness of our room's perimeter.

Anna looked at me, her head cocked to the side and

her eyebrows raised at an angle that begged for me to relax. "Jake, please don't worry." She sighed heavily. "We're on the fourth floor. It would take a great deal of effort for someone to get into our room."

I closed my eyes and took a deep breath, trying to force my heartbeat to slow and my sweat glands to stop leaking. It must have taken longer than I anticipated because by the time I opened my eyes, Anna's silhouette was slowly immersing into the tranquil pool.

"Well, you can stand there fretting about our safety, but I'm going to make the most of this honeymoon. With or without you." She trickled water up her arms and onto her chest. "But for the record, I'd prefer to be with you."

She was right. My fears were getting the best of me and ruining our honeymoon. I might have to sleep with one eye open, but if that meant keeping her happy . . . and safe, I'd do it.

I ripped off my shirt and kicked off my shorts. "Is it warm?"

"It will be." Her inviting words were enough to make me forget about my worries. If only for a few moments.

EVERYTHING ABOUT THE resort was perfect—the white sand beach, the friendly and attentive staff, the colourful gardens, the delicious food. . . . Everything except for that one missing wall. I kept envisioning someone sneaking into our room in the middle of the night. Creeping up beside us while we were sleeping.

"What 'cha thinkin' 'bout?" Anna kicked the sand as we walked along the beach.

My eyes adjusted to our surroundings and the beautiful Pitons in front of us. "Uhhh," I stammered, "just thinking about climbing those mountains with you tomorrow." I tried to look at her but found it difficult. Instead I squinted from the sun and slid my sunglasses over my eyes.

Anna stopped and pulled me into her. "Then why are you clenching your jaw and squeezing my hand like a vice-grip?" Only *she* would know what a vice-grip was.

I rolled my eyes and let my head fall back, the sun beating against my hot face. "You sure you like it here?" I returned my gaze to hers, searching for her wordless answer. "I mean, if it's not what you were expecting, we can always check out and find another resort on the island."

She pursed her lips and squinted her eyes. "Is it the wall?"

"You mean the fact that there *isn't* one?"

"Jake!" Anna threw her hands up in the air. "I'm sure it's safe! It *has* to be! This is a first class resort. *Celebrities* stay here!"

"I know. I know." I tried to convince myself. "It's silly. I just can't get my mind out of protection mode."

"No one knows where we are, baby." She playfully pulled at the drawstring on my shorts.

"We're never one hundred percent safe," I mumbled, trying not to let that be misconstrued as an argument.

"Okay." Anna pulled out her sulky voice. "If you want to leave, I'll support you on that."

I considered it, even though the look she was giving me made me feel like I was largely overreacting.

"You *are* my husband, after all, and this is our honeymoon, so I want you to be as happy as I am right now."

I sighed. She should be an actress. "Forget it. You're right. Celebrities stay here. It can't be that unsafe."

She jumped into my arms, knocking me to the soft sand beneath us. "Thank you, thank you, thank you! You won't regret this."

"Promise?" I took her face in my hands and pulled her salty lips to mine.

"How about I show you my gratitude?" she teased as she nibbled on my ear.

I searched the beach and quickly realized we weren't alone. In fact, we were mostly the centre of attention at this point. I cleared my throat and slowly sat up. Reluctantly. "Let's go check out our room again. Maybe I'll feel differently about it once we get back up there."

"I'm already there." Anna giggled as she pulled me

along the beach and back to our room.

ANNA WAS ASLEEP within seconds of closing her eyes. It took several hours for me, however, to join her in slumber. It was just after three in the morning the last time I looked at the clock. With Anna curled up beside me, I laid still trying not to wake her. The moon reflected off the water in our pool and cast a warm glow across her face. Her hair was swept neatly up onto the pillow and she breathed slowly with a permanent grin imprinted on her lips. I wondered how I could've gone all those years without noticing that she was the one for me. How could I not have seen that? Now I couldn't picture us apart. My life without her would be completely meaningless. Those were the last coherent thoughts I had before my eyes got heavier and heavier and finally closed.

I WOKE UP suddenly, startled by a noise. Frozen, with my arms locked around Anna, my eyes darted around the room, looking for any sign.

Then I saw it—something moving behind the armchair in the corner of the room where the glass wall met the stone wall. It was crouched low, maybe even lying down to stay inconspicuous. My heart quickened and my thoughts raced. Should I leave Anna's side to attack this intruder? Or should I keep her protected in my arms and wait for him to attack us? I decided to be proactive. Slowly, I slipped out of the sheets, keeping my eyes on the figure in the corner of the room. It reacted, knocking the lamp slightly. It was now my turn to pounce.

Obtaining record speed, I bolted across the room and dove onto the floor, wrestling the intruder to the ground. I was surprised when he didn't put up much of a fight and I suddenly realized that he could've been a decoy and that the real culprit was after Anna right now! I dropped him, ran back to Anna's side and flicked on the lamp beside her, keeping one fist tight and ready to attack. My eyes darted the room wildly.

"What are you doing?" Anna asked in her cracked, middle-of-the-night voice.

When I realized she wasn't in danger, I went back for the intruder. I picked up the armchair, which had toppled over in the tussle, and realized that our attacker was . . . a five-foot long iguana.

"Ew! What *is* that?" Anna rubbed her eyes to better focus.

"Ummm," I hesitated before telling the truth, "a dead iguana?"

"Gross! How did a dead iguana get into our room?"

"Ummm, I might have killed it?"

"Jake!" Anna gasped, holding the sheets to her face. "Get it out of here!"

MORNING CAME TOO soon, but when Anna finally

woke at nine o'clock, our bags were packed and I had already checked us out.

"What are you doing?" she asked, her voice an exact replica of how she sounded a few hours earlier.

"So I checked us out and we're going to finish our honeymoon at another resort." I kept my eyes focused on our luggage waiting at end of the bed.

"What?" I couldn't tell if she was more surprised or angry.

"I put a change of clothes for you on the bed. Get dressed. We're leaving." I grabbed our bags and headed for the door.

"Jake, wait!" Anna protested as she slipped on her housecoat. She caught up to me at the door and turned me to face her. "Have you . . . have you been crying?" She touched my face gently.

"No!" I defended, honestly.

"But your eyes—"

"That's what happens when you don't get any sleep." I turned away and faced the door, jaw clenched.

A minute passed before I felt her touch my hand again.

"I'm dressed," she said. "Let's get out of this hell hole."

CHAPTER 28

ALTHOUGH NOT QUITE as glamorous as the previous resort, our new room had four walls and not one, but two deadbolts on the door. There was a peace about this resort. Something that felt familiar and calm. I liked it a lot. I was happier here, and now I could focus on making Anna happy.

We grabbed our snorkelling gear and headed down to the beach. There were more couples around our age at this resort, which made it easier to blend in. I was sure there were whispers behind every coconut tree and cabana at the last resort as to how two teenagers could possibly afford such a vacation.

We took a catamaran a few minutes out to where the snorkelling was apparently unbelievable. I dangled my flippers into the warm water and adjusted my mask appropriately.

"You first," Anna prompted.

"How about together," I suggested. "Hold your

breath!" I hopped off the catamaran and pulled Anna in with me.

"No, Jake!" I heard her protest, but we were already on our way into the water. When we came back up for air, she splashed water in my face. "Jerk! What if a shark or something was down there waiting for me!"

I laughed. "Is that why you wanted to send me in first?"

Anna took a deep breath and lowered her face into the water, doing a complete circle, then came back up. "We're clear. Nothing around."

"Then let's go see some fish."

We swam for over an hour, witnessing some of the most beautiful sights I had ever seen. Schools of colourful fish would swim right up to us and take bread right from our hands. Although I was initially nervous about taking Anna into the ocean to go snorkelling, it was on her "must do" list for our honeymoon, and since she hadn't protested about us leaving the last resort, I had to give her this one.

Suddenly I saw Anna waving vigorously and pointing to something behind me. Her eyes were lit up with excitement rather than terror, so I immediately relaxed as I turned around to witness the most remarkable sight—a pod of dolphins swimming toward us.

We watched in amazement as they swam in circles around us, almost protectively. Anna took out her underwater camera and snapped some pictures. They stayed with us for quite some time until I discovered the real reason they were swimming in circles around us. . . . A shark was lurking on the outside trying to get in!

With Anna busy taking pictures and marvelling at our surroundings, I gently took her hand and began swimming toward shore. The dolphins, thankfully, followed us in, not letting us out of their circle. Eventually, only thirty feet from shore, the shark gave up and turned back. Once we were able to touch bottom, the dolphins left us too.

"That was amazing!" Anna exclaimed as I pulled her to the beach. "What are you doing? Why are you pulling me so hard?"

A group of people had formed around us on the shore as I sat down to catch my breath.

"Are you guys okay?" one guy asked.

"Man, you are lucky to be alive right now!" I heard another say.

Then a loud announcement came over the megaphone. "This is a second warning—everybody out of the water. There is a shark in the water. I repeat, everybody out of the water."

Anna held up her hands to the crowd with a sweet, innocent smile on her face. "It's okay. They were just dolphins. They're harmless."

The blank stares that were returned to her caused a

confused expression to reach her face. "There were only dolphins out there, right Jake?"

I took her camera from her hand, still trying to catch my breath, and flipped through the pictures that she took until I found one that showed the shark lurking in the background. "*That's* why the dolphins were circling us."

Her face drained of colour as her eyes widened with horror. I wrapped my arms around her and held her head to my chest and said, "Well, we can check snorkelling *and* swimming with dolphins off your list. What's next?"

WE SPENT MOST of the evening in the hot tub by the main pool. The ocean waves could be heard lapping at the shore while the palms rustled in the breeze above us. The air was thick with a cool, salty mixture that was intoxicating and relaxing.

"I'm still freaked out about the shark today," Anna admitted after a long silence.

"Yeah, it was pretty crazy." My stomach turned. To think that I agreed to this snorkelling trip against my better judgment and it could've ended so devastatingly. When we were in the water, scenario after scenario played through my head over how I could've become the bait over Anna.

"Do you think those dolphins actually *knew* what they were doing, or do you think it was just pure coincidence?"

"No, I definitely think their purpose was to be there to protect you."

"Us," she corrected.

"However you want to look at it."

"Yeah, I agree. I don't believe in coincidences. I think everything happens for a reason. Everyone and everything has a purpose."

I nodded.

"Do you . . . do you think this sort of stuff will always happen to us?"

"That's my fear," I said honestly.

"Well, at least we're fulfilling our purpose, right? So whatever happens, we have to leave it in God's hands." Spoken with such confidence.

"What do you think our purpose is?"

"Well, I don't know what *yours* is. I guess only *you* can know that. But I really believe my purpose has something to do with being with you. That might sound silly, but when we got married, I really felt like my mission was complete." She paused and I felt her eyes studying my face. "Don't get me wrong, I still have a desire to do a lot more good in this world, but I don't know. It's weird. Being with you makes me feel complete. Like it's finished."

I slowly nodded, feeling my eyes getting heavy and wondering if this was going to turn into another full-fledged "the true meaning of life" discussion.

"You're tired. Let's go to bed," she offered.

"We can talk about this in bed," I suggested, hoping not to have offended her.

"Sure. Or we could just go to bed. I'm tired, and looking forward to climbing into bed with my husband." She smiled suggestively.

That woke me up. I helped her out of the hot tub and we were on our way back up to our new honeymoon suite.

AFTER MUCH DELIBERATION and a bit of argument, it was decided that we wouldn't free climb the extremely steep Petit Piton mountain, but rather hike the safer Gros Piton. Even though it was larger, there were no fatalities recorded to date, unlike the steeper one. And given our track record so far, and it only being the third day of our honeymoon, my vote was for safer.

The two-hour hike to the top of the mountain was a good workout, considering we hadn't seen the inside of a gym in over a week. We started the climb with four other couples, all of which only made it to the halfway point. Anna and I pressed on through the steep trails and made it to the top without much difficulty. The views from the top were absolutely amazing. It felt like we were on top of the world. Free and untamed.

"This reminds me of the feeling I had when I walked down the aisle," Anna said as she sat down on a rock and peered out into the ocean. "Such an overwhelming sense of peace."

I nodded and sat down next to her. "I remember feeling the same way."

"Jake, I can't tell you how happy I am." She laid her head against my shoulder.

"It's impossible to put into words. I know."

"It's like ever since we finally finished ignoring the fact that we were right for each other, everything started to fall into place. Earth aligned with heaven and my purpose was fulfilled."

"I kind of wish you'd stop saying that, though," I admitted.

"Why?"

"I don't know. It sounds like you feel like you don't have anything else to live for or something." I wrapped my arms around her and pulled her onto my lap.

"It's not like that," she began. "It's weird. I just feel complete. But I still have so much life to live." She stroked a strand of hair from my forehead. "I can't wait to go back and live in our new home with you. Go on missions together. Raise a family eventually. I want to do all these things. I dream about them every night. You and me. Always. Forever."

I took a deep breath of the clean air on top of that mountain and I believed every word she said. Every part of it sounded perfect and just as I had imagined it too. Must have been destiny. *Must* have been . . . or maybe it was just a pleasant dream to carry us through to our true fate.

ZIP-LINING THROUGH THE rainforest was also on Anna's "must do" list. I, too, had always wanted to go zip-lining, but as we stood on the side of that cliff overlooking the rainforest and trusting our fate into the hands of minimum wage employees who mindlessly clipped our bodies onto the cable, I started second guessing myself.

"It's not too late to back out, you know," I mildly suggested as we neared the front of the line.

"Don't be scared, baby. I'll go first if you want," Anna teased.

"I hardly think so." I stepped in front of her. "I'll go first so I can catch you on the other end."

"Fine," she sighed.

My heart began beating wildly with excitement as I watched myself get clipped onto the cable. I had dreamed about this moment—soaring above the rainforest at an incredible speed. The ride didn't disappoint at all. The wind rushed through my hair and I let out a hoot of laughter nearly the whole way. What a rush!

I turned just in time to see Anna's take off. My palms began sweating uncontrollably and my heart thudded against the wall of my chest. Anna screeched as she started spinning out of control, twirling and twirling. We had been taught to just tuck our legs in and head down if this happened as there wasn't much she could do to correct it. She came into the landing extremely fast and I was thankful that I was there to act as a barrier between her and the tree trunk that she was headed for.

"That was *so* scary!" Anna shrieked as I helped unclip her from the line, her body trembling. "That was insane!"

I was relieved. Firstly, that she was safe, and secondly that she seemed to be as ready as I was to turn back and go relax safely on the beach.

"Let's do it again!" I heard her laugh with excitement.

I watched her skip down the walkway and to the next boarding plank. "You sure, babe?" I called after her.

She was.

WE SPENT THE last four days soaking up the sun and lounging on the beach or poolside. Anna had completed her "must do" list, so she was satisfied. At one point, we were taking a leisurely swim in the pool when we saw a lady playing a game of tag with two small children. I noticed that this caught Anna's attention and she treaded water as she watched the playful game with a beautiful smile on her face.

"I just can't wait," Anna finally said as she swam over to me. "I just can't wait to adopt our own."

Brakes on! "What'd you say?"

"Well, of course we'll get settled into our new house first. And make sure there aren't anymore big missions coming at us for a little bit. But after that, yeah, I'd like to have our own kids." She wrapped her legs around my waist and looked at me suspiciously. "You want kids too, right?"

"Yes, of course! But that's not what I heard you say. You said you wanted to adopt?" I studied her face for some insight into her mind.

"Well, we *could* have kids naturally if you were dead set on it, but I figure why bother when there are so many children in the world that need a home."

"Oh, is *that* what you figure?"

"Babe, I didn't mean to upset you. I don't mind giving birth, but I definitely think we should look into adoption too. Even in our own community. Think of the life we could give children. There are so many babies, toddler and kids waiting to be adopted. It's just really sad."

Even though I was slightly caught off guard on this discussion, there was no way I could be upset with her. She had the biggest heart. Full of love. And to be honest, the idea of adopting a child brought a warm feeling over me. I liked it.

"How about we have a child naturally first, and then we'll adopt a couple. Do you like that idea?" she asked.

"You're unbelievable," I said, kissing her wet nose. "How did I end up with someone as fantastic as you?"

She giggled and laid back in the water. "It was fate."

So far I liked fate. So far.

CHAPTER 29

BEFORE I KNEW it, the honeymoon was over. We reluctantly packed our bags and headed to the airport. Although I was slightly sad about leaving, I was really looking forward to starting our new life back at home. We had discussed so many ideas about what we would do to our new house. It was strangely exciting to think about doing yard work and renovations. I could already envision both of us sitting in the library—Anna curled up by the fireplace reading a book while I sat at the desk flipping through top-secret files.

"I have to admit," Anna began as the plane started to take off, "I'm really excited to get home."

"I was just thinking the same thing," I said, taking her hand in mine. I ran my fingers over her wedding band and felt like the luckiest man in the world to be married to such a beautiful, talented, caring woman.

The couple sitting across the aisle from us was the same couple that went on the zip-lining tour with us.

She and I made eye contact, and where I thought a polite smile and nod would've sufficed, she apparently thought differently.

"Hey!" she shouted with a wide smile and a bit too much enthusiasm. "Hey! It's our zip-lining buddies!" She nudged her partner for his reaction.

Oh, boy. One of those.

Anna leaned over me and returned her excitement. To be courteous, no doubt. "Fancy meeting you here. Are you guys from Canada too?"

"Yes, we're from Toronto, actually. I'm Krista. This is Will." She extended her hand and we made introductions.

"How was the rest of your vacation?" Anna asked politely. "Did you enjoy St. Lucia?"

"Oh, yes!" Krista exclaimed. "We stayed at a most beautiful resort. Jade Mountain. Have you heard of it?"

Our first resort. I grinned and looked at Anna.

"Yes," Anna answered. "We actually stayed there for the first night of our honeymoon."

"Really?" Krista looked puzzled. "Why only one night?"

"Ummm?" Anna looked to me for assistance.

"I didn't care for it," I answered truthfully. "Too quiet."

Krista nodded slowly, seemingly expecting more of an answer, but she didn't get one. "I see," she finally said. "Well, if you would've stayed a little longer, it definitely livened up a bit."

"Oh yeah?" Anna said.

"Yes! It was the craziest thing. The local police and security came barging through the resort around three o'clock in the morning on Tuesday, waking everyone up. *Apparently*, a little old couple staying on the fourth floor were attacked and nearly killed!"

My heart stopped. Fourth floor. That was our floor. What are the chances?

"Do you . . ." —I cleared my throat—"Do you know *why* it happened?" I tightened my grip on Anna's hand.

"Not for sure, but I heard that the lady told the police that the attacker wasn't really looking for them. That when he saw the couple's faces, he seemed to be expecting someone else, I guess. Then he took off."

"What room?" Was all I could get out. My mouth was dry and I could vaguely taste blood.

"412," Will answered, his first words of the conversation. "I remember hearing people talking about it that night. We were room 312, that's how I remember. It happened right above us."

Room 412. That was *our* room.

I turned back to Anna who was literally as white as the clouds billowing past the window behind her. Her lips were pale and dry, her eyes glossed over. I wrapped my arms around her and held her close. Rocking her slightly.

"It's okay," I whispered in her ear. "It's okay."

"That was supposed to be us," she cried into my shoulder.

"But it wasn't."

"Because of you, Jake." Anna pulled away and looked hard into my eyes. "*You* saved us. You have a gift for that. You're so intuitive. You seem to just *know* things." She buried her head back into my chest and cried. "That poor couple," she sobbed.

"Anna, don't worry about them right now. They're fine. This will just be a good vacation story for them." I pulled her hair off her wet face. "We have bigger issues. Someone knows where we were. *Who* would know that?"

I racked my brain, thinking about who had access to that information. *We* didn't even know where we were going until we got there. Was someone at the airport and overheard us? The only person who knew where we were going was our travel agent and . . . wait a second . . . Dad! Dad wrote down our travel agent's name. He could've easily used his position to find out any information from her files. He would've known. He was so adamant to find out where we were going. He did this. He tried to kill us. But why?!

No sooner had I come up with this conclusion when a deafening sound and an abrupt jolt rocked the plane. I instinctively grabbed Anna and held her as the plane rocked and teetered. The flight attendants hurried past us and disappeared at the front of the plane. The plane took a nosedive and started flying straight down. Down. Down. Down. Screams of horror were heard all over the plane. An infant flipped through the air over some heads before a man reached up and caught it. Anna sobbed in my arms as I held her tightly. No words were exchanged between us because we knew what this was. Another attempt on our lives.

The familiar murmurs of Anna's prayers became my focus and I pinched my eyes closed and tried to filter out all of the excess noise as we focused together. She was praying for a miracle. I was praying for her safety. She prayed for the children. The terrified, screaming children.

The plane plummeted several thousand feet before it jerked back up and the pilot tried to make an unsuccessful landing.

The last thing I remembered thinking was, "God, keep her safe!" The last thing I remembered seeing was the front of the plane being ripped off and thrown over top of us while it burst into flames. And the last thing I remember feeling was Anna's body being ripped from my arms. I fumbled. I tried. But I lost her.

IT WAS DARK. And quiet. My head hurt just a little, and then a lot. And gradually I saw shades of grey and then the bright sun beating down on my face. The only sounds were of tiny muffled cries and the occasional call for "Mommy" or "Daddy." It was then that I realized where I was and what had just happened. I jumped up, not giving much mind to the blood pouring down the side of my face.

"ANNA!" I shouted over the sea of rubble, smoke, fire and people. "ANNA!" I cried again, fighting back the large lump in my throat that was restricting my voice.

I made my way through the bodies, all burnt beyond recognition, decapitated or just beyond repair. I caught sight of a little girl, probably three or four years old, rocking back and forth as she held her knees tightly to her chest. I fought the urge to run to her and heal her mind. Erase the horrific memories. But first I needed to find Anna.

I continued sifting through the rubble and bodies, occasionally coming across another child. One eight-year-old who had found his lifeless mother and was curled up beside her on the ground. Another toddler who was telling her daddy to wake up and pulling at his nose, not understanding that this time he wasn't playing.

Finally I found her. She was lying unconscious in the bushes with bloodstained clothes and a gash the size of my hand through her chest.

"Anna!" I gasped as I ran to her and tried to pick her up. That's when I noticed the piece of airplane protruding from her side. I lost my breath. I couldn't breathe no matter how much I forced myself to try.

Seeing her in that state, so close to death, if not already there. I couldn't move. All I could do was stare at her bloodstained face and cry.

"God, why have you abandoned me?" I screamed at the top of my lungs.

Suddenly I was aware of people shouting and sirens sounding. I spun around to see emergency crews searching the area.

"OVER HERE!" I shouted, calling them to Anna's rescue. I wanted so badly to fix her, but I didn't have the strength. I didn't know where to begin. I was too stuck on the fear of losing her.

Within minutes she was loaded into the ambulance. I jumped into the ambulance beside her and had some difficulty with the paramedics telling me that I had to catch another ride. Maybe it was the look in my eye or perhaps they were mind readers too, but there wasn't another word spoken to me as I took my seat next to Anna.

Before the doors closed, I looked back once more at the scene of destruction. Eight children were huddled together with emergency crew assessing their bodies. All eight children aboard our flight. The only apparent survivors other than us. She truly was powerful. I prayed for the images to be erased from their memories and the pain of losing their parents to be replaced with some form of forgiveness and love.

"HOW DOES SHE look?" I pressed the doctor the minute he finished his assessment later that afternoon. I found myself depending more and more on him for her survival since my own healing efforts weren't making a difference.

"Still the same," he said as he slung his stethoscope around his neck. He pursed his lips apologetically and left the room. I hated that we were stuck in a foreign country with foreign doctors and foreign, likely outdated, medical equipment.

I buried my head in the sheets next to her and cried. "I'm so sorry, baby. I'm so sorry." Her hand was still warm in mine, and her chest still rose and fell . . . even if it was only for the machines.

The sound of the door crashing against the wall sent me leaping out of my chair.

"Jacob!" It was Mom. She ran toward me and threw her arms around me. "My baby! Thank God you're okay!" She pulled away and looked me up and down, reassuring herself that she was indeed correct. Then she grasped my head in her hands and said, "You're exhausted. Look at you."

She slowly looked past me and brought her eyes to Anna, lifeless and colourless, sleeping soundly next to us. The tears immediately poured out of her as she collapsed in my arms. I wished I had it in me to console her, but it took everything just to hold her upright.

"Joanna, let's go for a walk and leave Jacob alone

with Anna," Dad spoke from the doorway.

My hands immediately clenched into fists. The blood rushed to my face as my eyes began to bulge and my teeth clenched until I heard a crack.

Before I could accuse him of anything, Dad pulled Mom from the room and they disappeared into the hallway. I wasn't about to leave Anna for one second, so I let him go. He'd be back. Couldn't hide forever.

I returned my attention to Anna and took a deep breath, summoning any and all power left inside of me to heal her. I positioned my hands—one on her head and one on her body. This time it would work. This time I would heal her. I had to.

A HALF HOUR later the door opened again. I stumbled from my position over Anna and fell into the chair, quickly bringing myself back to my surroundings. My vision was narrow and breathing erratic as my body fought hard at replenishing the energy I was extracting for Anna's healing.

Nick, Claudia, Noah and Rachel filed into the room and went right to Anna's side. Rachel and Claudia held her hands and cried as I watched the monitor screen for any variation.

"She's not going to make it, is she?" Claudia asked through tears.

"Why would you say it like that?!" I demanded, feeling a rush of adrenalin that allowed me to pull myself upright.

She wiped a tear that trickled down her cheek. "The doctor said that—"

"Screw what the doctor said! We're better than doctors!" I shouted.

"Can't you heal her?" Noah asked.

I answered through clenched teeth, "Don't you think I've been trying?"

"Maybe you're too close to her," Nick said. "Have you called Matthias? He's the only healer I know, other than you, who could fix this."

"I hadn't thought of that," I replied, suddenly perking up to the idea. "Can you do that for me?"

"Sure, man." Nick left the room with his phone in hand.

Maybe this was our answer. This would work. Matthias could do this. I healed his niece on her deathbed when he couldn't find the strength. He could do this for me. I knew he could. Our only obstacle now was time.

CHAPTER 30

EVERY MINUTE FELT like an hour as I waited for Nick to return with the news of when Matthias would be here. We were only a seven hour flight from home, so at best he wouldn't be here until the morning. I would have to trust her fate in the hands of the doctors until then.

"Any leads yet on who did this?" I stroked Anna's fingers gently as the anger brewed inside me.

"Not yet," Noah answered. "Ms. Peters is meeting with Interpol in the morning to hold a conference. They'll get to the bottom of it."

I concentrated on not squeezing Anna's hand too tightly as I thought about the monster behind this attack. The sound of the door opening behind me broke my concentration.

"Did you get a hold of him?" Claudia asked.

Nick looked down at the phone in his hands. "He, uh . . . he's coming, but he's in India right now so he won't be here until tomorrow night."

No one dared to speak. I swallowed hard but couldn't fight back the tears that followed. And feeling like an abandoned child, I fell to my knees and cried.

Anna, don't leave me. I need you, I thought. The pain tearing at my chest was unbearable. The only thing I wanted in this whole world was to have Anna sitting beside me. Safe and unharmed. Now she was lying lifeless on a hospital bed hanging on by a thread of luck.

"Jake, you should eat," Rachel said after several minutes.

I stared at her blankly, wondering if she was honestly suggesting I leave Anna's side to fill my mouth with useless food.

Claudia added, "What can we get for you?"

"Nothing," I answered.

There was a quick knock at the door and Anna's parents pushed into the room.

"We'll be downstairs in the cafeteria," Noah said as he put his arm around Rachel and headed for the door. "Call me if you need us before we get back."

I sat back and watched in agony as Mr. and Mrs. Taylor cried and prayed over their daughter.

"Jake, you look terrible," Mrs. Taylor finally said, acknowledging my presence. "You need some food or something. Can we get you anything?"

"Nothing," I said. "I'll eat when she eats."

Hours passed and when daylight came again, my eyes burned. There were no more tears in my body to cry. No more strength to be angry. I needed everything left inside me to think positive thoughts for Anna's recovery.

I followed Anna's bed down to the lab for more cat scans and tests. A few hours later, I found myself sitting back in Anna's room, holding her hand and waiting on the words of the doctor to bring Anna back to me. Anna's parents, Nick, Claudia, Noah and Rachel stood around the perimeter of the room, waiting for the same good news that I was.

The doctor looked uncomfortable as he flipped through Anna's file and cleared his throat. My eyes flickered to Claudia for a prelude to his message, which I instantly regretted as I saw her bury her face into Nick's chest and begin sobbing.

"The damage to her brain is beyond repair. The internal bleeding has spread to her lungs and I'm so sorry to tell you that she only has a day or two at best."

Silence.

My heart and breathing quickened. "Can't you do more?"

"Even if we could, she would be paralyzed from the neck down—"

"Then do it!" I begged. "You have to *try*!"

"Jake, we've tried. If we opened her up right now, she wouldn't make it out alive."

"Can't you . . . Isn't there . . ." I stumbled but I couldn't find the words.

"Is there *anything* else you can do?" Mrs. Taylor hoped.

"I'm so sorry. I suggest you say your good-byes now." The doctor turned and left the room. Not another word spoken.

My body was frozen. My mind was numb. No thoughts entered my head. No words left my mouth. I'm not sure how much time had passed, but when I finally became aware of my surroundings, Anna and I were alone again.

"Baby," I whispered in her ear. "Baby, please wake up. I . . . I don't know how to heal you, so I need you to heal yourself."

She was silent. Motionless. I lifted the sheets and crawled in the bed next to her, careful not to hurt her. I rested my head above hers and touched my lips to her head, kissing it softly.

I closed my eyes and rested, for the first time in over twenty-four hours. Although she felt colder than normal, and her arms weren't wrapped around me too, I was comfortable.

I felt my body drifting to sleep. It was a strange sense of relief so I let myself go. So tired of crying. So tired of fighting. I just wanted to sleep. Right here, next to Anna.

My subconscious took up right where my conscious

left off. Anna's eyes opened and she rolled over on her side to face me. An overwhelming joy filled my heart as I felt the warmth return to her hands.

"I missed you," I said, stroking her hair from her eyes.

"I've always been here," she answered, her delicate eyes penetrating mine. "I'll always be here with you."

"Does this mean you'll be okay?" I knew she would. Something told me she was going to be perfectly fine.

"Of course I'll be okay, silly," she answered with a giggle. "I'll be more than okay. I just hope you will too."

"What do you mean?" I searched her face for an answer as her words weren't coming fast enough.

She stroked my face and kissed my lips, then whispered, "I'll be waiting for you. I love you so much, Jacob."

"Anna?" The scared feeling returned to paralyze my body. "What are you talking about?"

"I found my purpose," she said with a smile.

"What do you mean? What is it?"

"My purpose is . . ." she whispered as her eyes closed.

"Your purpose is *what*, Anna?" I pressed, sitting up slightly, urging her eyes to open with my voice. "Your purpose is *what*?!"

Her smile froze and a glaze covered her eyes as her last words fell from her lips. "It is finished."

A soft hand touched my face. I suddenly woke up and followed the arm to its owner. It was Mom. Looking down at me with such concern in her eyes.

"Honey, it's time to get up," she said quietly as she continued to stroke my face.

I scanned the room and found all of our friends and family standing there, holding their coats and bags. Ready to go.

"Is she okay?" I asked, confused, my attention returning to Anna who was still lying beside me.

There was a silence and I noticed the restlessness in the room.

"He doesn't know," Claudia whispered.

Mom pulled me up and wrapped her arms around me as she cried. "She's gone, baby. She's been gone for hours."

The familiar feeling of stillness took over my body as two men cloaked in white came in, draped a clean white sheet over my wife and rolled her out of the room. I couldn't move as the nightmare gripped my life. I failed her. I couldn't save her like she saved me. I was stranded.

MY FEET CARRIED me. Out of the room. Down the hall. Past Matthias who was running through the front door—a little too late, apparently. Down the sidewalk and along the boardwalk next to the vast ocean. I didn't know where they were taking me, but I didn't care.

Anywhere in this world would be better than where I
was. Nothing was important anymore. Nothing
mattered. Life without Anna wasn't worth living. I
wanted to die. I wanted to be where Anna was.

Suddenly I was aware of the pain that gripped at
my chest and the coldness that filled my lungs. I was
floating, and it became very clear why. . . . I was
drowning.

I'm coming home, Anna.

THERE SHE WAS. Standing in her wedding dress,
greeting me with the most beautiful smile. We held
each other for what seemed to be eternity. In her warm
arms, I was finally home.

SOME PEOPLE BELIEVE that, before you are even born,
you are the writer of your own destiny. You assist God
in creating your own challenges, assigning your own
personality traits, and even deciding when and how
you will die. All of the obstacles that you create are
designed to bring you to your purpose in life. It is also
believed that déjà vu is a sign that everything is going
according to God's plan. Your plan.

Here is a sneak peek at the series finale:

REPRIMANDED

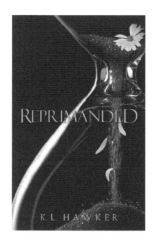

AFTER SAYING GOODBYE to his one true love, Jake struggles with returning to his new home and old life without Anna. But when strange things begin to happen, Jake secretly begins to look for missing pieces of an intricate puzzle, while his friends question his sanity. Soon Jake discovers that he's not the only one keeping secrets. With nothing to lose, Jake wages war between old and new alliances in an effort to uncover a thick plot, discover *his* purpose, and bring justice to the Defiers . . . before time runs out.

Turn the page to read the prologue to Reprimanded.

PROLOGUE

I WAS ALONE now, except for, of course, Jake who was fighting for death on life support, and Nick who casually leaned against the wall next to me, watching my every move and worrying that I blamed myself.

This isn't our fault, he thought loud and clearly. He knew how to make his thoughts vibrant when he meant them for me. He was becoming quite good at making them fuzzy when they weren't meant for me, too. Sometimes I appreciated it.

Claudia, this is not your fault, he repeated again, more staccato than before, and making it clearer that he knew I blamed myself more than I blamed the both of us.

I slowly turned my eyes from Jake's face and tilted my head toward Nick. "If we would've told him, this never would've happened. Look at him—he's on life support. This is *completely* our fault."

"We can't look at it that way," he challenged, his deep voice even and sure.

"You weren't in his head after his mother told him

she was dead. He was drained. Disconnected. His only thought was death. I could've stopped him. I should've stopped him. . . . I should've told him."

"Please don't blame yourself, Claudia. He'll pull through this. I promise."

"What good are we to anyone with this secret? We made a promise to each other as a group—no more secrets. Now look where we are." The burden of this secret weighed heavily on my shoulders. It was suffocating me. I wanted to let it all out. I wanted everyone to know. I wanted to rewind time and change the outcome.

"Claudia," Nick grabbed my arm and turned me to face him. His grip was firm and although I didn't think it was possible to feel more pain, I did. "Get a hold of yourself," he warned. "No one is to find out about this. Jake will get through this. All will be back the way it was soon enough."

I let myself fall into the chair next to Jake's bed and cried in my hands. *How could this all be happening?*

"She's safe now. The Defiers can't harm her where she is," Nick said, touching my shoulder lightly.

"But look at *him*." I gestured toward our friend lying comatose in a hospital room in a foreign country. "It doesn't matter where she is or how protected she is—what matters is that he can't live without her. And now look—he might not make it! We could've prevented this. We should've told him."

"Not an option, Claudia. What's done is done."

"He could've protected her. She was safest with him."

"Obviously she wasn't," Nick said, carefully reminding me of the devastating plane crash.

I reached out and held Jake's hand.

"Claudia," Nick started, crouching down next to me. "Promise me you won't tell anyone. This is for the best. You need to trust me on this."

I stared at Jake's face. The pain was obvious even when he was unconscious.

"All we need is time right now," he continued. "In time, it will come out. Jake will realize it was all for her protection. He'll forgive us."

I pressed my head into Jake's arm as Nick's words repeated in my head.

Please, baby, he thought.

I sucked in a deep breath and sat tall, clenching my jaw. "Okay," I said as I let out my breath. "Okay." I nodded and looked at Nick whose pain was evident by the dark circles around his eyes and the paleness of his skin.

Thank you, he thought. *This is for the best.*

I didn't like it. In fact, I hated it. I hated lying. I hated keeping this secret. But if it was the best thing for our group, I had no choice. For now.

ACKNOWLEDGMENTS

My first thanks will always be to God. Discovering my purpose was such a powerful moment for me—just as He meant it to be. I thank Him for my gift.

Thank you, my dear husband, for your endless support of my dreams and desires—no matter how crazy.

Thank you to my three wonderful children. You three inspire me daily and I love you so much!

Thanks, Mom, for modelling the perfect being—happiness, positivity, selflessness. You are an angel and I wouldn't be where I am without you.

Thanks, Dad, for encouraging my love for travel, and for keeping all of my short stories from the early years. How fun it has been to re-read my first creations.

Thank you to my first readers—Annette (one of the best friends a girl could have), Krista (the best sister a girl could have, although my childhood self might disagree), and Janet (an amazing mother-of-a-sister-in-law with a keen eye and giving heart). I appreciate all you've done.

Thanks to my brothers, Paul and Trevor. One who helped inspire Jake's character, and the other who taught me how to defend myself. Can you guess who is who?

And last, but certainly not the least, a big thank you to my awesome fans! Every single message I receive from you literally warms my heart and makes me smile. I pray that, no matter how old you are, you will always find time to pick up a book and escape to another world.

K.L. HAWKER lives with her husband, three children and faithful Golden Retriever in Halifax, Nova Scotia. When she's not writing, she enjoys photography, playing the piano, and travelling the globe with her family.

Join K.L. Hawker on Facebook and follow along on her adventures. www.facebook.com/klhawker.

K.L. Hawker's website is
www.klhawker.com

19301108R00191

Printed in Great Britain
by Amazon